HIGH PRAISE FOR
BILL MOODY AND
THE SOUND OF THE TRUMPET

"Bill Moody's characters have life and soul . . . Telling their stories, Horne gives us what we came for . . . a taste of a time when jazz was king."
—*The New York Times*

"Moody's like a skilled arranger—he gets all the little details right."
—*Twin Cities Reader*

"Fascinating insider information on various aspects of the jazz world. A must for jazz fans."
—*Booklist*

"A refreshingly unique who-done-it . . . The mystery is well done and the glimpse into the world of the collector is most interesting."
—*The Midwest Book Review*

"Evan Horne is a welcome addition to the genre . . . Moody's first-hand knowledge of the music world is a real plus."
—Jerry Kennealy, author of *Vintage Polo*

Other Evan Horne Mysteries by Bill Moody

THE SOUND OF
THE TRUMPET

An Evan Horne Mystery

BILL MOODY

A DELL BOOK

Published by
Dell Publishing
a division of
Bantam Doubleday Dell Publishing Group, Inc.
1540 Broadway
New York, New York 10036

All the characters and events portrayed in this work are fictitious.

ISBN: 0-440-22194-3

Reprinted by arrangement with Walker and Company

Printed in the United States of America

Published simultaneously in Canada

February 1998

WCD   10 9 8 7 6 5 4 3 2 1

How can we ever say for certain
someone that played
like Clifford Brown could play
could really be said to have gone away.
—Jon Hendricks

The basic difference between classical music and jazz
is that in the former the music is always greater than
its performance—whereas the way jazz is performed
is always more important than what is being played.
—André Previn

Acknowledgments

THANKS FIRST AND FOREMOST TO CLIFFORD BROWN for all the great music.

A number of people contributed their expertise to this book, not the least of whom are Walt Blanton, for special insights into Slick Stuff valve oil and trumpet cases; Jack Montrose, for his generous personal knowledge of Clifford Brown and life in general; Stan Dunn at Concord Records, for how the record business really works; Captain Tom Mapes of the Santa Monica Police Department, for keeping me procedurally accurate; and the very helpful folks at the Institute of Jazz Studies, Rutgers University, for archival material on Clifford Brown.

Special thanks to my little brother Doug for support, stories, and his behind-the-scenes view of record collectors.

Finally, thanks to Michael Seidman and George Gibson for giving me the opportunity to write about jazz and allowing me to do my own books—and Kimberley Cameron of Reece Halsey, for being far more than a dedicated agent.

And then, as always, there is Teresa.

INTRO

WITH MY DEAD HAND, I PUT THE TONE ARM ON THE record and listen to my live hand.

The title of the album is Arrival—Evan Horne, recorded, unfortunately, just before CDs became commonplace. There were fewer than two thousand copies printed. In my euphoria at accomplishing a lifelong dream, I gave away all mine, except this one, to friends and relatives.

I could try, but tracking down another copy would be difficult if not impossible. It's unlikely that collectors would have one, and according to the record company, a small label that was gobbled up by a bigger one, there are none in stock. To have some copies made from the master tape in the small numbers I want would be very expensive, even if the master could be found. Tapes get lost, misfiled, or just disappear.

It's been years since I listened to it. There are things I would do differently, tunes I would eliminate or add, arrangements I would change, but generally it stands up well. It got a flurry of airplay on some jazz radio stations, a couple of good reviews—of the promising-new-talent variety—but disappeared into obscurity in relatively quick fashion. Still, I have this copy, proof that I once recorded with my own trio.

I listen to a couple of other tunes, then carefully return the record to its sleeve. I glance at the photo of myself on the cover, seated at a grand piano, the bassist and drummer standing behind me. My smile reflects the hope and pride I felt at that moment. I wonder what the next one would have been, if there had been a next one.

I don't usually yearn for the good old days, but on this January night in Venice, California, with cold air and fog nudging my windows, I'm in the mood for the past. I pull out some CD reissues of Miles Davis, Dexter Gordon, Bud Powell, and Bud's brother Richie playing with the Max Roach–Clifford Brown Quintet.

Brownie's tone is as pure and clean and cool as a mountain stream. I wonder—as do all jazz musicians, especially trumpet players—what he would have done but for that rainy night on the Pennsylvania Turnpike when his car went off the road and a great talent was lost forever at age twenty-five.

Had Miles Davis died at the same age, there would be no recordings beyond Birth of the Cool. *No* Kind of Blue, *no collaborations with Gil Evans, no quintet with Wayne Shorter, Herbie Hancock, Tony Williams, and Ron Carter.*

I've never met a trumpet player who doesn't speak in reverent tones about Clifford Brown. His recorded legacy is small, to be sure, but studied and emulated by anyone who's put a trumpet to his lips. Lee Morgan and Woody Shaw are gone, but some of Brownie's disciples are still with us. Freddie Hubbard and Wynton Marsalis owe a lot of notes to Brownie.

I pour myself another Dewars on the rocks and listen to the final strains of "Joy Spring," imagining what it must have been like to be Richie Powell feeding chords to Brownie with Max Roach's cymbal beating down on us relentlessly, Harold Land standing in the wings making people forget—

at least for the moment—Teddy Edwards, the original tenor player in this band. Sonny Rollins was soon to follow.

One thing I'm sure of, I wouldn't have wanted to be Richie Powell in that car with Brownie. I had my own automobile accident. I survived, but my hand didn't, and maybe that's made me who I am today.

Someday, I hope I'll know for sure.

CHAPTER
ONE

I WAKE UP SUNDAY MORNING, JUST BEFORE THE PHONE rings, feeling the effects of too much Scotch and not enough sleep. I mumble what I know must be an incoherent hello into the phone.

"Evan? I wake you up?"

"Ace? No, I just haven't had my coffee yet."

"Sorry. Listen, get a shower and some coffee, and I'll call you back in about a half hour."

"What's up?"

"We'll talk then. I've got a job for you."

I pause and gaze out the window that affords me a sliver of a view of the Venice boardwalk, already filling up with early-morning joggers and walkers even though the sky is slate gray, the air cool.

"Ace, I'm still not playing, you know."

"It's not a gig, but it's something you'll be interested in. Thirty minutes." The phone goes dead before I can protest further.

I hang up the phone and drag myself to the bathroom and stand under the shower for ten minutes wondering what Ace has in store for me.

Dr. Charles "Ace" Buffington is my good friend at the University of Nevada, Las Vegas. The last time he called, it *was* for a gig. Cocktail piano at a shopping mall and research into the death of saxophonist Wardell Gray. It turned out to be much more than research in a lot of ways, but it had its upside. I also met Natalie Beamer, a policewoman who was now pursuing the law instead of criminals.

I wrap myself in a heavy terry cloth robe and get some coffee going while I scan the *Los Angeles Times* and survey the chaos of my apartment. I'm about half packed up and know I'm going to miss living in Venice. Progress has made its way to this corner of L.A., and developers have bought up the remaining houses on my block for a new set of condos. The demolition ball is swinging toward me. Time to move on.

I'm on my second cup of coffee when Ace calls back. "Evan? Better now?"

"Much. What's up? How's the book going?" My help with the Wardell Gray project had turned into a book for Ace, one that even his own department could not ignore.

"Great. You are now talking to a full professor."

"Congratulations, Ace. Stick it to them."

"Oh, don't worry. I plan to. How are things with you?"

"Let's cut to it, Ace. You don't call me on Sunday morning without something in mind. If it has anything to do with playing piano, forget it. If it has anything to do with investigating, *really* forget it."

Ace laughs now, but my run-ins with Anthony Gallio were not funny then for either of us. I managed to uncover a lot about Wardell Gray's death, and a lot more about Las Vegas mob types.

"No, nothing like that. This one is easy. What do you know about Clifford Brown?"

"One of the all-time great trumpet players in jazz. He was killed in a car crash in the fifties. Great loss to jazz, trumpet players still talk about him. End of story."

"Not quite. What would you say if some previously unknown recordings of Mr. Brown had been discovered?"

"I'd say they would be very valuable to certain people. Record companies, for one. They'd probably be released on CD to the great joy of all concerned, especially a number of trumpet players."

"Exactly," Ace says.

I take a couple of sips of coffee and light a cigarette, a foul-tasting menthol that I hope will encourage me to quit. Ace is a record collector and on the fringe of the wild-eyed serious fiends who, according to Ace, will do anything to secure a rare find. But as far as I know, there are no undiscovered recordings of Clifford Brown. That would be a big story.

"You've found something?"

"Maybe," Ace says. "At least, I know someone who thinks they have, and that's the job. Piece of cake for you."

"That's what you said about researching Wardell Gray."

"This is different. Tragic, yes, but there was nothing suspicious about Brownie's car accident. I've got a collector friend, really serious one, who thinks he may have come into some Clifford Brown. These guys are really secretive though, spooky really. Anyway, he wants some preliminary confirmation that this tape might actually be Clifford Brown."

"And?"

"As I said, he's really secretive. He doesn't trust hardly anyone when it comes to rare recordings, but he trusts me enough to contact you."

"To do what?"

"Come to Las Vegas, listen to the tape, and tell him if you think it's really Clifford Brown. All expenses paid, and a nice fee for your trouble. You can stay with me for a few days. I'm between semesters, so we can hang out a little."

"Wouldn't it be better to have a trumpet player listen to the tape? I play, or did play, piano."

"Maybe, but I don't know any trumpet players I can tell this guy I trust. You can at least tell enough to satisfy him he may be on to something."

I should know better, but I'm intrigued. Hadn't someone found some old John Coltrane tapes in a closet at Atlantic Records? A visit with Ace would be nice. Listen to a tape and get paid for it. Why not? "When is this supposed to happen?"

"If you're free, the sooner the better. This guy wants to move on this right away. Can I tell him yes?"

"Oh, I'm free." Natalie has been putting in ten-hour days at Loyola Law School, wrestling with contracts, torts, and real property. Except for weekends, I hardly see her.

"Great," Ace says. "I'll FedEx a ticket."

"Hang on, I might drive up. I've got a new car I'd like to try out on the road."

"Suit yourself. We'll reimburse you when you get here and settle on a fee. He'll go for at least five-hundred dollars."

"We?"

"Yeah, this guy and I are kind of—partners."

"Ace?"

"Yeah?"

"Are you telling me everything?"

I spend the rest of the morning packing up more boxes, discarding some things, mulling over whether to keep this or that, realizing finally with some surprise that my life can be contained in a few boxes and a couple of suitcases. I have two more weeks to go on the lease before the bulldozers move in, and I've been looking around for a new place. Nothing so far has appealed. After Friday's doctor visit, I'm not even sure I want to stay in Los Angeles.

Around noon I change into some presentable clothes—jeans, sweater, and my favorite cord jacket—and head for my lunch date with Carol Mann, my erstwhile therapist. The accident that maimed my hand led to psychological counseling with Carol's group of similarly damaged musicians. We officially stopped the sessions long ago, but Carol and I had become friends and stayed in touch. Occasionally, like today, we manage lunch or dinner.

My new car isn't really new except to me. When my Mazda was stolen and gutted—the cops think by a chop-shop operation—I endured some sticker shock looking for a new one. When one of Cindy Fuller's stewardess friends got married and moved to Boston, I was offered her babied and well-cared-for 1989 Chevy Camaro. It was too good to pass up, saving me the hassle of shopping and haggling with a dealer. I wouldn't have chosen a Camaro, but now that I'm used to it, it fits me well, and it's fun to drive.

I nose it out of the carport behind the apartments and head up Venice Boulevard for the 405 Freeway.

Traffic is light, and the throaty rumble of the Camaro's engine is comforting as I roll north to Brentwood, taking the Sunset exit. Carol has chosen a nouveau, fifties-style diner for our nontherapy-therapy lunch. I surrender my car to the valet parking attendant, a blond kid in white shirt and red bow tie with admiring eyes for the Camaro.

"Don't get too excited," I say, getting out of the car.

"No, sir."

Inside, I find Carol already there. She waves from her table, and I see she's purposely avoided the patio smoking section even though there is one, a rare thing these days in southern California. Everyone wants me to quit.

"Sorry I'm late," I say, taking a chair opposite her and glancing around the room. "Very L.A."

"You're not. I'm early," Carol says. "And be nice, I'm buying." She's dressed nearly as casually as I am in jeans, turtleneck sweater, and a denim shirt open at the collar. We hardly glance at the menu before a waiter slides into my line of vision. He's tall, thin, probably a UCLA student.

"Hi, I'm Steve, and I'll be your server today. Can I get you one of our appetizers, some sautéed mushrooms perhaps, a mini pizza?" He smiles at us both expectantly.

"Well, Steve, I'm Evan your customer, and I don't know what I want yet, since I haven't looked at the menu. A Bloody Mary would be nice if you can manage that. Carol?"

"Yeah, that would be fine," Carol says, blushing slightly. Steve gives me a glance and withdraws.

"My, aren't we cranky today."

I shrug. "I just get a little tired of the hustle these

days. Waiters don't know you, but they want to establish a relationship before you sit down."

"I take it your visit with Dr. Martin didn't go as well as you hoped."

I reach for cigarettes on reflex, then remember we're in nonsmoking. "I can't seem to win, Carol. Physically, Martin says I check out fine. The tendons and nerves have healed and responded well to the therapy—too well."

"What do you mean?"

"Focal dystonia."

"Come again?"

"Martin says it's called repetitive motion stress disorder. This is all new stuff apparently, still a lot of research being done, but I guess I qualify as a textbook case. It seems I overcompensated, practiced too much, and I've tired the muscles. A common mistake is to play through the pain. That's what I did, tried to come back too soon, and I sure felt the pain on that Las Vegas gig."

"So what's his advice?"

If it's possible to smile ironically, I try. "A period of relative rest, which for me means staying off the piano. Once the pain subsides, I can start practicing again gradually."

Carol nods and sighs for me. "Now that you mention it, there's a doctor in Monterey doing research on this. I think I remember reading something about it." She reaches across the table and touches my wrist. "I'm sorry, Evan, I really am."

I try a smile again. "Don't be, I guess—"

"All right, here we are." Steve, our friendly waiter, is back, balancing two Bloody Marys on a silver tray. He sets them on the table, rearranges the vase of fake flowers and the salt and pepper shaker, and begins a well-rehearsed routine about the day's specials. "We have a very nice poached salmon and—"

"Tell you what, Steve, how about a club sandwich with fries, and we'll skip the specials, okay?"

"But the lady—"

"That's fine," Carol says, arching her eyebrows at me. "I'll have the shrimp salad."

"Excellent choice," Steve says.

"And how is that, Steve?"

"I just mean—"

"I'm just kidding, Steve."

"No, you're not." Steve departs in a huff.

"Wow," Carol says. "What is that all about?"

I ignore Carol's question and take up where I left off. "As I was saying, I guess maybe I'm not supposed to play piano for a while, maybe not in this lifetime."

"So what are you doing?"

I take a long pull of the Bloody Mary. "Moving, for one thing, and it looks like I'm going up to Las Vegas for a few days to listen to some tapes."

"Tapes of what?"

"We still have doctor-client privilege working here, right?"

"Of course, if you want."

"It's probably not that big a deal, but someone thinks they've found some recordings of Clifford Brown, the trumpet player." I fill Carol in on Brownie and Ace's offer, barely finishing before Steve warily approaches the table with our food. Not a peep out of him as he sets it down. He addresses Carol only.

"Can I get you anything else?" Carol shakes her head no. Steve withdraws without looking at me.

"That wasn't so hard, was it?"

"Watch, he'll be back in record time." As it turns out, it's less than two minutes.

"And how are we doing here? Everything okay?"

"Well, Steve, I don't know, since I've hardly had time to even taste this sandwich."

Steve mumbles something and stalks away.

"Wait'll we have coffee. I'm willing to bet Steve was trained in the school that says never let the level of coffee go a half-inch below the rim before offering refills."

"We'll be lucky if he comes back," Carol says. "I'm taking you to Burger King next time."

Natalie is waiting on the front steps when I return. She's in old sweats and running shoes, her hair tied back in a ponytail. "Nice lunch?" she asks. Her eyes are hidden behind sunglasses.

"Yeah, okay." I sit down next to her. "What are you doing here? Don't you have a class or something?" The winter sun has finally broken through, but there's a chill in the air.

She takes off her glasses and looks at me. "I got your message. You didn't think I'd let you go to Las Vegas without saying good-bye did you?" The smile in her eyes is full of mischief.

"It's only for a few days, no big thing."

She nods. "I know, it's just—I've been walking on the beach, thinking. You're going to miss this place, aren't you?"

Down near the boardwalk, I can see the late-afternoon skaters and joggers. Always something going on. "I suppose. What were you thinking about?"

"That we're not seeing enough of each other."

I start to speak, but she cuts me off. "I know, it's me,

law school, I'm always trying to catch up." She takes my hand in hers, meets my eyes with a level gaze. "Move in with me."

"No."

"No, just like that."

I see the hurt in her eyes. "No, not just like that, but I'm not ready to jump into a situation forced upon us because I have to move. You're busy with classes, I'd just be a distraction, and I don't want that."

"Maybe you need a distraction."

"That's why I'm going to Las Vegas."

Natalie sighs and shakes her head. She knows me well enough not to push this discussion any further. "Okay," she says, "but while you're hanging out in Vegas with Ace, think about it, okay?"

"Okay, I'll think about it. How much time have you got?"

The mischief returns in her smile. "I don't have a class until eight."

"Tonight?"

"No, silly, in the morning."

INTERLUDE
June 25, 1956

Rᴵᴄʜɪᴇ Pᴏᴡᴇʟʟ, Bᴜᴅ'ꜱ ʙᴇʙᴏᴘ ʙʀᴏᴛʜᴇʀ, ᴄᴀʟʟᴇᴅ ꜰʀᴏᴍ up front. "Brownie, you awake, man?"

Clifford Brown opened one eye and moved his hand to the trumpet case on the seat beside him, slowly becoming aware of his surroundings, the warm, humid air blowing in the window, the car radio playing some big band. "Yeah, I am now," he said, pulling himself upright.

He leaned forward, resting his arms on the front seat, and peered out the windshield at the darkening sky. He followed the patches of blue for a few moments as they tried to outrun the somber dark clouds that seemed to keep up with the speed of the new Buick. He checked the speedometer. The needle on the dial hovered around sixty. "Where are we, man?"

"Few hours out of Philly," said Richie Powell. "You hungry?" He barely turned his head, knowing how prudently Brownie liked him to drive, heedful always of Brownie's concern. "I don't want you drivin' like you play piano," Brownie often said.

Car accidents were always on Clifford's mind when

they were on the road so much. He either drove himself or slept as much as he could, letting the hum of the
tires on the highway, the drone of the engine, act as
relaxers. As long as his eyes were closed, he felt like
everything was okay.

He wished now they were still in California with
LaRue and Clifford Jr., but the road was reality if they
wanted to keep this band together. Like Max always
said, "We gotta go where the gigs are, Brownie." Chicago was next. Harold Land was gone, but they had
Sonny Rollins now on tenor.

"Yeah, I could eat something. We got time?" He
leaned back in the seat again and rolled down the window, taking in the early summer air that smelled of
rain.

"Oh yeah," Richie said. "We got us plenty of time."

"So let's stop. Wake your old lady up," Brownie
said, tapping Richie's wife, Nancy, on the shoulder.
She was slumped against the window, still sound
asleep.

Brownie rubbed the sleep from his own eyes and
leaned back against the seat, thinking about the Philly
gig at the music store. It was to be kind of a homecoming for him. Just a jam session really, playing with some
of the old guys, seeing some friends. Art Blakey, his old
boss from the Jazz Messengers, had promised to drop
by. Then on to Chicago, meet up with Max, Sonny,
and George for the gig there, and another triumph.

He opened the trumpet case on the seat, took out
his horn, and blew silently into it, fingering a solo to
the tune on the car radio. He caught Richie watching
him in the rearview mirror, a slight smile on his lips,
shaking his head. He knew what Richie was thinking.
You practice even when you don't practice.

Well, that's the only way he knew how to do it. It's what had brought him back from the first accident. Almost a year during which no one thought he'd live, much less ever play again. But here he was, coleader of the Clifford Brown—Max Roach Quintet, hottest group in jazz, and he was only twenty-five. Whatta those doctors think about that shit? Dizzy knew. He'd come to visit Clifford many times in the hospital. Yes sir, Clifford Brown had come back. To Lionel Hampton, Tadd Dameron, Art Blakey, and finally to Max. But long drives still unnerved him, at times filled him with dread. He promised himself someday he'd travel on planes all the time, first class. No more of these car rides. He glanced out the window at the landscape rushing by.

There were so many things he wanted to do. He and Quincy Jones had talked about it a lot. Not just the music, but the business as well. Someday they would do it all, arranging, composing, movie sound tracks.

He ran his fingers over the trumpet. There were a couple of small dents, but this horn he'd never give up, even if he was picking up some brand-new ones, specially designed for him at the Conn factory in Elkhart.

He knew from the night Miles played "My Funny Valentine" on his trumpet—maybe that's why he'd never give it up—that it wasn't the horn. Miles, walking right in on his gig in the middle of a fast blues, rain dripping off his head, so high he'd hardly been able to stand up, but he'd put his mouthpiece in Brownie's horn and made everybody cry.

Brownie shook his head, thinking about that night. Damn, if Miles ever straightened up, what could he do? And Sonny Rollins was another one, but he'd been on Sonny, trying to convince him he didn't need that shit.

Brownie had never needed it. The music was enough for him.

His eye caught a sign flashing by. "Turn on your lights, Richie," he said, aware now of twilight settling around the big car like sheer black cloth. "Let's try that diner up ahead."

"I'm cool with that. Come on, Nancy, we got to eat. Get yourself together," Richie said to his wife.

Clifford Brown put his horn back in its case, nodded, let his thoughts take him to other places. Yeah, everything was cool.

He felt the tension begin to slide out of his body as the car began to slow.

CHAPTER
TWO

WHEN I WAKE UP, NATALIE IS GONE—BACK TO CLASS, the books, study groups, finding out if being a lawyer is better than being a cop. I lie in bed, slightly disoriented, trying to decide if I really want to get up and drive to Las Vegas. It's not too late, I could always call Ace and tell him I've changed my mind, but I've done too much of that lately.

For weeks I've been unfocused, lethargic, unable to dredge up much enthusiasm for anything as I try to come to terms with the most recent development in the continuing saga of being a one-handed piano player.

No. Las Vegas will give me time to think about what I'm going to do next, and besides, this might be a good time to get out of L.A. The O.J. Simpson trial starts tomorrow. I throw off the covers and hit the shower. If I get going, there won't be time to change my mind.

There are two ways out of Los Angeles if you're driving to Las Vegas. Interstate 10 through downtown and the industrial areas of Santa Ana, Carson, toward San Bernardino until the connection with I-15. The alternate route is straight up the 405 toward Palmdale, and the Pearblossom Highway, a two-lane strip full of curves, dips, and bumps that make it seem like a mini-roller coaster. Some of the dips are so deep that cars disappear for a few seconds, and that's just when some-one decides to pass. I won't drive it at night. Eventually it deposits you at Victorville and a more northerly con-nection to I-15. It's a roundabout route, but somehow it makes the trek into Las Vegas seem shorter.

I like to drive alone, leave when I'm ready, take whatever route comes to mind, stop when I feel like it. With one small bag and a box of cassette tapes in the car, I decide to avoid downtown and go the desert route. I'm curious to see how the Camaro handles Pearblossom.

I wait for the morning rush to be over before I ven-ture out after breakfast. By the time I hit the foothills in the north end of the San Fernando Valley, the traffic is light. The Camaro seems more than willing to hit the open road. I take the Palmdale cutoff. Pearblossom awaits.

Clifford Brown keeps me company on the tape deck. It's been a while since I've listened to him carefully, but if I'm going to make some kind of educated guess with this tape Ace had, I'd better bone up. I'm amazed at the sophistication of Brownie's playing at such a young age, and automatically compare it with my own at that age. Not a chance. Brownie already has virtuoso tech-nique, amazing ideas, and a sound as pure and clean as a snowflake. For once, the critics are right. Brownie's style harkens back to Fats Navarro and can easily be traced right through Lee Morgan, Freddie Hubbard, and Wynton Marsalis.

"Blues Walk" is playing as I come into the first sec-tion of the rolling Pearblossom Highway. Passing trucks and motor homes is a breeze. The Camaro seems to have its own mind as I bear down on Victorville with the sun starting its descent behind me. The gas gauge looks fine, so I make the looping turn onto 15 and merge with the traffic bound for Barstow.

I put a new tape in the machine, Brownie with some guys from Philadelphia, all of them trying hard to keep up, but Brownie blazing the trail for any of them to follow if they dare. I've read the notes and learned that three of the tracks were done the night before he was killed. What would any of them have thought if they'd known this was Clifford Brown's last night on earth?

They do "Walkin'" and "Cherokee" at an even faster clip, performances that must have left the audience breathless. I'd heard somewhere that Brownie's motto was, Play every time like it's your last. Well, he did, certainly on this cut. I play both sides of the tape, getting the sound of Brownie's trumpet in my head.

Halfway between Barstow and Baker, something catches my eye in the center median, a flash of color in the otherwise drab sand and brush. I check the rearview mirror, pull over into the far right emergency stop lane, and reverse, checking the oncoming traffic and searching the median. Another couple of hundred yards and I spot it.

I turn on the flashers and get out of the car while Vegas-bound traffic whizzes by me. It takes a minute or two, but I finally find an opening and dash across the highway to the median.

In a carefully cleared-away area is an arrangement of flowers, fresh enough to have been placed there today. There's a crude cross—two sticks bound together with string—stuck in the ground, a pitiful marker left by a loved one.

Somebody was killed on this spot. A tourist, headed for a good time in Las Vegas, or just a business trip to Barstow? In all the times I've driven to Las Vegas I've never seen anything like this. There's no name, just the flowers and cross.

Sobered by this discovery, I keep the Camaro in check. By the time I reach Baker through this seemingly endless desert and mountainous terrain, I'm ready to stop, stretch, and get something to eat.

Baker boasts the world's tallest thermometer. It juts up from the desert floor so high you can read it from the freeway. I take the main exit and cruise along the frontage road, which houses a collection of gas stations, fast food places, convenience stores, and a couple of real restaurants. What do people do in Baker? I wonder as I pull in for gas. I think about asking if anyone here knows who the flowers are for.

"Nice wheels," a kid in work pants, boots, and dirty T-shirt says as he takes my credit card. He walks around the car, taking in the new paint, wide tires, and low-slung body. "Had it long?"

"About two weeks." I sign the credit card slip and move off slowly. I can see in the rearview mirror he's still watching me.

After some coffee and a sandwich at Bun Boy, I make my way back to 15 for the long climb to Halloran Summit. Semis lumber up the slow lane, spewing exhaust, while newer, faster cars than mine hum past me silently, unhampered by the steep grade. I feel like I'm in a plane as I start down the other side. Probably ten miles or so ahead, I can make out the hotels and casinos at the Nevada state line. The barrenness of the desert is never more awe-inspiring than after the urban sprawl of Los Angeles.

I have one more tape of Clifford Brown with Art Blakey's Jazz Messengers, his last gig before teaming up with Max Roach, and even there Brownie is a standout. Anyone remotely interested in jazz has to wonder about the loss of so many musicians at such young ages. The bassist Scott LaFaro, who made all those great recordings with Bill Evans, also killed in a car accident at twenty-five. Dave Lambert, one third of Lambert, Hendricks, and Ross, hit by a truck one rainy night while changing a tire. Add the drug and alcohol deaths, and the count is devastating. Dizzy was right. Bebop is serious music, and people have died for it.

As the last strains of "Jordu" fade, I have Las Vegas in view. The incongruous pyramid of the Luxor Hotel shoots up out of the desert but seems out of place by several thousand miles. Just past Blue Diamond, with the lights of the hotels casting a neon glow over the desert, the freeway becomes clogged with evening rush-hour traffic. I exit at Flamingo and follow the familiar route to Ace Buffington's home in Spring Valley. Just over five hours if you don't count the stop at Baker.

I pull in the driveway and catch Ace waving from the door. He's in his between-semester uniform—baggy dark blue sweats, tennis shoes that were once white, and a KUNV baseball cap.

"Hey, I'm impressed," Ace says, walking around the Camaro. "I guess you won't be needing the VW. This is really nice. Reminds me of my high school hot rod days."

"How you doin', Ace?"

"Dr. Charles I'm-a-full-professor Buffington, at your service." He pulls himself to attention.

"Hey, that's right. Congratulations." No matter what happens with the tape, I'm glad I've come.

"Thanks," Ace says. "Come on, grab your stuff. I've got a couple of cold Henry Weinhards. You probably need one after the desert."

We go inside. Nothing has changed since I was here last, and Ace has my guest-house apartment all ready. It's just cold enough for a fire. Ace gets one blazing while I quench my thirst with a beer and wander around the house. There is still evidence of Janey, Ace's wife, in photos on the piano, but Ace seems to be adjusting okay.

Over our second beer, I fill him in on the latest medical report.

"Oh, I'm really sorry, Evan. What are you going to do?"

Ace doesn't even flinch as I light a cigarette. Good question. I can't practice now, at least for a while, until the muscles are rested. Then I have to take it very slow. "Frankly, Ace, I've run out of options."

"I know what you mean. Hey, it'll work out. How's that cop friend of yours?"

"Danny Cooper? Fine, still keeping Santa Monica safe."

"And Natalie?" His eyes are twinkling.

"She's fine too, and no, we're not getting married, so just relax."

He puts up his hands. "Okay, okay, just checking." He stands up suddenly. "I almost forgot. Got something to show you." He goes in his office and comes back with a book. "How about that?"

It's a blue paperback. Printed on the top are the words

Advance Uncorrected Proofs
Death of a Tenor Man
Dr. Charles Buffington

"This is great, Ace. When do you get the real thing?" I flip through the pages.

"Couple of months. Look at the acknowledgments, right there, just after the title page."

I turn to the page and see:

> For my good friend Evan Horne,
> without whose assistance this book
> could not have been written.

I look up and see Ace beaming at me. "How about that, huh?"

"That's really nice, it really is. You must be very proud. How is the department taking all this?"

Ace's smile turns to a frown. "About the way you'd expect. I thought I knew academics, but this crew—" He shakes his head in disgust. "I got an advance copy of the cover, put it up on the department bulletin board. Gone the next day, just disappeared."

"You're kidding."

"No, I'm not. Bastards. I gave a reading, and the department members, except for a few close friends who are enjoying me sticking it to them, were conspicuously absent, including the chair."

"Well, they can't take this away from you, Ace. Fuck them."

"My sentiments exactly." Ace drains his beer and sets the bottle down. "You're hungry, I hope. I've got one of my special casseroles in the oven, and a nice bottle of red to go with it."

"Sounds good to me."

Over dinner we get around to what Ace calls my "mission." "It's really nothing," Ace insists, but I still have the feeling he hasn't told me everything. "This guy will play a tape for you, and all you have to do is tell him your best-educated professional-jazz-musician opinion whether or not it's Clifford Brown."

"Like a blindfold test?"

"A what?"

"Blindfold test. Leonard Feather used to do them for *Downbeat* magazine. Get some famous musicians, play various selections, and see if they could identify the players."

"Right, only all you have to do is confirm it's Clifford Brown."

True, I think, but in many of the blindfold tests I've read, some awful mistakes have been made by famous musicians.

Ace gets up to get us both coffee. I light a cigarette and think about that. "This friend of yours, he's sure it's Brown on the tape?"

"Well, yeah, of course. He just wants confirmation."

"Based on what? Is this guy a musician? By the way, who is this guy?"

"A musician? God, no. He doesn't care whether or not it's jazz or R&B. If it's valuable, he wants it." Ace pauses before looking at me again. "I can't tell you who he is."

"Why not?"

"Because I don't know."

"You don't know?"

"Look, Evan, these are very serious collectors. They're obsessed, paranoid, highly secretive. If this *is*

Clifford Brown, they could be very valuable tapes, right?"

"Of course. I know the immediate market would be every trumpet player in the world. Clifford didn't record very much."

"Exactly, so you can see the need for security."

"Security? What do you mean?" Here it comes, the part Ace hasn't told me.

"I can't tell you who it is because I don't know. This is all through my partner, who is also very secretive. Look, I've got a fair collection, everything back to some ten-inch acetates, but I'm an amateur compared to these guys. Everything is dependent upon secrecy. They don't want word to get out that this even *might* be Clifford Brown until they get absolute verification."

"Depends on how it's put."

"How what's put?"

"You remember the Howard Hughes scam? The writer Clifford Irving had a publisher believing he was meeting with Hughes, doing a biography. When they finally demanded a sample of Hughes's writing, Irving thought it was all over. The publisher hired some handwriting experts and said, 'We have no doubt that this is Hughes, and we want you to confirm that.' "

Ace suddenly gets it. "Oh, I see, if they had said, 'We don't believe for a minute this is Hughes,' that's what the experts would have confirmed. Psychological edge, yes, I see."

"Exactly. Okay, I'm supposed to be objective in this, so this mystery man will simply play me the tape, and I tell him yes or no. This will only be my opinion. I don't want whatever deal they try for to be dependent on my opinion."

"Essentially that's it. We pay your expenses here and five hundred dollars."

I watch Ace carefully. Something is still not right. "What else, Ace? You're still not telling me everything."

"Well, as I mentioned, there is the security thing."

"What security thing?"

"You'll be picked up by someone and taken—" Ace starts laughing.

"What's funny?"

"Nothing, just that you mentioned a blindfold test."

"And?"

"You won't know where you're going until you get there."

"Why won't I know?"

"They'll probably blindfold you."

Despite Ace's assurances that the blindfolding is merely a formality, I realize I have a lot to learn about record collectors and the lengths they will go to. Of course, if this tape I'm to verify really is of Clifford Brown, it will be worth a great deal of money. Because of his early death, Brown's recorded legacy is relatively small. The discovery of new recordings will set the jazz world on fire.

To relax me, Ace suggests we take in some live music at the Riviera, one of the new Las Vegas jazz venues, but I'm not so sure I want to go nightclubbing.

"C'mon," Ace says. "Don Menza is there with a quartet, and his guest tonight is Cedar Walton. You can go from there to the meeting. I'll call them from the Riv for the location."

"This is sounding more like a James Bond deal all the time."

"Stop worrying," Ace says. "This will be a piece of cake. What could go wrong?"

We get to the Riviera after nine. Menza and company are already under way, and Cedar Walton is given plenty of solo space. An alumni of the Jazz Messengers, Walton is playing better than ever, the crowd is appreciative, and there are a number of musicians I recognize in the audience.

"Pappy Dean ever come by here?"

"I've never seen him," Ace says. "The last time I talked to him he and Louise were doing just fine."

"What does Alan Grant think of this?" I ask indicating the stage. Menza, a fiery tenor player, has just ripped off several choruses of "Just Friends" and managed to play several hundred notes in the process.

Ace shrugs. "This has been going on for some time, but I gather it hasn't affected Grant's thing at the Four Queens." Ace looks at his watch. "Back in a minute. I've got to make that call."

I listen to the rest of the set, and then a guy who introduces himself as a KUNV DJ takes the stage to introduce the players and tell us about next week's attraction.

"I'm Don Gordon, thanks for coming to Jazz on the Strip."

As the curtain drops, Ace slides into the booth next to me. "Okay, we're all set. They want you to meet at a place called the Inn Zone. It's over on Decatur and Flamingo. Easy to find."

"Will you be blindfolded too?"

"Me? No," Ace says. He looks a little sheepish. "Didn't I tell you? You're going alone."

CHAPTER
THREE

THE INN ZONE, AS ACE TELLS ME, IS A SPORTS BAR. Pulling into the parking lot a few minutes after eleven, I park and go inside, feeling a little silly when I remind myself this is all only to listen to a tape that might possibly be Clifford Brown. Jazz at midnight.

Straight ahead, there are a few people at the bar nursing drinks, playing video poker machines, and glancing up occasionally at the TVs situated all over the bar and in the walled-off dining area to the left. A couple of pool tables take up the right side of the room. The balls are racked, but nobody's playing.

I take a booth facing the door, order some coffee from a waitress who seems surprised to find someone in the dining area, and watch the silent television screen, which is showing a rerun of a Lakers game. I don't see any record collector types around, but Ace assured me they would find me.

About eleven-thirty, a guy who looks like he might be an accountant walks in, takes one quick look around, and comes directly to my table. He's got short brown hair, combed straight back, and wears baggy slacks, a white shirt, and thick glasses. I figure him for mid- to late forties.

"I'm Ken," he says, sliding into the booth. He grabs one of the plastic menus and signals the waitress, a blond with a curly perm. She refills my coffee and takes his order for a draft beer and a basket of chicken fingers.

"Mild, medium, or hot?" she asks, popping gum and scribbling on a pad.

"Medium," Ken says quietly, turning his attention to me after she's gone.

"I trust you had a good trip from L.A."

"Yeah, fine. I trust you're sure I'm Evan Horne."

"I wouldn't be here if I didn't. Charles described you very well." Ken's eyes are all over the bar, as if he's looking for someone. "You'll have to leave your car here, but we'll bring you back. I hope that's not too inconvenient. We do appreciate you doing this. It's very important, you know." Ken has suddenly become very earnest.

The waitress returns with Ken's order, and I watch him wolf down a basket of fries and fingers, dripping with grease. He carefully dips the last piece in a plastic container of ranch dressing, licks his fingers, and shoves the basket aside. He glances at his watch. "Well, shall we go?"

"Fine," I say, getting up.

Ken pays the check, and we go outside. There are only a few cars in the parking lot. He takes me to a dark green Buick in the far end of the lot. A few feet from the car, another man gets out, but I don't get a good look at him.

"Wait here," Ken says.

I watch the two of them confer briefly, then Ken

opens the back door and motions me inside. I slide over, and he joins me in the backseat. The driver never looks back but hands something over the seat to Ken. It's a black sleep mask with an elastic band. "I'm sure this was explained to you," Ken says. "Would you please put this on?"

I do, and only then does the driver start the car. Ken checks the fit. I assure him I can't see, and we're off. I feel ridiculous sitting in the backseat with a Lone Ranger mask on and wonder what anyone would think if they looked inside the car.

For something to do, I try to keep track of the number of turns the car takes, but I lose count and realize the driver may be trying to confuse me. Ace was right, these guys are really serious. I estimate about a fifteen-minute drive before the car slows and stops. All I recognize is the sound of gravel crunching under the tires.

Ken opens the door and takes my arm. "Watch your head," he says as I get out.

He shuts the door and leads me by the arm. We stop, and he evidently presses some kind of doorbell. A few seconds later I hear the car start and drive away. There's a buzzing sound, and the gate or whatever it is clicks open.

"This way," Ken says. We walk maybe twenty or thirty feet, then up several steps. A door must already be open, because we go right inside.

"Hello, Mr. Horne," a voice says from my left. I cock my head in that direction. The voice is friendly, well modulated, and much lower pitched than Ken's.

"Hi. Nice to meet you."

The stranger laughs slightly. "My name is Cross. We're going to go down some stairs."

With Ken still holding my arm, we walk a few more

steps, and then come the stairs. I've counted twenty when Ken says, "Just to your left." A few more feet, and we stop. Ken removes the mask. "You can just sit right there."

I'm in front of a black leather couch that faces dual reel-to-reel tape decks and two large speakers. There are some other chairs and a couple of lamps. Cross, if that's really his name, the man who greeted me, goes to the tape deck, puts on headphones, and listens for a moment. He rewinds the tape, takes off the phones, and looks in my direction.

The lighting is very dim—one desk lamp aimed at the tape deck, casting shadows over the rest of the room. I can't make out the man's features clearly. I wonder if it's deliberate or simply a trick of the shadows playing around his face.

Cross is taller and heavier than Ken; he wears a sweater and slacks and some kind of boots. He too wears glasses, thicker than Ken's, that glint off the light from the tape decks, and his dark wavy hair is parted on one side. His face never comes into focus. I can see his jaw moving as he chews on something—gum, breath mints, or antacid tablets.

"Please forgive all the what must seem to you unnecessary precautions, Mr. Horne," Cross says, "but this is a very important project. Now, if you're comfortable, we can begin and get you home quickly. Can we get you anything—a drink?"

"No, I'm fine. Is it all right if I smoke?"

He glances at Ken, who nods approval. Ken brings an ashtray and sets it on the coffee table in front of me. I take out my cigarettes, light one, and say, "Okay, I'm ready, but there's just one thing."

"Yes?" I feel Ken tense beside me.

"I want you to understand this will be just my opinion. I'm not a trumpet player."

"Of course. I appreciate that," Cross says.

I find myself trying to memorize the room, wanting to savor the moment, like some game show contestant about to choose Door Number Two. I realize I might be among the first to hear some previously unknown recordings of one of the great jazz-trumpet players.

Besides the tape decks, floor-to-ceiling racks of records, tapes, videos, and books cover the two adjoining walls. I'm sure I'll never be back to this place, and I remind myself I wouldn't be here now without Ace's okay. But these guys are creepy.

Cross presses the play button. There are a few seconds of hiss as the tape begins to roll, then music. An eight-bar drum solo comes on first, mostly hi-hat cymbals that are soon joined by bass and piano in two choruses of a blues tune.

The great jazz players all have a very strong identifiable sound, usually a combination of tone and technique. Max Roach is no exception. He's known for his melodic solos and also for the tightly tuned, high-pitched tom-tom sound that is so much his trademark.

At the beginning of the third chorus the trumpet enters like a crackling brushfire sweeping down a hillside. I can't help but feel elated. The trumpet player sounds so much like Clifford Brown it's uncanny. Within eight bars, I'm sure it's him. He plays the line, then solos for four choruses. The technique, the ideas, the sound, everything is there. He roars through the changes, leaving ashes in his wake.

Next, the piano solos for a couple of choruses, but it doesn't sound like Richie Powell. Competent, but no match for the smoking trumpet. The bass is muddy;

simple lines that a modern bass player would not play. He walks for a while, then there are some four-bar exchanges with trumpet and drums.

It sounds like Brownie, but the drums definitely aren't Max Roach. It's just not his sound, unless Max is playing on a borrowed set. The drums are much lower pitched than the way Max was always recorded, and the cymbals are cloudy, not the high, bright tones I'm looking for. I can't tell if it's the recording quality or not.

The whole band plays the line again twice and ends it short, as was the style in the fifties. The entire cut is probably not more than four minutes, but it's enough for me. I lean back on the couch and close my eyes, hearing that sound in my head.

Ken walks over and hits the stop button. Both men look at me expectantly. "Well, Mr. Horne, what do you say?" Ken says.

I stub out my cigarette in the glass ashtray. "If that's not Clifford Brown it's his double, somebody who can really imitate him, and I don't think that's possible."

Ken and Cross glance at each other and breathe an almost imperceptible sigh, but I sense some kind of tension between the two men.

"You're sure?" Ken says.

"Well, you want my opinion, I'd say yes, absolutely. Can I hear some more?"

They exchange glances again. "Of course," Cross says.

Cross presses the play button again, and for nearly an hour, I'm listening to Clifford Brown in full flight. The big, fat, buttery sound, clean lines, awesome technique, and breathtaking emotion make your hair stand on end. I'm just as convinced, however, that it's not

Max Roach on drums, and it's certainly not Richie Powell on piano. But for my money, it's definitely Brownie.

When the tape ends, I stand up and stretch. "Could I get a drink of water or a Coke?" I ask.

"Of course," Ken says. I hear him go upstairs while Cross rewinds the tape. I wonder what's happened to the driver.

My mind is racing with questions. Where and when were these tapes done? Where did Ken and Cross get them, and what are they going to do with them? But Ken, when he returns with a soft drink in a can, won't say a word.

"Obviously, at this stage we can't reveal any of that, Mr. Horne. I'm sure you understand, perhaps better than we do, the value of these tapes. Record collectors are a very competitive breed, and record companies very careful. We want to be first with this find."

"You mean there are more?"

"Oh yes. We have two all together."

I sit back and let that sink in. Two tapes. Enough for a multi-CD package that is going to make these people a lot of money. These are probably master tapes, previously undiscovered, unreleased—who knows, maybe just misfiled and found now. Clifford Brown. Any record company would drool over these.

"So is that all?"

"No, we'd like you to listen to the other tape as well, or at least some of it."

It's much the same, and nothing I hear makes me think anything different. There are standards, blues, and some tunes I don't recognize, but it's all the same band, and it's all Clifford Brown. The sound of his trumpet echoes in my head even when the tape comes to an end. I stand up and look at my watch.

"Well, congratulations, you've got quite a find here."

Cross rewinds the last tape but leaves it on the machine. The other one he carefully places back in one of the tape boxes.

"There's one other thing," Ken says. "Something we'd like to show you."

Ken and Cross exchange that look again. It's something I can't quite read, as if Ken looks to Cross for approval of everything.

Ken says, "There's a trumpet."

"A trumpet?"

"Yes. Would you like to see it?"

I sit down again as Ken sets a case on the table in front of me. It's scarred and battered, a light gray with black piping. Some of the fiber threads are hanging loose, and there are a few gouges in the finish, as if it's been dropped or scraped or shoved into the corner of a car trunk hundreds of times.

I don't know what I expected to see. A shiny horn in red velvet? Not this one. When I open the case, a pungent odor drifts out. The case reeks with gasoline or kerosene. I take out the horn, turn it over, and look at it from every angle. The metal has oxidized, and there are a couple of small dents near the bell.

Inside, I can make out the initials *C.B.* etched into the metal in some kind of fancy script. The valves are sticky but they work, and the mouthpiece is missing, but sometimes trumpet players keep that separate or carry it around in their pocket. A very old trumpet that hasn't been played in years. I set it back in the case and close it, shaking my head.

"Are you saying this is Clifford Brown's trumpet? This is unbelievable," I say, looking from Ken to Cross. I don't know if it's really Brownie's horn. I'm certainly no expert on that, and I don't know if his initials were engraved on his horns, although I remember a story about him picking up some new ones before his last gig.

Ken can't help but smile as he removes the case and confers again with Cross, then comes back over to stand by me.

"Would you excuse us for a few minutes, Mr. Horne? We have something to discuss briefly, something concerning your fee, if you don't mind. Then we'll take you back to your car."

"The fee? I thought that was decided on already. My friend—"

Ken smiles reassuringly. "Nothing to worry about. We're talking about a bonus. We're not easily fooled, Mr. Horne, and we don't think you are either. If in fact these tapes—and the horn—are indeed genuine, we would naturally want to reward you for your expert opinion. At the least your fee would be doubled. Now, if you will come with me, please?"

I'm not happy about this part, but I can see at least from Ken's expression—I still haven't seen Cross clearly—that they're not kidding.

I suddenly flash on them not letting me go, keeping me here until they make a deal, something I hadn't thought about because I guess I really didn't expect these tapes to be the real thing. From their point of view, I could be a liability now, but I reason that Ace must have vouched for my integrity. Still, something tells me I should just leave now. I never did listen to myself well enough.

Ken leads me off to another room, adjacent to the tape room. "We won't be long." He crosses the room and turns on a small TV.

He shuts the door behind him. I sit down, staring absently at the television, amazed at the music I've just heard. A few more minutes pass before I look at my watch. I get up and roam around the room restlessly, wondering what's taking so long. I'm ready to get out of here, go back to Ace's, and crash.

Over the sound of the TV, I hear voices from the other room. Ken and Cross and someone else I don't recognize. The driver? I turn the sound down on the TV and listen at the door. I can't hear what they're saying, but one voice is louder than the others and it's clear they're arguing about something.

"Listen!" one of them shouts. Cross? Then one of the tapes begins playing, much louder than before. All the voices get jumbled and lost in the music, then silence except for the tape. I try the door. It's locked. Then, two other sounds, clearly audible: a shout and some kind of banging noise on the floor.

And more sounds: too much like gunshots.

I reach for the doorknob and twist. "Hey, what's going on?" I rattle the door, then hear the lock click, and suddenly the door crashes back on me, knocking me down. I turn and glimpse a face just as something cracks down on my head. I'm not out entirely, but there are points of light before my eyes as I get to my hands and knees. When I touch my head I feel blood, and from somewhere in the distance I hear a car start and drive off.

I get to my feet slowly, feeling a little dizzy. I go in the other room, heart pounding, adrenaline pumping. The Clifford Brown tape is still playing full-blast. Ken is sprawled on the floor, his arms spread out, his white shirt soaked crimson, and his glasses askew on his head. I check for a pulse and hear him moan slightly.

"Hang on, I'll call nine-one-one."

Now what? I look around for a phone, but there's not one down here. I run upstairs, only now aware of the size of this house. At the top of the stairs there's a small table with a phone on it. I grab for it, hit the three buttons.

"Emergency services," a female voice says.

"I need help, and an ambulance. A man's been shot."

"Is he still conscious?"

"What? Yes, he was a minute ago."

"What is your name, sir?" Same calm voice.

"There's no time for this. He's hurt bad."

"Where are you, please?"

I suddenly realize I have no idea, and there's no number on the phone. "Hang on."

I drop the phone and run out the front door. The yard is bathed in light, surrounded by white wrought-iron fencing. I look above the door, on the gate, but I can't see any numbers. Doesn't matter, I don't know the street. I throw open the gate. We're two houses from the corner. I run down and check the street signs, but it looks like I'm in some kind of compound, one of those walled housing estates. I can see a sign, Rancho Bonito, lit on a white wall that opens into the street.

I sprint back to the house and grab the phone. "Rancho Bonito, I think west of Decatur."

"We're responding now," the voice says.

I slam down the phone and rush back down the stairs two at a time. Ken hasn't moved. I check his pulse again. Nothing. The music is still playing. I go to the tape player, press the button, and glance around for the other tape box, but it's gone. My foot bangs into the trumpet case in front of one of the speakers, right where Ken had put it after showing it to me.

For a moment I blank. I just have my hand on it when I hear a car skid to a stop outside. There was no siren, but I think I know who it is and why he's back.

I grab the trumpet case and duck back into the room I was in before. No place to hide here, but there's a window high up on the wall. I get it open, knock out the screen with the trumpet case. I throw the case out, drag a chair over, boost myself up, and crawl through the window. I'm on the side of the house, near a three-car garage. Still carrying the case, I run for the back of the house.

Seconds later, I freeze. Sirens, and they're getting louder.

Somebody else has heard them too. I hear a car start and roar off, then the sirens are louder and I see the glow of spinning red-and-blue lights. Above me, the drone of a helicopter, its spotlight sweeping toward the house.

Why, I don't know, but I drop the trumpet case behind a hedge and walk toward the front of the house. Three black-and-whites with lights flashing are near the gate. "Over here," I yell, waving my arms over my head.

Two cops approach cautiously with drawn guns. The others crouch by their units.

"Put your hands where we can see them," one of the cops yells. Three flashlights blind me.

"I'm the one who called," I say, raising my hands.

"Down on the ground. Do it now!"

I stretch out on the grass, and seconds later I'm on my knees and handcuffed.

Another car skids to a stop, and a man in jeans and a windbreaker walks over.

"What have we got here?" The voice is all too familiar. A few seconds later I'm looking at Detective John Trask, Las Vegas Metro Homicide.

CHAPTER
FOUR

"WHAT THE FUCK ARE YOU DOING HERE?" JOHN Trask doesn't look as if he's at all happy to see me back in Las Vegas.

"It's a long story," I say. My head is throbbing now. "There's a guy downstairs who's been shot."

"Check it out," Trask says to one of the uniformed cops, "and take the cuffs off him."

The paramedic truck has also arrived, and suddenly this quiet residential neighborhood is teeming with people and cars. Ken's neighbors, with the security of police now on the scene, have decided it's safe to venture out to see what's going on. One of the uniformed cops is putting up yellow crime-scene tape around the perimeter of the house; another is telling everyone to go back to bed.

"There's nothing to see here," he says. Of course— that's why there are three police cars with lights flashing, an ambulance, and at least one plainclothes detective among the officers milling around in the front yard.

As the paramedics rush past us, Trask says, "I hope you didn't touch anything."

"Just the phone," I say. "I need to sit down." I realize I've been running on adrenaline, and I'm coming down fast.

The paramedics are back up quickly. "What have we got?" Trask asks them.

"Dead, gunshot, looks like two bullets, close range," one of them says, walking slowly back to the truck. "I'll call for the coroner."

"How about him?" the other one says, nodding toward me as he notices the blood on my forehead.

"Yeah, check him out."

The medic kneels beside me. His black nameplate says Mike Daniels. He flips open a metal case and adds to the porch light with his own flash, shining it on top of my head. "Must have hit you pretty hard."

He dresses the wound with something that stings, but is very cool. He adds a soft bandage and tape. "You'll be okay. Any dizziness?" He shines the flash in my eyes.

"Not now."

"Do you want to go to the hospital?"

"No, I'm fine. I need to stay here."

"Okay. I'll need you to sign a release." He folds up his case and heads for his truck as Trask comes back.

"I need you to come with me," Trask says.

I feel drained now. Staying up half the night, being hit on the head, and having virtually witnessed a murder have left me bone-tired and slightly unsteady on my feet. I follow Trask back downstairs.

There are two uniformed cops near Ken's body. "Just wait right here," Trask says. I stare at Ken while someone takes flash pictures and Trask calls for the forensics team on his cell phone. Trask has me sit down on the couch; now it seems hours ago that I was just listening to music here.

"Tell me what you did here, and if you touched anything besides the phone upstairs."

I look around the room. "I don't know. This table, the Coke can." I glance at the tape deck. "The stop button. The tape was playing when I came out of the other room." I run everything down from the time I arrived.

"You were brought here blindfolded?" Trask is incredulous. "That's going to help a lot on the other guy's car."

"I know, it sounds silly."

"Silly?" Trask says, looking at Ken's body. "Does that look silly to you?"

I explain the rest, but Trask wants to hear it from the beginning. "Can we go upstairs?" I ask, wanting to get as far away from Ken as possible.

We go back up to the sparsely furnished living room–dining area, just off the main hall, and sit down at a large oak table. "Now, let's start again. Why are you here?" Trask asks. He flips open a notebook and begins to write.

I go over it all from Ace's first phone call Sunday morning, leaving out nothing except the trumpet case, which I assume is still outside behind the hedge. Trask's eyebrows go up when I mention Ace's name.

"Professor Buffington. Great. So these guys are record collectors? Jesus."

"Yeah. I was supposed to verify some tapes as being genuine."

"And did you?"

"Yeah, well, I think so. That's when they made me wait in the other room."

"Why?"

"I don't know. They said it had something to do with my fee."

"Your fee? You do this professionally? I thought you were a piano player."

"I am—I mean I was—I'm not playing now. This was just a one-time thing."

"Okay, we'll come back to that," Trask says. "You say they were arguing? Ken and the other guy? Could you hear what they were saying?"

"Not really. The door was shut, and the music was playing loudly."

"And then you heard the shots."

"Right."

"And you didn't get a good look at the guy who shot—Ken, what's his last name?" Trask flips through the pages of his notebook.

"I don't know."

"You don't know." Trask sighs in frustration. "You let somebody bring you to his house blindfolded, and you don't know his name. Is this his house?"

"I don't know. Probably. Professor Buffington probably knows."

"All right," Trask says. "I'm going to want to talk to him too."

"I'll call him."

"Do that," Trask says. He flips his notebook closed. "Tell him to meet us down at Metro."

Trask goes back downstairs, following the forensics crew, who have just arrived and are pulling on latex gloves. I dial Ace's number, not surprised when he answers on the first ring.

"Evan? Where are you? I thought you'd be back hours ago."

"Just listen, Ace. There's been a problem. Ken is dead, he's been shot. I'll explain everything when I see you. Get right down to Metro. Lieutenant Trask wants to talk to you, and I hope you have some answers for me too."

There's a long pause. "Oh, my God. Ken dead. Of course, see you there."

I hang up the phone as two guys carry Ken out in a black bag, Trask close behind. Through the front door I can see a small crowd behind the police tape; the first light of dawn is fighting for dominance with the street and house lights.

"All right, let's go," Trask says to me. "My crew will be a while down there."

"Wait a minute—the tape."

"What tape?" Trask stops, turns, and looks at me.

"On the machine. Clifford Brown. You should take it."

"Why?"

"Because that's what this is all about."

Riding in the front seat with Trask, I take very careful notice of the area as we drive away, memorizing street names and counting turns. I realize we're only about ten minutes from the Inn Zone. Working Las Vegas is up and clamoring for space on the clogged streets as Trask pulls onto the expressway for the ride downtown.

"Fuck this," he says, attaching a red light to the roof and barreling up the on-ramp. Despite the emergency light, we get tied up briefly at the I-15 interchange. When we pull into the parking lot at Metro and go upstairs, Ace is already there, eyes red, looking disheveled in jeans and a sweatshirt and tennis shoes, as if he hasn't slept much.

"Come with me," Trask says, pointing at Ace. We walk past a maze of desks manned by detectives, who glance up quickly from typewriters and telephones, and back to one of the interview rooms. "Have a seat," Trask says. "I'll be back in a minute. You guys want some coffee?"

We both nod yes and sit down at a gray table in two folding metal chairs. As soon as the door is closed, Ace starts in.

"Evan, what happened? This is crazy. You say Ken was shot?"

"Ace, I hope you've got some answers. Trask is going to want to know everything, and so am I. Who were those guys?"

"Ken Perkins, he was the one who was shot. My God, he's dead?" Ace doesn't wait for my answer. "The other one, he's the one who had the tapes, is from out of town, made the initial contact with Ken. I don't know his name. Ken wouldn't tell me, just that he was a major collector." Ace looks at me. "You've got to believe me, Evan. I had no idea something like this—"

He doesn't finish the sentence. The door opens, and Trask comes in, carrying two coffees in Styrofoam cups.

"All right, gentlemen, let's get to it," Trask says. Ace fills in the blanks in my story. Trask says little but makes a lot of notes while we sip coffee. Finally, he sits back in his chair and looks at us both.

"You're telling me that this is all because somebody found some tapes that might be of a trumpet player who was killed in a car crash in 1956? What is it with you and dead musicians, Horne?"

"I guess that's what we're telling you," Ace says, "although there was nothing suspicious about Clifford Brown's death."

"Well, we can all be grateful for that, can't we?"

"The point is," Ace says, "if they're genuine, these tapes would be worth a great deal of money."

Trask shakes his head. "No, the point is, someone has been murdered. Valuable to who?"

"Record companies, for one. You see Clifford Brown didn't record very much during his short lifetime, and—"

"Save the aesthetics and music history for one of your classes, Professor," Trask says. He shuts his notebook. "I'll need a full statement from both of you. Where are you staying, Horne?"

"With Ace."

"Okay," Trask says. "This is an ongoing murder investigation, Horne, so—you'll excuse the cliché, Professor—don't leave town."

Ace nods and looks sick. We give our statements separately to a police stenographer, a middle-aged woman wearing glasses on a chain, who types up my account of the shooting as if it's nothing more than a grocery list. It's nearly ten before we get out of there.

Trask is nowhere to be seen as we walk out past the detectives. He's probably back at the Perkins house. "I'll take you to your car," Ace says as we go back down to the parking lot and get in his red Jeep Cherokee. He drives in silence, his elbow on the window ledge, his hand cradling his forehead.

We go back north on I-15. In the distance, the mountains to the west are topped with snow, and heavy gray clouds hover around the peaks. Neither of us speaks until we get to the Inn Zone and pull around back, where the Camaro is still parked, apparently untouched.

"Evan," Ace says, as I get out of the car. "I'm so sorry about this. If I'd known—"

"Let's talk about it later, Ace." I slam the door of the Jeep and head for my car. All I want to do is sleep. As soon as it's dark I've got a trumpet to pick up.

I wake up disoriented. It's either early morning or twilight. The shadows that cast themselves around the patio doors are wide and dark. I look at my watch. Just after four. I sit up in bed suddenly, hoping for a moment I've dreamed everything, but when I switch on the radio and catch the tail end of a story about a shooting, I know I haven't.

I stand in the shower for several minutes, thinking about what's next. Call Natalie and Danny Cooper, maybe. I need some quick advice. I grab a pair of jeans, a T-shirt, and a dark sweater out of my bag, pull on some socks and running shoes, and go to the main house to look for Ace.

I find him at the kitchen table, staring out at the pool. It's covered with some kind of quilted plastic cover. A mug of coffee is beside him.

"Got some more of that?"

"Sure." Ace gets me coffee and takes a carton of half-and-half out of the refrigerator.

I sit down with him, fix my coffee, and light a cigarette. "We have to talk, Ace."

He nods. "I've been sitting here thinking about Ken," he says quietly.

"How well did you know him?"

"Not very well, really. We did a couple of deals together, some not especially valuable records." He looks up at me. "God, Evan, I was never in this for the money. It was the music I was interested in. You know that. You know what I've got in my collection. I was just excited that this might really be Clifford Brown."

"I know, Ace, I know. But Ken?"

Ace shrugs and shakes his head. "Ken was part of a very serious network of collectors. He was a very secretive guy, never talked about his finds, as he called them. But this deal, this was the most excited I've ever seen him." Ace gets up and pours us both more coffee, then stands leaning against the sink.

"What about this other guy? He seemed to be calling the shots."

Ace nods. "I guess he contacted Ken, told him about the tapes."

"And that's where I came in?"

"Right. I guess before they did anything more, they wanted to be reasonably sure that it was actually Clifford Brown on those tapes. Then they could estimate their worth, get the word out to collectors, or go directly to a record company." Ace stops and looks at me. "Was it Brownie?"

Was it, or did I just want it to be? To have something new of Clifford Brown out and available was an exciting prospect. "I'd have to say yes, it sure sounded like him to me. You think the other guy just wanted to cut Ken out of the deal, they argued, and it got out of hand?"

"Possibly. These guys are crazy," Ace says. "I guarantee you he wouldn't have cared about it for the music. It would be because it was a rare find and worth a lot of money."

"Suppose it is Clifford Brown on those tapes. How valuable would they be? Do you have any idea?"

Ace shrugs and begins to pace around the kitchen. "What if somebody found those stories Hemingway's wife lost in Paris, or some paintings by Georgia O'Keeffe no one knew about?" He stops and points his coffee cup at me. "They'd be worth a lot, enough—"

"To kill for."

"Yes," Ace says quietly. "With these guys, I think they would."

I think about that for a moment, letting it all sink in. Still, despite what Ace and I thought about jazz, Clifford Brown was not Ernest Hemingway or Georgia O'Keeffe, although at some point, if there's any justice, Louis Armstrong or Charlie Parker or Clifford Brown might be considered as important an artist.

"I know what you're thinking," Ace says, "but remember the discovery of the Charlie Parker tapes, the Dean Benedetti collection?"

"Vaguely. Wasn't he the guy who followed Bird around, recording him in clubs?"

Ace sits down again and assumes his professorial persona. "Dean Benedetti was an alto player, just like Bird, but he idolized him. Recorded him, got drugs for him. He made the recordings on metal-based disks and early paper tape, so the quality wasn't that good. Sometimes he ran the mike from the men's room at clubs. When Bird died, Benedetti drifted out of music altogether, left the tapes with his brother, and moved to Italy.

"He died two years later. His brother didn't do anything with the tapes until they came up in conversation with a writer in the early eighties. It was about 1988 that he started negotiating with some record companies and finally sold them to Mosaic Records."

"How good are they—the sound, I mean?"

"Not very," Ace says. "I read something about one of the sessions being done at the Onyx Club in New York. Benedetti had the recorder beneath the bandstand, directly under Max Roach's drums, but it didn't matter. He caught Bird when he was clean and playing well, even if he did virtually shut off the machine during the other solos. The point is, they were undiscovered tapes of Charlie Parker. I've got the set right there in the other room. You can listen to them if you like."

"So if these tapes are of Clifford Brown, with the better sound and all, they could be worth even more, right?"

"Exactly, and there's probably more we don't know about, because they didn't keep very good records of recording sessions in those days, and tapes get misplaced, misfiled."

Or sessions get done and never released. I've talked to many older musicians who don't even remember doing some sessions. But if these tapes were really of Clifford Brown, when had he done them, and where?

"You know about the Coltrane tapes Atlantic found?" Ace says, breaking into my thoughts.

I'd forgotten about those. Somebody at Atlantic Records was assigned to clean out a closet. "What about these boxes?" the guy asked his boss, when he came across some unlabeled tapes. It turned out they were reels of stuff John Coltrane had done in the fifties. They're now a multidisc CD set called *Heavyweight Champion*.

"I hope that guy got a raise."

Ace nods. "They should have made him a partner. There are also some rumors about some Bill Evans tapes made at the Village Vanguard by some doctor and his wife who made every gig. Evans didn't even know they were recording. The doctor's wife had a recorder in her purse, and they always sat at a front table. Only one who knew was Max Gordon, the owner."

"What happened to those?" That's a collection I'd like to have.

"I read they were turned over to Orrin Keepnews at Riverside Records."

"Turned over?"

"Well, sold, I imagine, and of course, very valuable."

Even more so if they also included Bill Evans's piano. I don't have a piano, but maybe I have Clifford Brown's trumpet.

And by now, the guy who killed Ken Perkins might know I have it.

CHAPTER
FIVE

ACE DOESN'T FEEL LIKE COOKING, SO WE HAVE PASTA and a carafe of red house wine at a small Italian restaurant in a strip mall next to a Lucky Market on Rainbow. Viva Trattoria is small and cozy, family run, with checkered tablecloths, candles in Chianti bottles, and smells wafting from the kitchen into the dining area.

The food is good, and miraculously the waiter—one of the sons, according to Ace—doesn't continually hover around our table, even though we have the place almost to ourselves.

Over cappuccino we continue to talk about the Clifford Brown tapes and Ken Perkins's death. I light one of my generic menthols, and Ace wrinkles his nose.

"What are those?"

"Not my regular brand. I'm trying to quit."

"Well, good for you."

On our second cup of coffee, I get to what I'm really thinking about and raise the possibility that I might be charged with something.

Ace scoffs at the idea. "I don't see how you can be,"

he says. "You told Trask everything, just how it happened. What could they charge you with?"

I hope Ace is right. I don't think I'm a suspect—Trask seemed to accept my account of things—but he is certainly going to want to talk to me again once he's had time to go over my statement and whatever evidence has been collected. It could go wrong.

"What if he comes up with some scenario like I realized how valuable the tapes were, I decided I wanted a bigger fee, Ken and I argued, Ken or the other guy pulled a gun, there was a struggle, the gun went off, and—"

"No," Ace says emphatically, slapping his napkin down on the table. "You stayed there. It was you who called the cops. The other guy, the killer, left, and you certainly didn't hit yourself on the head."

Instinctively, I touch the bandage. The only residual effect is a slight headache. "I hope you're right, Ace, but there's only my word that there was another man, and I didn't actually see the shooting."

Ace says no again. "I'll testify to that if necessary, that there was another man. I got you into this, Evan, and I think my standing in the community is sufficient for me to be a very good character witness. Besides, you have a track record with Trask over the Anthony Gallio thing."

"Yeah, I guess so. That was kind of fun, putting Gallio away and helping to save the Moulin Rouge." Ace is right, of course. I just wish I could be more convincing, even to myself. "We need to find that guy, Ace."

"We?" Ace looks panic-stricken. "Are you nuts?" He looks around the room, realizing his voice has become louder. In almost a whisper, he leans across the table and says, "He killed Ken Perkins, Evan, and that is business for the police."

"Okay, okay, but there is one other factor to consider. What if the tapes are phony, and Ken got cold feet and was killed because he wouldn't go through with the scam?"

"But you said—"

"I know what I said. I was convinced, but I'd sure like to listen to the remaining tape again."

"You think Trask would allow that?"

"I don't know, but I'm going to try. In fact, I'm going to see if he'll make a copy of it for me, and I need to convince him to have the tape analyzed."

"What do you mean, analyzed?"

"Look, it should be relatively simple to determine if this brand or type of tape was being used in the fifties. If not, then the whole thing is bogus, some kind of scam to defraud other collectors or a record company. If it is tape from the fifties, then maybe it's genuine, or maybe someone is being very clever."

Ace gazes into space for a moment, then shakes his head. "No, I don't buy it. They'd have to, what—just by coincidence find tapes with a guy who could imitate Clifford Brown perfectly, well enough to fool you, anybody? You said yourself that would be virtually impossible. And why choose Clifford Brown? Why not Miles Davis or Chet Baker, someone more well known?"

I've been thinking about that, and I already have an answer. "Look, Ace, if there were some unreleased, undiscovered recordings of Miles or Chet Baker, that would be great, but they both recorded a tremendous amount of material. The CD reissue business is big, but most of the stuff they're releasing now is from record companies. After Atlantic found those Coltrane master tapes you told me about, I imagine most companies are digging through their vaults right now looking to see if they have stuff they didn't know they had. No, the first thing to do is have the tape analyzed. Then we go from there." There are several possible explanations, but I'll have to work on them a bit more. I still leave out the fact that there's also a trumpet that I have to retrieve.

"I don't know, Evan. I think you're asking for trouble."

By the time we get our check, Ace looks totally exhausted. He glances at his watch. "I'm going to turn in early," he says. "You be okay?"

"Don't worry about me, Ace. I'll find something to do."

Maybe Ace is right. Am I asking for trouble again? Or, as Carol Mann told me, maybe my pursuit into investigations is more than simple curiosity. Maybe it's a psychological ploy to distract me from facing the fact that I can't play piano and maybe never will again.

I find myself identifying with Clifford Brown more and more. He had a near-fatal accident that almost ended his playing days, but he came back to a brilliant, albeit short, career. So far I hadn't done that yet.

But more and more I'm coming to the conclusion—especially since my own accident—that choice is an illusion. We always do what we have to do, which explains why once we're back at the house, I stand outside on the patio for a few minutes, smoking, listening to the wind, turning over everything in my mind.

The air is cold. Probably more snow at Mt. Charleston. A slight breeze ripples the pool cover and rustles tree branches. Do I have a choice? Rational thought tells me I should follow Ace's lead, go to bed early, and see what tomorrow brings.

But that other voice is powerful, always trying to lead me in another direction, like the Robert Frost poem "The Road Not Taken." The last lines have always struck me with the sense they've been written for me. "I took the one less traveled by, and that has made all the difference." I always seem to be drawn to the less-traveled road, whether it's a career in jazz or asking why when everyone else wants to give up.

I leave a message for Natalie, with no details, and decide to try Danny Cooper in the morning. I slip out of the house, make sure my flashlight is working, then drive back to the Perkins house, finding the street with little trouble. The homes are fronted by a high white wall that is well lit and faces the street. I drive inside, past the house, and down to a cul-de-sac at the other end, checking out the houses as I pass.

Turning around in the cul-de-sac, I pull in behind another car and shut off the lights and engine. The Perkins house is dark except for the outside lights, which are probably operated by sensor. Some of the yellow crime-scene tape still hangs from the gate, fluttering in the breeze, and there's a red seal slapped on the front door. The police have had all day to finish their work, but they'll probably be back.

I check the street for cars not belonging to residents, but there don't seem to be any that look as if they don't belong. I smoke a cigarette and wait a few minutes more before I grab my flashlight and get out of the car. I stay on the opposite side of the street, walking past Perkins's house. No one is out walking their dog, no visitors; it looks as safe as it will ever be.

Crossing the street, I walk quickly around the side of

the house, away from the front lights, only now realizing how large the house is. I find the window I went out, and the hedge. I pull it back from the house and snap on the flash for a second, shielding the light with my body, and reach behind the hedge.

Nothing there. No trumpet.

I look again, shining the light behind the hedge in both directions, thinking I've mistaken where I dropped it. I check all along the side of the house, but no trumpet anywhere. Now what? I stand for a minute in the yard, watch a light go on in the house next door. I go back to the car, my heart beating hard, and sit there for a few minutes smoking, waiting, thinking, contemplating something that other voice is trying to convince me to do.

Where is the trumpet? Did the police find it? Did someone else beat me to it? Or is it—in the house? I know I can't leave without seeing for myself. I want to see inside the house once more. Not that I think the police missed anything, but I want to recapture the scene, clear up the fuzzy images in my mind.

I go back to the house.

The broken screen is still dangling where I knocked it out the night before, and no one has locked the window. Maybe nobody even knew it was unlocked; all the activity would have been in the room where Perkins was shot. It opens easily, and I climb through. There's just enough light from the street to make out the shadows of the TV and other furniture. I cross the room and run the flash around in the music room. The flash sweeps over the outline where Ken's body was and the dark stains on the carpet, but everything else looks the same. There's nothing to see, or I don't know where to look.

I turn off the flash and stand in the darkness, trying to get something clear in my mind. When I've got it, I sit down on the couch, facing the tape decks, and point the flash across the room at one of the speakers. Perched in front of it is the trumpet case, just where I'd first seen it last night. Unless Trask comes back to the house, no one will miss it. That's it; time to get out of here.

I go back out the window, shut it behind me, and after checking the street, get to my car and put the trumpet in the Camaro's trunk. Getting back inside the car, I light a cigarette and sit there a few minutes, running things through my mind, thinking I've missed something.

I'm just about to leave when another car comes around the corner and does exactly what I did twenty minutes ago. It drives by the house slowly. I slide down in the seat as it passes me and turns around in the cul-de-sac. Back in my direction, past me, it parks near the corner, opposite the entrance to the compound.

I raise myself up just enough to see a man get out of the car. No doubt, it's Cross or whatever his name is. He walks up to the front door, opens it with a key, and walks right in, breaking the red seal. I sit up straight now to get a better look at his car. A Pontiac, late model. With one eye on the house, I walk in a crouch to his car and kneel down to get the license plate, memorize it, and trot back to my car. I write down the number on some scrap paper and wait.

Five minutes later Cross comes out of the house. He looks around then goes to his car. I watch him for a few minutes; he's doing just what I did—waiting, thinking, trying to decide what to do next. He's obviously come back for the trumpet and is trying to figure out what happened to it.

A minute later, he starts his car and pulls away. Time for my second stupid idea of the night.

I follow him.

He turns left out of the compound, then takes the first right at the traffic light. We're on Oakey now, headed east. I keep a couple of cars between us. He turns right on Rancho, then again on Sahara, then immediately turns on his signal to go left. I pull over and stop, knowing he's headed for the Palace Station Hotel.

The traffic on Sahara is heavy, so it takes me a couple of minutes to make the same turn into the Palace Station parking lot. There are people out headed for the casino, walking to their cars, or jockeying for a parking space. I cruise around for five minutes before I find his car in the covered parking garage, but now I see it has a rental agency sticker on it. Behind me somebody honks, and in the rearview mirror I see the familiar hands-up gesture that means "Are you going to park or what?"

I pull away and try for a spot nearer the hotel entrance, find one, and shut off the engine. Now what? I don't like leaving the trumpet in the trunk, and I don't want to go inside, call the police. Cross could spot me in a second. For once in my life I wish for a cellular phone.

I get out of my car and walk back to the parking garage, checking over my shoulder every few steps, but I don't see anyone except for some people going to their cars, carrying buckets of quarters. When I get to where I think Cross left his car, it's gone. I check two or three rows on either side, but I have the right spot; the car's just not there now.

Back in my own car, I sit for a moment, then slam my hand against the steering wheel. Nice going, Horne. All I can do now is go back to Ace's house and call in the license plate.

Back at the house, I see I won't have to call the police. They're already there, two black-and-whites. One is in the driveway, the other at an angle at the curb.

Two young Metro cops in tan uniforms, one blond, one dark-haired, are standing in the living room with Ace. The blond one turns to me; the other one is writing in a notebook. Ace, in pajamas, is sitting hunched over in a chair, staring at what's left of his record collection.

I take a quick look around. Records and CDs are all over the floor. Some of them have been smashed. Boxes of reel-to-reel tapes are open; some of the tapes are pulled off the reels and strung around the floor.

"Ace, what happened?"

"Are you staying here, sir?" the blond cop asks me. "I'll need your name, please."

"Yeah, Evan Horne. I'm a friend of Professor Buffington."

He takes down my address in L.A. and asks me where I've been. "Doesn't look like a robbery," he says, turning back to Ace, who hasn't spoken.

Ace and I exchange a quick glance that neither of the cops catches. "How did they get in?"

"Looks like the patio door," the blond cop says. "No windows broken, anything like that." That was me. I must have left it unlocked.

"I was sound asleep," Ace says. "Something woke

me up, some noise. I thought I heard music, figured it was just Evan. When I came out here I found this." He points to the mess in front of his stereo.

"Probably kids," the blond cop says. "Looks like vandalism to me." He nudges a broken 78rpm record with his foot. "Any of these valuable?"

"Just to me," Ace says. He picks up one of the records and reads the label. "Louis Armstrong and the Hot Five on Decca."

"Oh yeah," the other cop says. "Didn't he do 'Hello Dolly'? My mother used to have that one." The blond cop shrugs; Ace rolls his eyes at me.

"Okay, Professor Buffington, I guess that's all we can do for now. When you get everything straightened up, if you could make a list of anything that's missing and drop it off at the Spring Mountain Substation that would be helpful."

"Sure," Ace says, looking at me again.

"All right then, gentlemen," the dark-haired cop says. "We'll leave you to it."

I show them out and promise to lock all the doors and windows. When I come back in the living room, Ace is sitting in the middle of the floor sifting through records, tapes, and CDs. He looks up at me, a pained expression on his face.

"Who would do this, Evan?"

"I think we both know, Ace. He was looking for the other tape, must have connected you to Ken Perkins. He knows you knew Ken." I join Ace on the floor and look at some of the smashed records. Most of the 78s are Armstrong, Bix Beiderbecke, Fatha Hines.

"Some of these are replaceable," Ace says. "The good stuff wasn't here."

"What do you mean?"

"Thank God a friend of mine persuaded me to put the real collector's items in a safe deposit box at my bank. I didn't have much, really, but at least they're safe."

I breathe a sigh of relief. "Ace, I'm sorry, I think I left the patio door open."

"Doesn't matter. Whoever did this would have got in somehow. You just saved me a broken window. By the way, where did you go?"

"Ken Perkins's house."

"What?"

"Hang on a minute. I've got something to show you." I go out to my car, get the trumpet, and bring it back inside. I sit it on the floor near Ace and open the case. "What do you think?"

Ace's eyes get huge. "Oh my God. You're not going to tell me that's Clifford Brown's trumpet."

"I'm afraid I am."

Ace picks up the horn and turns it over in his hands as carefully as if he were handling the Hope diamond. He runs his hands over it, turns it in every direction, and pauses only when he sees the letters *C.B.* inscribed inside the bell. He pushes down on the valves, then puts it back in the case and takes a deep breath before he says anything. He leans back and folds his hands together across his chest.

"Do you have any idea how valuable this is?"

"I could guess. Twenty-five thousand?"

"Double that, at least. In an auction, with the right people involved, it might bring a hundred thousand."

The way Ace is staring at me, I know he's serious. "This is what whoever broke in here tonight was looking for, isn't it?"

"No, I don't think so. He was looking for the tape

on the off chance you might have gotten it. He probably figures the police have it."

"And why don't they? How did you get the trumpet?"

I tell Ace and watch his expression turn to panic. "You went back in the house? Tonight?"

"It was right where I first saw it. I didn't mention any trumpet in my statement. Probably one of the uniformed cops found it outside where I left it and simply returned it to the music room."

"But, Evan, that's evidence."

"Not if the police don't know it is." Strictly speaking, that's true, but I have removed something from a crime scene. Still, it doesn't belong to Ken Perkins. It belongs to his killer.

Ace shakes his head, still trying to comprehend. "Do you think that's really Clifford Brown's horn?"

"That's something I want to find out."

Back in the apartment, I put on one of Brownie's cassettes. I listen for a minute but don't recognize the tune. When I check the box I smile to myself; it's called "Clifford's Axe."

I try to imagine that this is the horn that played those notes. The trumpet still bothers me. Is the tape fake and the trumpet genuine, or is it the other way around? I run my hands over the cool metal, the horn that maybe Clifford Brown himself once held, put his lips to, and made jazz history with. The enormity of the trumpet's potential value still hasn't hit me yet.

I open the case, trying to discern the message it has for me, trying to picture the scores of trumpet players I've watched as they put their horns away for the night. The smell of oil is still very present, almost like kerosene. What else is in this case? I take the horn out of the case. There's a small compartment, held closed with a snap, where most guys keep a bottle of valve oil, an extra mouthpiece, cigarettes, a phone number hastily scrawled on a napkin.

There's no mouthpiece, but there is a small glass bottle. When I hold it up to the light, shake it, I can see there's maybe a sixteenth of an inch of liquid inside. The lettering on the label is worn off in places from being handled hundreds of times. I can only make out a few letters of the brand name. "—ick Stu—" The rest of it is too smudged to read. I set it aside and explore the case further. In some instrument cases I've seen another traylike storage compartment, which lifts out.

I feel around inside. The lining is worn and frayed, and on one side it's coming away from the side of the case. I pull it back gently and find another treasure I imagine Cross didn't even know about.

A once-white postcard, now slightly yellowed but still intact. On one side is a black-and-white photo of the Ambassador Hotel in Los Angeles. When I turn it over, I realize Ace might be right about the contents of this case.

The name and address are virtually unreadable, smeared with what appear to be dark rings, coffee cup stains, or maybe valve oil. The message, however, written with a flourish, is very clear.

Dear C.B.,
Thanks so much for lending your not inconsiderable talents to our musical family on such short notice. I adore your sound, and of course,
We love you madly, D.

No signature is needed to know who the writer was. And the message, a gracious gesture, so typical of this man who knew what it would mean to a young musician. Probably done over room-service coffee, before checkout, dressed in a robe, the famous bags under his eyes puffier than usual. Even the large *D*, done with a sweeping flourish, was unnecessary.

The writer's closing line was his musical signature as well. The song played, the words spoken at the end of every concert around the world.

We love you madly.

What I hold in my hand is a postcard written to Clifford Brown from Edward Kennedy "Duke" Ellington.

CHAPTER
SIX

I HAVE SEVERAL THINGS TO FACE WHEN I WAKE UP.
The first is finding a suitable safe hiding place for the
trumpet. Somewhere where I can have access to it, but
where Cross or whoever else is involved won't think to
look.

I work that one out in the shower. As for the other
things, I'm willing to bet Trask will be calling before
the morning is out if Danny Cooper doesn't beat him
to it. I can imagine a phone call between those two,
discussing their mutual acquaintance, the musician-
detective. I still haven't decided what or how much to
tell Natalie.

By the time I get dressed and walk over to the
house, Ace has everything pretty well under control.
Coffee is on, probably his second pot, and records,
CDs, and tapes are stacked up in neat piles on the living room floor. Ace doesn't look happy.

"Anything missing?"

"Far as I can tell, no," he says, glancing at the damaged pile that sits alone from the others. "There's
plenty of damage, though. That pile is for the trash.

This was sheer vindictiveness, Evan. There's no other word for it."

I agree. "How about anger and frustration? Whoever did this knew the tape wouldn't be here, but he had to go through the motions. Just confirming that made him more angry." I watch Ace scoop up the remnants of several 78s, some broken CD boxes, and hundreds of feet of reel-to-reel tape. "You don't have any idea who this guy was? Ken didn't tell you anything about him?"

Ace shakes his head. "Sometimes Ken acted like he was in the witness protection program, especially when it came to record collecting. Hell, for all I know, he was. I just don't know that much about him. He was never married, always lived alone."

"What did he do? I mean, aside from collecting?"

"I called him once at work, the accounting department at one of the Strip hotels, can't remember which one. The job was only to support his collecting. That was his real passion. You've got to understand, Evan, these guys are obsessive—books, stamps, whatever, they're always on a quest for a rare find and always looking over their shoulder, worried somebody's going to beat them to the Holy Grail."

"And what would that be?"

Ace stops and thinks for a moment, smiles. "In jazz? The only recording of Buddy Bolden."

"Buddy Bolden. Isn't he the trumpet player who went nuts, ended up in an insane asylum in New Orleans?"

"Right, played in the Storyville district."

"But I thought he never recorded."

"That's right, but there were rumors of a cylinder recording in the late 1890s. If it really existed, it's never been found, and it probably wouldn't be playable if it was, but of course that wouldn't make any difference."

"Okay, so with record collector types I gather it's more the rarity of the item than the music."

"Absolutely. They're also very competitive about it. There's a whole network. Special magazines—the Internet now plays a role. If you offer them a record, they want to know the color of the label, what's printed on it, when it was made. It could be Clifford Brown or some doo-wop group from the sixties."

I sip my coffee and try to imagine not being interested in the music. It makes no sense to me. "Do they ever get together, I mean in groups or meetings, that kind of thing?" I was already thinking of a way to track down the man who called himself Cross, maybe even a way to draw him out.

"Oh yeah," Ace says, smiling. "They have conventions several times a year. The big one, I guess it's still going on, is held in, of all places, the parking lot at Capitol Records in Hollywood. But get this, it starts early Sunday morning, but people arrive earlier every year, when it's still dark. They bring flashlights; some even wear those miner's hard hats with the light on them to comb through offerings. Bids are made, deals are done right there."

"Have you ever been to one?"

Ace shakes his head. "No, I stick to the magazines, personal contacts for stuff I'm looking for. It's too weird for me." Ace pauses and looks at me. "You'll get an idea of what I'm talking about if you go to Ken's funeral."

I hadn't thought about that. Cross is probably long gone and wouldn't dare show up at that, but I might pick up something useful. "How many of these collector types you think will show up?"

"Once the word is out that Ken was killed, they'll flock here. Not to mourn Ken so much as to get a lead on what he was killed for. They'll all know it was for something big, believe me."

I leave Ace to his cleanup and wander outside with my coffee. The sun is bright, but it's still cold. The steam comes off my coffee and mixes with cigarette smoke. On days like this it's hard to imagine the oppressive summer heat of Las Vegas.

I hear the sliding glass door open behind me. Ace is holding a cordless phone. "Your friend from Santa Monica," Ace says.

I sit down at the patio table. "Coop?"

Lieutenant Danny Cooper has little time for the amenities. "Interesting fax I received this morning from Las Vegas Metro," Coop says. "It seems you've got yourself involved in yet another fascinating scenario. What is it with you and dead jazz musicians?"

"I'm fine, thanks, Coop. How are you?" No response. I picture Coop at his desk, glaring at the phone. "Okay, that's what Trask asked too. Look, there was nothing suspicious about Clifford Brown's death. He died in a car crash forty years ago."

"But there's a lot suspicious about you being present when one"—I hear paper rustling as Coop searches for the name—"Kenneth Perkins was shot."

"It sounds silly, I know, but the truth often does."

"Just a minute," Coop says. "Let me get a pen. I want to write that down."

"Look, Coop, I was hired to listen to some tapes and give an opinion as to their genuineness. I didn't know any of this was going to happen."

"What happened—this Perkins guy didn't like your review, so he shot himself?"

"Funny. I suppose you'll be auditioning at the Comedy Store any day now."

"Valuable, huh?"

"Very, if they're genuine."

"Well, that's motive. You were there, so that's opportunity. Means is the other question. At least that's Trask's question. This fax was followed up by a phone call. We law enforcement types call it professional courtesy in the field. He asked for a character reference—whether you're a threat to society or should make a guest appearance on *America's Most Wanted.*"

"Trask knows better, and so do you."

Coop's voice changes. "I told him as much, but this is a murder, sport, and you were there. Don't fuck with this one, Horne. You're in over your head. Call me when you get back to L.A. if they let you out of town."

Coop hangs up before I can manage a comeback.

The second I turn off the phone, it rings again. "Evan Horne, please."

"Speaking."

"This is Detective Ochoa at Metro. We met during the Gallio thing last year."

"I remember." I also remember I didn't particularly like Ochoa. He was too slick, trying to look like a TV detective, and he'd asked Natalie out the first time they met.

"Good. Lieutenant Trask would like you to come down to Metro this morning. He has some questions about your statement."

"What time?"

"Ten would do it."

"I'll be there."

Well, there it is. At least I'll find out the extent of my involvement and whether or not I can remain among the free.

I make two other calls on Ace's cordless before I head for downtown, Clifford Brown's trumpet securely locked in the trunk. On the off chance that Trask asks about it, I'll have it with me. How I would explain it being in my possession is another hurdle.

The midmorning traffic is light as I retrace the route Trask took when I was with him in his car. I find a parking spot and go inside to a scene of organized chaos. After passing through a metal detector, I'm directed down a long hallway to the detective bureau.

Trask is at his desk, on his phone. He looks up at me, checks his watch, and motions me to a seat at his desk. Ochoa appears to be out. Trask grunts into the phone several times, then says, "Right, I got it," and puts down the phone. He looks at me for several moments like I've done something, grabs a file folder, and stands up. "C'mon, let's go back here."

I follow him down the hall to one of the interview rooms, the same one where Ace and I talked with him the day before. Same table and chairs. Ochoa is already there, looking as usual as if he just finished a shoot for *GQ*. He nods at me and stands leaning against the wall. Trask and I sit down, and there's several moments of silence while Trask reads from the file folder.

"We've got a couple of things we want to clear up regarding your statement, okay?"

"Sure, whatever."

"Okay. You say you didn't get a good look at the shooter, right?"

"No, the door flew open, he hit me, then he was gone."

"You don't know his full name, and you can't give us much of a description."

"No, he was always in shadows, like he didn't want me to get a good look."

"And you don't know if Cross is his real name?"

"How would I?"

Trask pauses a moment and looks up from the file. "Professor Buffington didn't tell you?"

I look from Ochoa to Trask. Both have a look of expectancy. "I don't think he knew either."

Trask closes the file. "I had an interesting phone call this morning, from an attorney, Perkins's attorney. Says your friend Professor Buffington is listed as executor of Perkins's will."

I don't have to try to look shocked. "What? Are you sure?"

"Buffington didn't mention it—you didn't know?"

"As far as I know, their only connection to each other was through record collecting, and that was minimal. Ace says he had very little to do with Perkins, that Perkins was a very secretive guy."

Trask and Ochoa exchange glances again. "According to his lawyer, Perkins had some very valuable items in his collection—extremely rare recordings, were his words."

"Well, that's what he did. That shouldn't be a surprise."

"What if I told you this lawyer says a good deal of Perkins's estate was left to your friend Professor Buffington?"

Trask has me again, and I'd bet Ace will be dumbfounded. I still don't see where Trask is going with this.

"You'll have to ask Ace about that, but I'm sure he doesn't know."

"Oh, don't worry, we'll ask him." Trask opens the file again, refers to something inside. "Perkins had only one surviving relative, a sister. She's flying in today to make funeral arrangements."

"Well, that should clear up a lot of things."

"We hope so." Trask looks at Ochoa. "Dave, can we have a few minutes?"

Ochoa shrugs but looks annoyed as he goes out and shuts the door.

"Look," Trask says, "we have very little going on this. We don't have a description of the alleged shooter, we have no gun, no prints, we don't even have his name. Then I find Buffington stands to gain a good deal from Perkins's death, and these tapes, if they're as valuable as you say they are, could be worth a lot more than the fee they paid you to listen to them."

"For one thing, I didn't get paid, remember? What are you suggesting? That Buffington and I had something to do with this?"

Trask shakes his head. "You, probably not. I checked with Danny Cooper, and he vouched for you pretty solidly, but I don't want your friendship with Buffington to cloud your thinking."

"Oh, come on, Trask. Ace is an English professor with a long-standing reputation in the community. Are you forgetting his help with Anthony Gallio?"

Trask shrugs again. "No, I'm not, but he did little more than let us use his house for a short time, put a tap on his phone. This is a murder investigation, and I just have to keep my options open."

I shift in my chair, uncomfortable with Trask's innuendo. I would stake my life on Ace's honesty. "You're all wrong on this, Trask, you really are. Ace would never be a part of something like this."

"Okay, let's go to something else—the tapes. You say there were two, right?"

"As far as I know. I only saw two."

"You think there might be more?"

"If they're genuine, I really doubt it. I'm not even sure these are genuine."

"I thought you said this was—what's his name— Clifford Brown."

"I could be wrong. They could be very good fakes."

Trask frowns. "I won't pretend to understand how this would work."

This is the opening I've been waiting for. If I'm reading Trask correctly, I'm not really a suspect, and neither is Ace. Trask is frustrated in having a murder on the books, and with almost nowhere to start, he's grasping at straws.

"Think of it as an art forgery. There would be tests made for the canvas, paint, and comparisons of the artist's genuine work, to determine if the paintings were genuine or copies. We can't do that with music except to listen to the tapes and try and determine if the artist is who it's supposed to be. Call it expert opinion."

"We've had an audio lab listen to the one that was left on the machine at Perkins's house—told us nothing. Good trumpet player, was all the technician said."

"Exactly my point." I lean forward, hoping I can sell Trask on my idea. "If this was really Clifford Brown, the tape would have been made sometime before June 1956. That's when he died in the car crash. That means the tape used would have to be vintage fifties. There must be ways to test the tape through the manufacturer, some kind of manufacturer's code, maybe even the makeup of the tape itself. Recording tape has improved vastly since then."

Trask thinks about that. "We don't have the facilities to run a test like that. It would have to go to the FBI lab in Utah."

"Fine, have the test made, but do one thing first."

"What's that?"

"Make a copy for me, a cassette." I throw up my hands and smile. "Think of me as the equivalent of an art forgery expert. I want to listen to that tape, maybe play it for some other people more expert than me who might be able to verify that it's Clifford Brown."

Trask leans back in his chair, runs his hands through his thinning hair, and allows himself a slight smile. "Danny Cooper said you might want to do something like this. What if it's not Brown on the tape, what then?"

"Then we know that this whole thing was a scam to dupe a record company. That's a whole other deal. I have some contacts you don't have for the music end of things. Let me try. It can't hurt your case to know exactly what you're dealing with."

Trask gets up and walks over to the window, then turns back to me. "Okay, we'll send the tape off to the FBI, and I'll have a cassette copy made for you, but that's the extent of your involvement, understood?"

"Absolutely, no problem. When can I get the tape?"

"I'll let you know." He puts up his hands. "I know, the sooner the better." I stand up. "So there's no reason I have to stay in Las Vegas. Some of what I've got in mind I'll have to do in L.A."

"You mean, are you a suspect? No, but you stay in touch with me, and I want a full report on what you're doing." Trask picks up the file folder. "There's one other thing."

"Yeah?" Here it comes; where's the trumpet?

"What's going on with you and Ochoa? He doesn't like you for some reason." I try not to show my relief that's all he wants to ask me.

"Search me, unless it's something to do with my girlfriend."

There's a knock at the door before we can finish. It opens, and Ochoa sticks his head in. "Lieutenant, you've got a call. It's Perkins's lawyer."

"Okay, be right there." Trask turns to me. "I'll call you about the tape. Remember, stay in touch."

I brush past Ochoa in the hall. "Good to see you again, Dave. Nice tie."

"It's Sergeant Ochoa," the detective says, glancing down at his tie.

Back in my car in the parking lot, I go over the conversation with Trask. I light a cigarette and sit for a moment, watching police arrive for work, suspects being brought in for questioning, allowing the luscious wave of relief to flood through my body.

Not even a mention of the trumpet. It hasn't been missed by anyone, and I get a copy of the tape as well.

But my triumph is shadowed with doubt. Is Trask simply hoping I'll come up with something by exploring possibilities in an area he doesn't know, find some lead in a dead-end case? Maybe I'm imagining it, but was Trask too receptive to my idea, too eager to cooperate?

The thought crosses my mind, especially his allusion to talking with Danny Cooper. Maybe he was going to sell me, and I saved him the trouble.

* * *

Coming up with a safe place for the trumpet while at the same time ensuring I don't make anyone else a target turns out to be easier than I thought. I've mulled over several possibilities. A storage locker at the airport or bus station? Leaving it with someone totally unconnected to the case? I even considered a band teacher I know who deals a lot with musical instruments. One more trumpet in his lockers wouldn't make a difference.

But as I find a parking space on Fremont Street and walk into the Silver State Pawn Shop, I know I've come up with the right solution. I pause for a moment and glance in the window. There's the usual array of jewelry, cameras, video and stereo equipment. It's the clarinet, like new, sitting in an open case, that clinches it for me. Hide it in plain sight.

Inside, there's a young couple looking at engagement rings. I wander around the shop, browsing over the many offerings, items unredeemed that are now for sale. How many stories are there here?

The clerk glances at me from time to time while he shows rings to the couple. Save money on a ring for other more important things. They look happy, in love, but practical.

"That's all I've got in that range," the clerk says, winking at me. He's thin, nearly bald, and probably in his mid-sixties. A jeweler's magnifying glass hangs on a chain around his neck. He glances at the trumpet case. "Be right with you," he says.

The couple talks quietly for a moment, turning away slightly. Finally the man says, "Well, thanks for your time. We'll check back with you."

Before they're out the door, the clerk scoops up the

ring boxes, replaces them in the locked glass case, and pockets a ring of keys.

"How can I help you?" He eyes the trumpet case as I set it down on the counter.

"Just want to see if I can get a few bucks on this." I open the case.

He takes the horn out, holds it with both hands like he's held one before, presses down on the valves. He wrinkles his nose, looks up at me, and smiles.

"What's that smell?"

"Valve oil."

He nods his head up and down. "Yeah. Awfully strong, though. I used to play a little myself," he says. "High school band."

I nod and watch him give the trumpet a cursory examination. "How much were you thinking of?"

I shrug, try to look hopeful. "I don't know." I tell him the figure I have in mind.

"Bad day on the tables, huh?"

"Yeah, something like that."

He fingers the valves again. "No mouthpiece?"

I hadn't even thought of that. I pat my pockets. "Yeah, I left it home, I guess."

"You probably got hurt, what with the strike and all, right?"

"Strike?"

"Yeah, Musicians Union strike. That's why there's no music in the hotels anymore."

"Well, I guess you know the whole story."

"Yep, sure do." He looks at the trumpet one last time and puts it back in the case. "Well, it's pretty old, needs some work and a shining up, but something tells me you'll be back for it."

For one scary moment, I think he isn't going to take

it. I look disappointed but agree to his price. He counts out the cash, and I fill out a form and take the ticket.

"Well, thanks," I say.

"Son, let me give you some advice, if you don't mind."

"Sure."

"You get some money together somewhere, come back, and get your horn and go back home, wherever that is."

"Oh, don't worry. I'll definitely be back."

I walk out to my car feeling sad. It's not even my horn, my instrument, but I think I can imagine the feelings of musicians everywhere who've had to hock their horns.

INTERLUDE
June 25, 1956

THEY WALKED TOWARD A BOOTH IN A BACK CORNER OF the diner, Brownie leading, Richie just behind him, his hand protectively on Nancy's arm. No problems, really. Just three pretty-well-dressed, road-tired Negroes in a restaurant, wanting some dinner. There were a few curious looks, but nothing to distress any of them. This wasn't Alabama, this was Pennsylvania, and tomorrow they would be in Indiana.

"Back Home in Indiana." Brownie couldn't think of a song title without running the chord changes through his mind or devising a new melody, his mind never at rest, working all the time. That's why he enjoyed— excelled at—math, why he was so good at chess and so knocked out to discover Max Roach was a great chess player as well as a great drummer.

Max had won the city championships in Brooklyn, but Brownie could beat him once in a while if Max was off his game. Brownie and Max were good together in so many ways, like brothers, especially with that big damn ride cymbal pounding behind him relentlessly on "Cherokee," driving him toward the edge every time they played. And damned if that motherfucker couldn't play melody on the drums. If you knew the tune, you could tell where Max was when he soloed. Brownie liked that, he liked that a lot.

"And how are you folks tonight?" the waitress asked, setting down three glasses of water, handing them menus. She looked tired too, Brownie thought, but neighborly. He awarded her one of his best child-like smiles.

"We'll be just fine with some coffee, ma'am. How is that beef stew I saw on the blackboard? Tasty, I'll bet."

"You'd win your bet, son," the waitress said, returning Brownie's smile. Like so many strangers, she warmed to him immediately.

"Sounds good to me," Richie said. "Nancy?" She was still studying the menu.

"I think I'll have the fried chicken."

Brownie and Richie both laughed. "Oh, you tryin' something different," Richie said, winking at Brownie.

"Yeah," Brownie chimed in. "Charlie Parker ain't the only one should be called Bird."

"Don't you laugh at me, Richie Powell," Nancy said, playfully slapping Richie on the arm. The gesture reminded Clifford of how much he missed LaRue. Well, he'd call her tonight, wish her happy birthday, tell her how much he missed her and the baby.

He watched the waitress write down their order, knew she was thinking, Who the hell is this Charlie Parker cat? One day everybody will know, he thought. Maybe one day everybody will know who Clifford Brown is too.

They talked and joked over dinner. The food was as good as the waitress's word, but they lingered long over several cups of coffee and cigarettes—Brownie stalling, Richie anxious to be gone, but leaving meant getting back in the car, getting back on the road. At least it was a short ride from here into Philly.

They paid the check, walked outside to the car, and stood nearby stretching, smoking, Brownie reluctant to get in.

"Well, come on, man," Richie said, looking at his watch. "Sooner we get to Philly, sooner you play this gig, sooner we get to Elkhart. Them trumpet cats will be gone if we don't get going. How many they gonna give you?"

"At least one, they said." Brownie nodded at Richie and Nancy, knew they were watching him, but not pressing. He ground out his cigarette. "I'll drive this time," he said.

Richie said, "Cool," and opened the door for Nancy.

CHAPTER
SEVEN

"YOU HOCKED CLIFFORD BROWN'S TRUMPET FOR FIFTY dollars?" Ace is beside himself, stalking around the kitchen, shaking his head. He stops and spins toward me, almost losing his balance. "A hundred-thousand-dollar horn?"

"A hundred thousand? Relax, Ace. In the first place, we don't know yet if it's Brownie's horn or how much it's worth. Besides, it couldn't be in a safer place. There's a security buzzer on the door and a steel gate across the whole front of the shop when it's locked up at night. Most importantly, no one knows it's there."

Ace isn't quite convinced. "But what if there was a robbery or something?" He's more under control now. "Evan, that could be a very valuable horn."

"Even if there was a robbery, no one is going to steal an old trumpet in a battered case. They'd go after the jewelry, cameras, TVs."

Ace smiles for the first time since I came back to the house. "No, I guess not. God, I wish I could tell someone about this." His smile suddenly changes to a frown again. "You have the ticket."

"Of course." For now, it's safely tucked in my wallet. "This way I can get at it if I need to, and nobody is on the spot."

"When would you need to use it?"

I had worked a lot of this out already. I find myself slightly doubting that the tapes are genuine. If they're not, and I can prove it, doesn't it follow that the horn would be phony too? "There are a couple of people still around who might be able to recognize the horn if it's Clifford Brown's. You can't play with someone every night and not know what his horn looks like. Max Roach for one, and there's Sonny Rollins, and Harold Land, who still lives in L.A."

"Right," Ace says. "I'd forgotten about him. He was the tenor player before Sonny Rollins. And wait"—Ace snaps his fingers—"Teddy Edwards. He was the first tenor player with Max's band. He was just at the Riviera last year."

"Great. Any other ideas you have, I'd like to hear." Ace is not only a collector but an amateur jazz historian as well. Jazz names come to him as easily as characters in a Jane Austen novel.

His good spirits sag quickly, though, when he gets back to the business of the day. "Did Trask tell you about Ken Perkins naming me in his will?"

"Yeah, this morning. You had no idea, I take it?"

"How could I? Not the remotest idea." Ace sits down and checks his watch. "I have a meeting with Perkins's lawyer and sister this afternoon. I've offered to help with the funeral arrangements. God, Evan, how did things get so complicated? I start off thinking I might play a minor role in verifying a great musical discovery, and I get us both involved in a murder investigation." There's pain and confusion in his eyes when he looks up at me. "I'm sorry, Evan, I really am. If I'd known—"

"Forget it, Ace. There's no way you could have known. The thing we have to do now is clear us both of any involvement in this. Meanwhile, I'm going to try and determine if that's really Clifford Brown on those tapes."

"Do I want to ask how you're going to do that?"

"Probably not, but I can tell you this. I have Trask's blessing and I guess the reluctant blessing of the Las Vegas Police."

"What do you mean?"

"Trask agreed to have the remaining tape analyzed, and he's making a cassette copy for me."

"What are you going to do with it?"

"There's a couple of people I want to listen to it."

I cross Las Vegas Boulevard at Sahara, giving the Strip lights one quick glance. The Sahara is remodeling, and to my left, Bob Stupak's Stratosphere Tower looks like it's nearly finished. I continue on to Eastern Avenue. The Hobnob is gone, given up entirely now to heavy metal, so Pappy Dean tells me, but Melrose, another of those out-of-the-way, unlikely places for jazz, has emerged as the new hangout. It's tucked away in a corner of a small shopping center next to a 7-Eleven. Parking is no problem—the lot is only about half full—but I'm early. It's only eight-thirty. The sign in the window reads Marv Koral's All-Stars.

Inside, the musicians are setting up under a bank of TVs that are the real attraction of Melrose, all tuned to different sports programs—two hockey games, an ESPN studio show, and the Lakers game from L.A. On Wednesday nights and Sunday afternoons, the TV sound is off and Melrose is transformed into a jazz club.

The bandstand is a small dance floor immediately in front of the TVs. There are dark green leatherette booths, and several tables jammed together are occupied by some early arrivals, who pay no attention to the soundless televisions.

In the corner, to the left of the TVs a saxophone player licks his reed, puts it in his horn, and blows a few tentative notes into a tenor. He smiles, says something to a short, dark-haired man rolling a set of vibes into place. The vibraphonist strikes one of the metal keys and leans in closer to listen, cocks his head as if he can't believe what he just heard. He tries again, seems satisfied, then does a series of fast runs that make the mallets only a blur in his hands. He looks familiar, but I can't place him.

I take a stool at the bar, which takes up one entire wall, and order a draft beer from one of the lady bartenders. They're all dressed in black pants and white golf shirts. The other end of the bar opens into a separate dining area with a dozen or so tables and booths. At the bar small groups of people are talking, laughing, telling stories, glancing around the room to see who's there, who's not.

By nine the pianist is adjusting the controls on his electric piano and the drummer—clearly the oldest member, with thinning gray hair and thick glasses—is seated behind his drums, craning his neck at one of the TVs. A sign hangs around his neck that says Out of Order.

Pacing around his instrument, the vibes player finally turns to the rhythm section and counts off a tempo. There's one false start as the bass player's amp acts up, but he quickly finds the problem, and they're off on a fast minor blues called "No Room for Squares."

The vibes player has the first solo. His hands flying effortlessly over the keyboard, he half sings, half hums—loud enough for me or anyone at the bar to hear—his lines, leaning in, now rocking back, then returning to the keys as if he's forgotten something. He brushes over the chord changes like a runner circling the bases after hitting a triple, carefully touching each base but veering outside the base path.

The rest of the band is tuned in to his route. They like what he's saying and rise to the occasion, even though this is the first tune of the night. He ends his solo with a flourish, backs away from the vibes, then suddenly leans in again for an afterthought, strikes one last key with the handle end of the mallet, and smiles and nods, acknowledging the smattering of applause. Taking two steps back, he holds the mallets on his shoulder like a soldier with a rifle, released from the present-arms command.

"Dude can play, huh, piano man?"

I turn at the voice of Elgin "Pappy" Dean at my shoulder. He smiles broadly at me, tilts the Panama hat back on his head. "How you doin', man?" His huge arms envelop me in a bear hug.

"Hey, Pappy. Great to see you, and you are, as usual, lookin' good." With the hat goes the tan suit, white shirt, and Miles Davis tie. Pappy stands back and holds out his hands to his sides. "Don't I always?"

I signal the bartender for another beer and a drink for Pappy as the tenor player shuffles up to the microphone to offer his story, the rhythm section cooking behind him.

"Who's the vibes player?"

Pappy gives the band a quick glance. "Dave Pike. Don't nobody grunt and groan and play vibes like that, 'cept Dave."

Dave Pike. Now I remember. Many years with Herbie Mann, lost for as long in Europe with the other jazz exiles—Chet Baker, Dexter Gordon. "What's he doing here? I thought he lived in L.A. now."

"Did," Pappy says, "thought he'd play some jazz in Las Vegas. He won't stay. Ain't nothin' here for a bebop vibes player like Dave Pike. He better go back to Europe. That's the only place they give a shit about jazz."

Pappy is right, and Las Vegas isn't New York or L.A. "So, how's Louise? Ace tells me you two are seeing each other."

Just the name brings a smile to Pappy's face. "She's fine, just fine, and we're gettin' along real good, real good. She can cook, too." Pappy shakes his head. "Not like my last old lady. She couldn't cook potatoes." Pappy laughs again loudly.

He sips his cognac, sets the glass down, and glances again at the band. "Now I know you didn't call me to ask about Louise, but I don't know if I *want* to know why you called."

"Don't worry, Pappy, nothing dangerous." I doubt if Pappy can help at all, but it's a place to start. "You know any trumpet players who sound like Clifford Brown?"

"Clifford Brown? Here comes that shit from the past again. I know lots of trumpet players who *want* to sound like Clifford, especially this young dude, Wynton Marsalis. Then there's Freddie Hubbard, who took his from Lee Morgan."

"No, I mean somebody else, somebody not famous maybe, somebody who could play so much like Clifford Brown you couldn't tell the difference."

We both look toward the bandstand. The piano player—dark complexion, graying curly hair—is hunched over the electric keyboard slicing off jagged lines from the blues before he hands things over to the bassist.

Pappy shakes his head and looks at me. "What are you into now, Mr. piano man detective? Your hand okay now?"

"It was, but I overdid it," I say, holding it out in front of me, flexing my fingers. I'd already decided to tell Pappy as little as possible, and nothing about the trumpet, at least for now. "Some guy thinks he's found some recordings of Clifford Brown that nobody knew about."

"You heard the tape?"

"Yeah, couple of times. Sounds like Brownie to me."

"But you think the dude might be pullin' your coat-tails?"

"Exactly, but I want to be sure."

"You got the tape?"

"I'm getting a copy from the police."

"The police?" Pappy sets his glass down, gets off the stool. "Bye."

"Wait a minute, it's nothing like that." I grab his arm. "The tapes were stolen. The police are just trying to find the owner." Pappy stares at me, holds my gaze for a moment, knows there's more. "Oh, hell, Pappy, the owner was killed, okay? They have no leads, and when I told them there was a possibility the tapes were phony, they agreed to let me look into it."

Pappy says, "Like I said, bye." He gets up again.

"Look, just hear me out. My part has nothing to do with the murder. I just want to know if the tapes are genuine."

"What you talkin' 'bout, murder? Damn, Clifford Brown, tapes, murder. Why you always into this heavy shit?"

"Just lucky, I guess."

It takes a few more cognacs and some heavy persuasion, but Pappy finally agrees to help, or at least listen to the tape. He sighs, runs a hand over his face.

"Okay, I owe you, man. Let me think about this. You goin' back a long ways again. I'll call you. You stayin' with the prof?"

"Yeah, same number."

Pappy sets his glass down. "Later, but one thing," he says as he walks away. "There was only one Clifford Brown." He walks off muttering to himself. "Wardell Gray, Clifford Brown, shit."

I stay for the rest of the set, listening to Dave Pike humming, moaning, groaning, literally talking to his instrument as if convincing it to do things it can't. He gives a clinic in bebop vibes. The drummer, apparently moved by his performance, periodically unleashes an almost inhuman moan of his own at the end of several tunes.

I massage my right hand with my left. When trombonist Carl Fontana ambles to the bandstand, the urge to join in is overwhelming.

Back at the house, Ace has already gone to bed. I let myself in and make a cursory check of the doors and windows. No more break-ins, and the record collection is back in order. I feel for Ace, who has lost some of his most precious recordings.

He's left me a note to call Natalie. I pour myself a drink and dial her number. This time I'm successful.

"How's Miss F. Lee Bailey?" I say when she answers. Her voice sounds sleepy, but then she's instantly awake and alert.

"Evan? What's going on up there? Ace told me what happened, and there was a story in the paper today about a murder of a record collector. Please tell me you're not involved."

"Afraid I can't do that."

There's a pause before she continues. "Oh, Evan, how? What happened?"

I give her the capsule version, and she listens without interrupting. Just one of the things I like about Natalie.

When I finish she says, "How deep are you going to get into this? You're not a witness, so I don't see how you can be much help to the police."

"I can help them with this tape, maybe determine if it's really Clifford Brown or not, maybe track down the musicians who made it if it's not Brown."

"How are you going to do that?"

"We have our ways."

"Evan, stop joking around. This is a murder you're talking about."

"Yeah, know a good lawyer?" She doesn't laugh. "Okay, I'm just going to poke around a little. The police have no leads, so the music is the only connection to the whole thing. That and these crazy record collectors."

"And you're just compelled to follow it through."

Now it's my turn to pause. It's suddenly become very important to me. I want to know if that's Clifford Brown on those tapes. "Yeah, I guess I am."

"When do you think you'll be back?"

"I don't know. Couple of days, maybe. I'm going to Ken Perkins's funeral, see who turns up there. Maybe I can connect with some of these collectors. Ace knows a lot of them."

"Call me as soon as you get back?"

"Promise. Get some sleep, counselor."

"It would be a lot easier if you were here."

"For me too."

Neither of us says good-bye, we just hang up.

I have one more drink and make a list of things I have to do. One is to call the Conn instrument company and find out what I can about Clifford Brown's trumpet, which is safely at the Silver State Pawn Shop. The second is to get some more information on Clifford Brown. Tim Shaw, who I wrote a couple of things for at *Blue Note* magazine, seems the most likely source.

The last thing I do is call the police and give them the license number of what might be Cross's car. I report it as abandoned at McCarran Airport by the rental company.

When I finally go to bed it's with thoughts of Clifford Brown, wondering what he would have thought if he'd known his name would come up in a murder investigation nearly forty years after his death. One thing I'm sure of:

Clifford Brown's music, that's the key to the whole thing.

CHAPTER
EIGHT

ACE IS IN A COAT AND TIE WHEN I WANDER OVER TO the house. He doesn't look either happy or rested. "Another meeting with Ken's lawyer and his sister this morning," he says.

"How's she taking it?"

"Very well, but she told me they hadn't had much contact over the last few years. Seems like she just wants to get it over with and go back home." Ace sighs and shakes his head. "I just can't believe he named me in his will. You know what he did? He left me records, my choice, any ten records from his collection."

"He must have had a reason. From what you tell me, most of these collectors aren't the most ethical types. He must have trusted you."

"Well, you're right about that, but I hardly knew him. Taking records from his collection just doesn't seem right. I know more than I wanted to about Ken, and I'm not the only one named in his will."

"What do you mean?" I pour myself some coffee and try one of the cinnamon rolls Ace has brought out.

"Ken owed money to several collectors—there's a

list. In lieu of payment, they get to pick out records too. I don't know, it's like looting someone's home after a tornado. It just isn't right."

"Well, if that's what he wanted."

"I know, I just hate to deal with these guys. Wait'll you see them. They'll be turning up here for the funeral, circling like buzzards."

"What about the rest of his things, the house?"

"Left it all to his sister. She's turning over the house to a realtor. She wants to sell his collection as well, and she wants me to run the sale."

I don't envy Ace his task, but I'm interested to see who turns up for the funeral, and I'm sure the police will be too.

"Well, I better get going," Ace says. "Talk to you later."

"Can I use your fax number?"

"Sure. The machine is in the office."

I spend the morning making phone calls. Tim Shaw at *Blue Note* promises to fax me some articles on Clifford Brown. "You working on something?" Shaw asks. I'd written for Tim over the past few years—reviews, insights on playing jazz piano, and a few profiles. "Clifford Brown is old news."

"Maybe. It's only Clifford Brown related. I just need some background material." I can tell from his voice that Tim thinks there's more to it than simple research.

"Okay, I'll send you what I've got in my files," he says, "but if there's a story, I want it first."

"You got it."

I also put in a call to the Conn instrument factory in Elkhart, Indiana. If I remember right, Brownie was supposed to get a new horn before his next gig with

Max and the band in Chicago. What I want to know is whether it was before or after the automobile accident.

I get transferred around to several people, but nobody at Conn seems to know anything. Most, it seems, don't even know who Clifford Brown is.

"That was what, forty years ago?" one guy in marketing says. "Nobody here was even working then."

"Any other ideas? It's important."

"Well, one of the designers—he's retired now, of course—I think still lives in the area. Saw him at a company picnic last summer. He'd be the one to talk to."

"How do I get a hold of him?"

"Let me check the personnel records, see if we have a current address. If we do, I'll have him call you."

"Thanks, you've been a big help." I leave him Ace's number and my own in Venice. When I get off the phone, the fax machine starts spewing out articles from Tim Shaw. I take the curling paper outside on the patio with another cup of coffee. The articles make for some very interesting reading.

There's a moving tribute from Quincy Jones, who worked with Brownie in Lionel Hampton's band, an interview with Max Roach, and some other short news items from various music magazines, most written within a year or two of Brown's death. Tim also included the liner notes from an album called *The Beginning and the End*, which I have as a CD reissue. Three of the tracks were supposedly made the night before Brown died; the notes claim that he was scheduled to pick up the new trumpet from Conn *on the way* to Chicago. Before the accident.

But an interview in another magazine with Billy Root, a saxophonist on that gig, contradicts the whole story. Root says that date was made months before the car crash. Tim has scribbled a note in the margin telling me Root lives in Las Vegas, so I can check that out myself. Thank you, Tim.

If Brown never made it to Elkhart, then what happened to the trumpet? If he did, was the trumpet picked up by someone at the scene of the crash, lost, misplaced, or perhaps never found until now? Another quote from Max Roach says a lot of companies gave the trumpeter horns. The articles raise more questions than answers. How many horns were there? In any case, I still don't know if the one at Silver State Pawn is Brownie's or not.

Around noon I call Metro; I ask for Trask but get Dave Ochoa instead. "There's supposed to be a cassette tape for me. You know anything about it?"

"Yeah, it's here, but you'll have to sign for it." Ochoa sounds bored and annoyed at talking to me.

"Fine, I'll be down within the hour."

"Eager, aren't we?"

I do my best to ignore Ochoa's sarcasm. "Has the reel-to-reel tape been sent off for analysis?"

"Yeah, Trask said to tell you it went out yesterday, to the FBI lab in Salt Lake City. Waste of time, I think."

"Why's that?"

"Nothing on it but music. What's that going to tell us?"

"Maybe nothing, maybe a lot." I hang up before Ochoa can say any more, glad I won't have to deal with him. My last call of the morning is to Pappy Dean.

"Damn," Pappy says, turning his head toward the speaker. "You tellin' me that's not Brownie?"

"I didn't say that."

He listens a couple of minutes, glances at me, and says, "Can we hear all of it?" He leans back against the seat and smiles as I head west on Charleston. "Got you a nice ride," he says, running his huge hands over the Camaro's seats. "This detective business must pay good." He winks and smiles at me.

"Just listen to the tape, Pappy."

Twenty minutes later we're in Red Rock Canyon. So close to the city, but another world from the Strip hotels and casinos. I stop and park at one of the view sites. It's several degrees colder up here, enough so I put on the Camaro's heater.

We listen to both sides of the tape, then get out of the car and walk over to a stone bench that faces the Spring Mountains. As the sun moves, I point out the caps of snow on the highest peaks and the movement of the sun, almost making the mountains change color before our eyes.

Pappy is not impressed. "I ain't into this nature shit," he says. "Critters out here." He points at a rabbit scurrying through the brush.

"So what do you think?"

"I don't know who the rest of the band is," he says, lighting up a long brown cigarette. "Bass player is sorry, but I'd swear that's Brownie. Caught him once with the Jazz Messengers, before he teamed up with Max Roach." He leans against the car, smiling, shaking his head. "Cat always played like it was his last gig." Pappy looks at me. "If this is Brownie, could be some long bread in it for somebody."

"That's what it's all about."

Pappy squints at the mountains. "Only thing you could do is check the solos."

"What do you mean?"

"Some of those tunes Brownie recorded with Max. See how close the solos come to your tape."

I hadn't thought of that. Brownie was an improviser of the first order. He wouldn't likely play the same solo, the same combination of notes. No jazz musician would, at least not one as good as Clifford Brown.

"Can you think of anybody who could do that, play that much like Brownie?"

"I don't know, man. Cat would have to have a lot of chops, almost as good as Brownie. Take a lot of time in the woodshed to sound that much like him."

Pappy has just described what every jazz musician goes through. I remember the hours I spent listening to Bill Evans's records, trying to sound like him, before I found my own voice.

"Brownie gave a whole lot of trumpet players something to think about." He turns to gaze at me, a smile on his face. "You got yourself a big job, piano man."

We get back in the car and head for Las Vegas, the tape playing again. The song is "Gertrude's Bounce." Pappy stares at the tape deck. "Damn, somebody put a gun to my head, I'd have to say it is Brownie."

"Nobody is going to do that, Pappy."

"Shit, hangin' around with you they might."

I spend the rest of the afternoon making more calls and listening to the cassette and other CDs and tapes I know are Clifford Brown. I waver so many times, and after repeated listening the tunes run together in my head. I can't tell the difference, especially on the few tunes that are the same. If this wasn't Clifford Brown, who was it?

Between listening and thinking, I also try to track down Billy Root, the saxophonist who had once recorded with Brown but disputed the story that the recording was done the night before Brown's death. No luck; he's touring in Europe and, according to his wife, won't be back for several weeks. She promises to relay my message if he checks in, but he's on the move.

I get luckier with Jack Montrose, another saxophonist who had written an entire album for Brownie when he was in California and knew the trumpeter's sound well. I explain what I want, and he agrees to see me.

"Sounds fascinating," Montrose says. "I'm leaving for California in the morning. Just finishing up some arrangements for a mini-festival. If you can make it about seven, we'll have a little time."

I copy down his address. "Seven is fine."

I know Montrose only by reputation, primarily as a composer-arranger, but when he greets me at the door, he reminds me that he was in the saxophone section for one of the hotel dates I'd played and conducted for the singer Lonnie Cole. Small world. Montrose was mentioned in the faxes Tim Shaw had sent me, so I knew that besides Brown, he'd written for and recorded with Art Pepper and Chet Baker and was a major force in the so-called West Coast jazz movement.

We settle in the den of his comfortable home. Montrose is soft-spoken and quick to smile, especially when talking about Clifford Brown. "He was a wonderful man, and a joy to write for. At a time when heroin habits were your credentials, Brownie was very refreshing."

We talk some more about the California scene in the fifties, and finally I pull out the cassette. "This is the tape I mentioned. I hope you can tell me if it's Clifford Brown."

Montrose puts the tape in his machine and settles in

a nearby chair, listening quietly. I try to read the expression on his face as the first few notes of the trumpet fill the room. Three tunes go by before he signals me he's heard enough.

"Are they all like that?" he asks.

"Yes."

He looks away, thinks for a moment. "That's really remarkable. You say these are from a master tape?"

"I'm not sure. That's what I'm trying to determine."

"Well," Montrose says, "I'd be hard pressed to say that's not Clifford Brown. I really would."

Now what? I'd hoped Montrose could tell me something more definite. "Do you think it's possible someone could imitate him so well nobody could tell the difference?"

"Well, that would depend. Sonny Stitt sounded so much like Bird at times people couldn't tell the difference. Charles MacPherson too. I think Clint Eastwood used him for that movie about Bird. As a musician yourself, I don't have to tell you that if somebody did, they would do it deliberately, not by accident. Even if you're influenced by another player, you don't want to sound just like him, right?"

Montrose laughs, thinking of something else. "Do you know the story of the invented pianist? As a pianist yourself, you'll appreciate this. Sometime in the fifties when there were so many records being made, a comedian who also played piano—I don't think I have to tell you his name—made a record. He invented a birthplace, a complete history, a name, that this was a great jazz talent who lived somewhere in the South but wouldn't go to New York. When the album came out it got rave reviews from all the hip critics. A new star in jazz, they called him."

"What happened?"

"He let it go on for a while, then confessed that he'd made up the entire story. The point is, he played just well enough to fool a lot of people. Maybe this trumpet player was doing the same thing."

Maybe he was, but that still didn't explain the time frame. This scam, if that's what it is, wasn't planned forty years ago. Based on the recording quality and the sound of the instruments, Montrose agrees with me that it was done in the fifties.

"On the other hand," Montrose says with a mischievous smile, "that might be Clifford Brown."

I let my head drop to my chest, wondering if I'll ever figure this one out.

"Don't forget," Montrose says, leaning forward to make his point, "record companies are coming up with forgotten tapes all the time." He looks away for a moment, recalling something else. "Do you read much?"

"Yeah, quite a bit. Why?"

"Just curious. I do too. You ever read *Invisible Man*, by Ralph Ellison? Lots of jazz in that book. Well, I just read that six new stories were discovered that he wrote in the thirties. Sitting in a box under his desk. There was no doubt they were Ellison's stories, they were written in his hand. See what I mean? It can happen." He holds his palms up and smiles broadly.

I nod, take the cassette out of the machine. "Well, thanks for your time."

"A pleasure," Montrose says as he sees me out. "I hope I've been a help."

I go back to Ace's house and play and replay the cassette until I'm sure that if I were pressed, I couldn't tell Clifford Brown from Herb Alpert. But there was something else Montrose said. It eludes me now, but I know it's important.

The service for Ken Perkins is more like a stockholders' meeting after the chairman of the board has died than a funeral. Ace spent the day before making arrangements with the help of Perkins's sister and fielding calls from collectors who knew Perkins or his collection. They'd been arriving like delegates to a convention.

"These are not mourners," Ace says, "they're vultures, come to pick over the bones."

According to Ace, the pickings are very good indeed. I don't recognize a lot of the records Ace is talking about, but he assures me that even a cursory inspection of the Perkins collection is enough to make any collector envious.

I hadn't seen Ace since the day before. He'd been holed up with Perkins's lawyer, going over the inventory of the collection, determining which collectors would get what records. Perkins apparently had it all on his computer.

"I don't think Ken's sister will have to hold an auction," Ace says. "She's had offers on virtually everything Ken has already."

"How did they know what he's got?" We stand outside the funeral home, watching the late arrivals. From the looks they give Ace, most of them know he's in charge of the collection. Some stop, shake hands with Ace, and mutter something like, "Terrible about Ken. Do you know if the copy of 'Earth Angel' is still available?" One or two are almost genuine with their condolences.

"See what I mean? They know mostly from Ken.

Collectors like to brag. That's part of the enjoyment," Ace says. "Either that or they've lost out to Ken on previous auctions."

Ace gets a signal from the funeral director that the service is about to begin. "I better go in," Ace says. "You coming?"

"In a minute." I arrived early after running out of people to call and tried to remain low profile while getting a good look at everyone in attendance. Not that I expected to, but I haven't seen anyone remotely resembling Cross. I watch the last few file past me. I'm about to go in when I see John Trask pull up in an unmarked car. He gets out and walks over.

"Quite a gathering," Trask says. "I take it Perkins had a lot of friends."

"They're not exactly friends." I explain what Ace has told me about the collectors.

"You mean they're all here for records? What kind of music did he collect?"

"I guess it doesn't matter. The point is, the records are rare and collectible."

"And I thought I'd seen it all." Trask looks around the full parking lot. "Let's take a walk, unless you're in a hurry to go inside."

I'm not anxious. I've been to two funerals in the past three years, both for people I hardly knew, even though I played a minor role in their deaths. "I can wait." I light a cigarette and follow Trask across an expanse of lawn.

"Interesting call logged in the other night. Anonymous, of course, from someone reporting an abandoned rental car at McCarran."

"Really?"

"Really," Trask says. He stops and looks at me for a

moment, trying to read my expression, then continues. We walk down an asphalt path to a small wooden footbridge built over a motionless stream. Trask stops and leans on the railing. "Turns out the rental car wasn't due back for another day. Guess the caller got confused."

"Must have," I say, not looking at Trask.

"The car was rented to a Bernard Dalton. Name mean anything to you?"

"Nothing. Should it?"

"Could have been the driver you told me about, the one who took you to Perkins's house."

"Or it could have been the guy who called himself Cross, to throw you off the trail."

"No, I think it was the driver, that's my gut feeling. I think this guy that calls himself Cross is too smart to have his name on anything."

Trask doesn't pursue it any further, and I'm grateful for that. "Thanks for the cassette tape," I say, more to keep him off the subject than anything else.

Trask nods. "Yeah, Ochoa told me you picked it up yesterday. Does it tell you anything?"

"Not yet. I played it for a couple of people, but so far nobody is convinced one way or the other. When do you think the master tape analysis will be back?"

"Hard to tell. We get in line with the FBI lab like anybody else. I'll let you know." He straightens up, hitches up his trousers, and tucks his tie inside his jacket. "We also found a trumpet in a case, outside the house in the hedge."

"A trumpet?" I get real busy fumbling for a cigarette, turning away from Trask to light it.

"That's what you used to break out the screen, right?"

I nod, exhale a cloud of smoke the wind carries away quickly. "Yeah, it was handy. Guess I forgot. What did you do with it?"

Trask shrugs. "Took a couple of photos. There were a few smudged prints, so we put it back in the house. You going back to L.A.?"

I try to make my sigh of relief inaudible. "Yeah, probably tonight." We walk back toward the mortuary. Near the entrance, Trask veers off to his car.

"You're not going in?" I ask.

"No, we don't know who we're looking for. If you pick up on anything, I want to know." Trask stops. "I don't like it, Horne, but you're all we've got. You and what might be the recordings of a dead trumpet player."

I go inside. There's a guest register, open on a podium. I run my finger down the list of names. No Cross, of course, nor Bernard Dalton, and no names that sound remotely familiar.

I stand near the back and look around the room. It's a closed-casket service with a very strange atmosphere. Everyone but Ace and Perkins's sister, who both sit up front, seems edgy, restless, more impatient than somber. There are a few obligatory remarks by the pastor, and it's all over in a few minutes. With the formalities concluded, several men converge on Ace.

He fends them off as quickly as he can, hands those that approach him a piece of paper, and checks their names off a list. These are the lottery winners, and they're smiling as they exit the chapel.

"Time to hand out the goodies," Ace says as he stops beside me. Perkins's sister is close behind. "Evan, this is Felicia Young, Ken's sister."

"How do you do," I say, taking her outstretched

hand. "I'm sorry for your loss." She's dressed in a dark suit. Her face is a mask. No sign of grief that I can see.

"Thank you," she says. "Are you a collector too?"

"No," Ace says quickly. "Evan's a pianist, sometimes a detective."

"Really?" she says, looking at me with new interest. "How fascinating." I can't tell if she's being sarcastic or just courteous.

"Evan, could you drop Mrs. Young at her hotel? I've got to take care of some business." He sweeps a hand toward the people filing out.

"Sure, be glad to. See you back at the house."

Felicia Young and I walk out to my car. When I open the door for her, she looks surprised. "Ken had at least two good friends," she says as we drive off.

"I really didn't know your brother, Mrs. Young. I only met him the night he was—"

"Killed? It's all right, you can say it. Ken and I weren't close at all, not for years. And it's Felicia." She rolls down the window a bit. "Do you mind if I smoke?"

"Not at all." I press in the lighter. She takes out cigarettes from her purse, lights one, and leans back in the seat. "Where are you staying?"

"Bally's," she says. "It's the only hotel I know here. My husband and I were out a few years ago."

We ride for a while in silence as I head up Eastern to Flamingo and turn left toward the Strip. "Charles tells me you were with my brother when it happened?"

"Yes, that's right."

"Did he say anything?" She shifts in the seat to look at me.

"No, I'm sorry, he didn't."

"No reason he should, I guess." She stubs out her cigarette. "Do you know why he was killed?"

"I think it was something to do with some tapes he came into. They could be quite valuable."

She shakes her head. "Jesus, killed over some music. It was always a thing with Ken. When he was a teenager he used to make lists of records he wanted, even called me once years later to see if I still had any of the old records I had when I was a teenager. Got mad when I told him I'd thrown them out."

I pull into the Bally's entrance and stop the car. "Do you want me to go inside with you?"

"No thanks, that won't be necessary. You've been very kind." She opens the door and starts to get out of the car, then turns back and touches my arm. "There is one thing you could do."

"Sure."

"I probably won't see you again, but Charles said you're sometimes a detective. I don't know what that means, but if you find out who killed my brother, I'd like to know."

"You'll be the first."

She manages a slight smile. "Thank you."

I watch her disappear into the hotel, head down. Her grieving will be done alone.

A sometime detective. I don't know what that means either.

INTERLUDE
June 25, 1956

Brownie drove, his eyes on the road, his mind drifting off, imagining how it might go at the Conn factory. There wouldn't actually be a ceremony, but he knew they would all be happy to meet him. They'd have records for him to autograph and warm handshakes while Richie and Nancy stood by beaming as the trumpets, laid out on a table covered with red velvet, were handed over. There would be new cases for each of them as well.

He would smile shyly, but inside he'd be overcome with joy. Maybe he would play these new horns too, carefully taking each out of its case, maybe blowing a few bars of "Joy Spring." Yeah, that would be perfect.

The car hurtled through the Pennsylvania countryside. Nancy was stretched out in the backseat, lost to the world in a deep sleep. Richie slumped beside him up front, dozing, smoking, occasionally making some conversation Brownie barely heard. He kept his eyes on the road, glancing every now and then at the dashboard, the radio on softly, the miles drifting by almost in a dream.

At dusk, the lights of Philadelphia glowing in the distance, they stopped for gas. There wouldn't be time later, Brownie reasoned. The truck stop was lined with big rigs, their engines idling ominously while the drivers rushed into the diner for coffee, past the busy bays of gasoline pumps.

Brownie felt rested even though he'd driven most of the way, riding on adrenaline, the only drug he needed, anticipating the gig at Music City. It would catch him, he knew, later tonight, after they were a few more miles down the highway. Then it would be his turn to curl up in the big backseat, and hope he wouldn't wake up till they were in Elkhart.

He got coffee in a paper cup for Nancy while Richie gassed up the car and joked with a trucker at the next pump. Nancy was smiling sleepily at him, standing by the car, stretching, yawning, rubbing her eyes.

"Girl, you slept right through," Brownie said, handing her the coffee.

"Have to if I'm going to drive the rest of the way tonight," Nancy said, squinting at the dials on the gas pump. Richie exchanged glances with Brownie and rolled his eyes. Nancy was a novice driver, with poor vision and barely able to negotiate a U-turn.

The attendant, dressed in a dark green, grease-stained Texaco shirt and pants, gazed at the Buick. He said, "Nice car. Where you folks headed?"

Brownie turned to him, smiled. "Philly. I'm playing tonight at Music City."

"Is that so?" the attendant said, taking the money from Richie, not knowing what Brownie meant.

"You cool?" Richie said, pocketing the change and glancing at Clifford.

"Oh yeah," Brownie said. He climbed into the back-seat and was asleep almost before the car pulled away.

CHAPTER
NINE

BY SIX I'M ON THE ROAD, CLIMBING OUT OF LAS VEGAS into the darkness, the glow of the Strip's lights growing fainter and smaller by the mile in my rearview mirror. The pawn ticket for the trumpet is in an envelope, taped under the front seat; the nearly empty bottle of trumpet valve oil is in the glove compartment. That should be one of the easiest things to check out at any number of music stores in L.A. Everything else is confusion.

Ken Perkins is dead, shot by someone maybe named Cross, who I never got a good look at. A tape that may or may not be Clifford Brown is all I have that's tangible. I run over several scenarios in my mind, starting with the premise that the tapes are genuine. If that's the case, how did Cross get them? Master tapes would have to have come from a record company or some recording studio.

Did Cross steal them, have someone steal them for him? How did he know about their existence? Is this simply another instance like the Dean Benedetti tapes of Charlie Parker, or the more recently discovered tapes of John Coltrane at Atlantic Records? Tapes of Clifford Brown lying around on a shelf somewhere, forgotten for years until somebody cleans out a store room or an attic and says, "What have we got here?"

A discovery of that magnitude would be big news, but as Jack Montrose said, "It happens."

On the other hand, what if the tapes are not genuine? How was it done, and who made them? Was there perhaps a very talented trumpet player—and is he still around—who could sound so much like Clifford Brown everybody would be fooled? Something Montrose said still bothers me, but I don't have it yet. A remark about the Clint Eastwood movie *Bird*. I've seen the film several times, and somewhere in a box at home I have the sound track. Maybe that will bring it into focus.

Traffic is light as I reach the Halloran Summit and start the descent into Baker, a cluster of lights four thousand feet below me. Another hour to Barstow, then a decision. On to I-10 and through downtown Los Angeles, or the more risky Pearblossom Highway at night? Dark curves, no lights, and all those dips where cars disappear for several seconds then emerge with blinding high beams.

I stop for gas and coffee in Barstow, smoke two cigarettes, pace around the huge parking area. A procession of resigned truckers in jeans and flannel shirts or parkas, baseball caps or cowboy hats, gas up, check their huge rigs, and run inside for steaming paper cups of coffee. I go over everything in my mind, but I'm still not clear on so many things. Finally, I give up and get back in the car. I know I'm stalling.

On the road again, I decide the best course of action is to go, at least for now, on the assumption that whether the tapes are genuine or not, they had to be made somewhere. I'm guessing Hollywood.

I can start with some recording studios that were in operation in the fifties. I've heard all the stories about small studios that were around then, some legitimate, some not. They would grab a group from one of the many clubs, get them over to record after a gig when the musicians were tired, drunk, or both, and pay them a few bucks. Then the sessions were forgotten, the tapes lost and put away for years.

Clifford Brown was in L.A. then, that much I know. Maybe that's when the sessions were done—scheduled for release at some later date, or held back after the car crash? It was done by many record companies. A forgotten musician becomes a star, and old tapes are hauled out to capitalize on his newfound fame.

It is a place to start, and I feel better with some plan in mind, so much so that when I get to Victorville, I turn off on 18 and take the Pearblossom plunge across the desert toward Palmdale and the Los Angeles interchange.

I tune in to a talk show for distraction but find myself hardly listening, gripping the wheel tighter as I take the first series of dips and curves, keeping the speedometer needle on sixty. There are patches of snow littering the desert, and the air blows cold through the open window.

At the Palmdale cutoff the road flattens out and widens to two lanes. I relax a little, knowing the freeway into the San Fernando Valley is not far off. But then, at a traffic signal, I notice a car behind me I think I've seen before, possibly when I gassed up in Barstow. A white Pontiac or Oldsmobile.

I pull away from the light and stay in the right lane,

giving the car an opportunity to pass. It doesn't. At the interchange he allows some space between our cars but stays right with me all the way into the north end of the valley, no matter how often I change lanes or speeds.

The Camaro's windows are tinted dark, so it's impossible to see the driver's face. My eyes flick from the road to the rearview and side mirrors. Cross? Bernard Dalton? Or just my imagination working overtime? One way to find out.

The traffic is more congested now as we reach the interchange with the Ventura Freeway. I watch for an opening to my right, and at the last minute I veer across to the Santa Monica exit, cutting off two cars, horns and squealing tires in my wake, but the white car continues on.

I merge with the San Diego Freeway traffic and climb up out of the valley. At the top of the hill, I exit at Sunset and take surface streets home to Venice. No tails, no strange cars all the way.

"What are you looking for?" Natalie asks from the bedroom doorway.

"Something I've got to find." I sit in the middle of the floor, surrounded by boxes, books, CDs, and tapes.

"Well, I gathered that," Natalie says, "but it's almost midnight."

"It's here someplace." I've been through three boxes of tapes and books already, but my packing was without any system. I stop for a minute and look at Natalie, standing in the doorway watching me. Bare feet, a baggy UCLA sweatshirt that hangs down well over her waist, almost hiding the black panties. Her hair is brushed loose around her face. I called her as soon as I got in, and she came right over. "Aren't you cold?"

She looks down at her bare legs. "A little." She raises her eyes slowly. "You could warm me up."

She comes in and sits on the bed. "What are you looking for?"

"A cassette of the *Bird* movie." I dig around in the boxes and finally find it near the bottom. "Here we go," I say, holding it up. I take the tape out of its plastic box. "Do me a favor and put this on."

"Yes, master." She stands and gives me a mock salute.

I take the liner notes out also, follow her into the living room, and sit down to read while the music begins. I'm through half the notes, listening to Bird. I play "Now's the Time," then slap my knee. "That's how they did it," I say. "Yes."

Natalie doesn't know what I'm talking about. "How they did what?"

"The tapes, that's how they made them."

Natalie sits down on the couch next to me. "Will you please tell me what you're talking about? Have you got anything to eat here? I'm hungry."

"What? Yeah, sure, help yourself," I say, continuing to read how the music was done for the film.

"How about some bacon and eggs?" she calls from the kitchen.

"Yeah, sounds good. I'll make some coffee." I come up behind her, put my arms around her waist. "I think I've got it."

"Not yet, you don't." She pushes me away, smiling. "I've had a long day of studying. I'll cook, you tell me what this is all about."

I sit at the kitchen table while she gets things going.

I've already told her about the cassette and most of what's happened in Las Vegas, but I realize I've developed an automatic habit of editing what I say, depending on who I'm talking to. I have told her my doubts about Clifford Brown being the trumpet player on the tapes.

"It was something Jack Montrose said that got me to thinking, but I couldn't figure it out until now. There," I say. "Hear that? That's Charlie Parker." The tape is now on a tune called "Cool Blues."

She pauses, a fork in her hand over the skillet, listens for a few moments. "So? That's who it's supposed to be, isn't it?"

"Exactly. That's the real Charlie Parker, not someone imitating him."

Natalie still doesn't get it, but is curious about my grin. "You are going to tell me, aren't you?"

"Okay, that's Charlie Parker, but it's not any of the guys who played with him—Al Haig, Curly Russell, or Stan Levy. That's Monty Alexander on piano, Ray Brown on bass, John Guerin on drums."

"Didn't we just see Brown and Alexander a few months ago at the Jazz Bakery?"

"We sure did."

"So how—"

"It's all right here," I say, holding up the liner notes. "Clint Eastwood had a choice. He could make a movie about Charlie Parker and use someone so good at imitating him—Charles MacPherson, for example—or somehow use recordings of the real Charlie Parker. He managed to track down some old Bird recordings, air check tapes, then—using filters and some process I don't fully understand—eliminate everything but Bird's sound. Then he brings in this rhythm section; they listen to Bird on headphones and record their parts. When it's all enhanced, mixed, it sounds like Bird playing with a modern rhythm section."

Natalie stops, one hand on her hip, and turns the bacon. "Forgive me for asking, but could anyone tell whether that's Charlie Parker or, what's his name, Charles MacPherson?"

"Probably not, unless you're a musician or an audiophile. The rhythm section gives it away, but Eastwood could tell, and he wanted Charlie Parker, the real thing. It would have been much easier, saved a lot of time, to just use MacPherson. He is on some of these cuts, but most of it's Bird."

"So if I've got this right, you're saying that with the alleged Clifford Brown tape, whoever was responsible did it in reverse?"

"Alleged Clifford Brown tape. I like that. You know, for an aspiring lawyer you're pretty smart."

My head was swimming with the details, but it could work that way. With today's recording capabilities it wouldn't be too difficult to take a Clifford Brown solo from any of his recordings and mix it with a rhythm section sound isolated from whomever they had recorded with. It would sound like Clifford Brown because it was Clifford Brown, and it would sound like it had been done in the fifties.

Everybody—record companies, me, for example— could be convinced that these were previously unknown recordings of Clifford Brown.

Natalie listens to me explain it all again while we wolf down the bacon and eggs and toast. Over the second cup of coffee, I play portions of the *Bird* tape again and point out the differences in sound. "Monty Alexander was ten years old when Bird died. Guerin is primarily a studio session drummer, but notice how clear the sound is."

The more I explain it to Natalie, the clearer it becomes to me. This is how it could be done, and I am starting to appreciate the thoroughness of the man who calls himself Cross, the man who I think shot Ken Perkins.

Natalie listens quietly, watches me work it out. "I don't want to burst your bubble, but isn't it still possible that the cassette you have from the master is in fact Clifford Brown, and the whole thing was recorded before he died?"

"Yes, of course it is, but this at least proves there is also a way to fake the tapes and proves to me I'm not crazy. I'll know for sure when the tape Trask sent to the FBI for analysis comes back."

Natalie leans back in her chair and folds her arms in front of her. "I've got just one more question. Can we go to bed now?"

"I thought you'd never ask."

Long after Natalie falls asleep, I lie awake, hearing the cassette in my mind, hoping the FBI report tells me that type of recording tape could be purchased today at any Tower Records store.

Natalie is gone again when I wake up, and again it's the phone that wakes me.

"We need to talk, sport."

"Coop? It's kind of early, isn't it?"

"Not for us civil servants who protect you from the ravages of crime. We're usually up before noon."

"Noon?" I roll over and glance at the clock. "I've got things to do."

"Yes indeed," Coop says. "The first of which is to

meet me and buy me lunch while I advise you on the policies of reciprocal cooperation between the Santa Monica police and Las Vegas Metro. You with me, sport?"

"Yeah, I'm here."

"Get your butt down to Santa Monica Pier. I've got something to show you."

Coop hangs up before I can ask him what. It's never straightforward with Coop. He always holds something back, but at least I know I'm not in any trouble with Las Vegas. Coop's call would have been different if I was.

Santa Monica Pier has always been one of my favorite places. I spent a lot of time there as a kid, and it's been used as a backdrop for so many movies and TV programs that it's one of the most recognizable landmarks in southern California. The carousel at the edge of the pier brings back a lot of memories—riding those wooden horses, the faces of my parents a blur as I go round and round, the promise of a hot dog and a snow cone when the ride is over—just as vivid to me today.

I nose slowly down the steep incline and find a spot in the city parking lot. Coop is leaning on the rail, watching some of the fishermen that still haunt the pier, their lines in the dark water below, tackle boxes and plastic buckets at their feet. Some things never change.

"I don't see your fishing gear. This a new hobby for you?" Coop turns toward me, looking like he's been caught doing something he shouldn't. "That's me, centerfold for *Field & Stream*." He's in jeans, a windbreaker, and running shoes.

"Little out of uniform, aren't we?"

"Even us dedicated civil servants get a day off now and then. Let's take a walk," Coop says. "We'll be dining alfresco."

We stroll down to the end of the pier. Not many people out today, and those that are have their collars turned up against the cold sea air. There's the smell of fish, the ocean, and hamburgers frying on a grill at one of the small takeout places.

I buy us a couple of hot dogs and Cokes, and we take a seat on one of the benches bolted to the asphalt at the end of the pier. Below us, the dark green water laps against the pilings. It looks cold. We've both been here, done this many times before. Coop inhales his hot dog and drinks off his soda before I'm half finished with mine. Afterward I light a cigarette and wait for Coop to reveal his secrets.

"Tell me about this jazz consulting you did that turned ugly. You didn't give the tape a bad review, I hope?"

Coop's wit is lost on most people. He has a reputation for being abrasive at times, but there's no one I'd want in my corner more. It's been like that since we were in high school together.

I go through the whole story for him, not minding at all, since each telling clarifies things for me. Like the good cop that he is, Coop saves his questions and insights for later. Sometimes he cuts right to the core of things.

"Have you considered that Trask is taking advantage of your obsession—all right, eagerness—to determine if this musician on the tape is genuine by using you?"

"The thought crossed my mind. I wouldn't exactly call it an obsession either."

Coop gives me a look and frowns at my cigarette. "What are those filthy things you're smoking?"

I take one last drag and crush it out. "A new brand, thought they might make me quit."

"Well, if you're smoking those, I'm sure you won't mind one of my cigars." He lights up a long, thin cigarillo and turns toward me on the bench. "I don't exactly agree with Trask's methods, but he's a solid cop, and where we all are sometime or other: a murder with no leads. Otherwise you'd be entirely out of the loop, sport. You know that, don't you?"

"I know that. I'm not trying to catch a murderer, just verify a recording, but Coop, you know they're connected."

"You have a theory, I trust, and you're going to share it, try it out on a brilliant criminologist."

"Well, now that you mention it." I sit forward on the bench and stare out to sea. Somewhere on the horizon the sun is peeking through the dark sky, the wind whipping up whitecaps, blowing across the pier.

"I think this guy Cross somehow came into these tapes and planned to run a scam on a record company. The money would be good, but I don't think he was going to do it for money. These guys are really obsessive. The whole thing is to have something no one else has."

"But it went wrong somewhere along the line."

"Very. Either Perkins got cold feet, even if they did fool me, which I'm not entirely sure of, or there was some disagreement on the split if the scam worked. Maybe the argument just got out of hand, and Perkins's death was accidental. I don't know."

Coop continues to smoke, gaze out to sea, follow the flight of some gulls that hover overhead. "Why is it so important to know if the tapes are genuine? Bogus or not, there was a murder." Coop puts his eyes on me now. "Forget the accidental death routine. You don't shoot somebody accidentally twice."

"Okay, it was murder. Why is it so important? I don't know, it's just something I have to do. If Cross made the tapes or stole them or whatever, there are other people involved. If I get close, maybe some of them will come out."

"Or maybe Cross will come out and go after you. He's going to think you'll figure out how he faked the tapes, if they are fake." Coop pauses, lets that sink in. "There's a general rule about murder. If they've done it once, they're capable of doing it again. Keep that in mind, sport."

"You said you had something to show me."

Coop nods and takes a computer printout from his jacket. "Trask faxed this to me early this morning."

I know what it is as soon as I glance at it. The FBI logo is right on the top of the page. There are a lot of numbers and evidence citations, some technical stuff about magnetic particles, but the good part is near the bottom. The lab test analysis conclusively shows the tape was manufactured in the fifties. Comparison tests were made on currently available similar recording tape, and all tests were conclusive.

The tape I listened to couldn't possibly have been recorded this decade, much less this year, unless Cross found some leftover stock.

"This is awfully fast service, isn't it? Trask said something about having to get in line like everybody else with the FBI lab."

"Usually takes weeks," Coop says, "unless it's given

some kind of special priority. I wonder how that came about?" There's a trace of a smile on his face.

I get up and walk over to the railing, look down at the water below. One hot summer's day, when I was in high school, on a dare, I jumped off this pier just to see what it would feel like. Coop had followed me in, thinking I'd fallen, but it was me who saved him. I turn around and face Coop. "This doesn't prove anything."

"Doesn't it prove what you wanted it to?" Coop says. "These tapes—at least that one—were made in the fifties. I don't care how carefully this Cross guy planned it, he didn't start then, so maybe the tapes really are genuine." He asks me the same question that's been running through my mind. "Is it possible for someone to imitate a musician that convincingly?"

Pappy Dean thought so, as did Jack Montrose. In my own first hearing of the tapes I had been convinced immediately. Now I don't know if I am or not. My theory about the murder fits a lot better if they're fake.

Coop stands up and joins me at the railing. "There's not much I can do here but keep your good name alive, such as it is. The murder was done in Vegas. Unless there's a crime committed here that's connected, my hands are tied," Coop says. "Dare I ask why you don't just drop it? You're in the clear, you can just walk away from this."

"No, I can't, Coop. You know that."

Coop shrugs. "You never can."

We walk back to our cars, each with our own thoughts. We get to the Camaro first. Coop walks all around it. "Well, you finally got a car like you wanted in high school. Imagine cruising Santa Monica in this."

I get in, roll down the window. Coop leans on the roof. "Thanks for the info."

"You're going to be busy, sport."

"How's that?"

"You've got to find some out-of-work trumpet player who likes to record like someone he isn't."

CHAPTER
TEN

I START WITH RICK MARKHAM AT PACIFIC RECORDS. I did him a favor once, and now it's his turn. Maybe in the process I'll again save him money. He actually sounds glad to hear me when I call, although I have to run an obstacle course of secretaries, assistants, and several "he's on another line" routines.

"I'll hold," I say, with the last one, then spend the next four minutes listening to Michael Bolton moan and whine through his latest hit. There's another dream concert for Coop. Michael Bolton and Kenny G.

"Evan, is that really you?" Markham asks, when he finally comes on the line. I can visualize him in his spacious office, spinning in his huge chair, juggling calls and visitors.

I'd been put off by Markham when I'd found his half brother Elvin Case during the Lonnie Cole episode. But I'd alerted him to some possible discrepancies in Pacific's own stock. He'd been grateful, even offered me a job. I don't think he was surprised when I declined.

"I need a favor, Rick, just some information really."

"Glad to help if I can," Markham says, with only a trace of apprehension in his voice. When I explain what I'm after, he's puzzled but interested in my request.

"That's not really my area of expertise. Tell you what, let me get my guy on that and we'll set up a meeting. How's that?"

"Fine, the sooner the better."

"You got it." At least he doesn't say, "Let's do lunch."

I only have to wait an hour for his return call. "How about tomorrow morning? Ten o'clock, my office."

"Thanks, Rick, see you then."

I kill the afternoon on a tour of music stores to see if anyone can identify the bottle of valve oil that was in the trumpet case, but most of the clerks are too young, have no idea of the brand or if it's still even made. They try to sell me other brands, larger bottles of new improved valve oil that, so they say, are far more effective.

Most of them gaze at my nearly empty bottle with the rubbed-out name, hold it up to the light, and shake their heads as if they are looking at a relic from another era. Some even say exactly that, which is precisely what I want to hear.

"I don't think they make it in bottles that small now," one guy at a store on Lincoln Boulevard tells me. "I know they don't make it in glass bottles."

"Are you sure?"

"I've never seen glass." He turns and reaches for a plastic bottle on the shelf behind him. "Here, try this stuff, it's our most popular oil." He sets a larger plastic bottle on the counter. The brand name is Al Cass. He touches the rubber dropper on top of my bottle, unscrews the cap, holds it up to his nose, then throws his head back quickly.

"Wow, smell that."

I already can, very strong kerosene.

"Used to be more kerosene content. You can still smell the new stuff, but not as much." He opens the new bottle for me to sample. He's right; the kerosene odor is still there, but much lighter.

"Any idea what the name might have been?"

He looks at the rubbed out label. "Ick Stu? Got me, man." He suddenly smiles. "Maybe Vanna White could figure it out."

"What?"

"You know, the TV show, *Wheel of Fortune*, the word puzzles."

"Yeah, maybe I'll call her."

"Sorry I can't help," he says, sliding the new bottle across the counter. "You should try this. Same stuff Wynton Marsalis uses."

"No, thanks anyway."

It goes like that all afternoon. I decide to try a couple of shops in Hollywood that cater to professional musicians, and maybe talk to some trumpet players who might have once used whatever this is. But that's all for tomorrow.

Around six I call my mentor.

Most people have had somebody in their life who represents a turning point, a time when things become clear, when someone or some event shows you the way to your own destiny. Sometimes it's a parent, a good friend, or perhaps a stranger who says just the right combination of things to open your eyes to what you've always been aware of but have never seen clearly. For

me that person was Calvin Hughes—Cal, to anyone he
allowed to enter his world.

I'd heard about Cal long before I met him. He was
one of those legendary underground figures that slide
around like shadows. I'd heard about him as I made my
way through the labyrinth of the jazz world. Like Art
Pepper, Cal had been one of the few white musicians
accepted on the bandstands of Central Avenue, which
in the fifties was the Los Angeles equivalent of Fifty-
second Street.

"You should have heard Cal Hughes with Dexter
Gordon and Wardell Gray," musicians would tell me.

By the time I was out of music school, a degree in
hand, armed with a lot of dreams and some optimism,
Cal had already quit playing years before. No reason
that anybody knew; he just quit. No one knew why,
and the legend grew, the jazz counterpart to the legend
surrounding writer J. D. Salinger. I learned through
the grapevine, however, that Cal occasionally took a
student. Not for the money—somehow, according to
the scant information available, he managed to survive
on a small inheritance, living in a tiny house in the
Hollywood hills. He rarely went out. You had to pass a
certain test to be accepted by Cal, but nobody seemed
to know what the requirements were.

One of them was apparently persistence. I tried for
months to make contact, sure that studying piano with
Cal Hughes would be my postgraduate work, but I was
rebuffed at every turn. Finally, coercing the address out
of someone who had once played with him, I simply
drove up to his house one summer evening and
knocked on his door. By that time, I figured I had
nothing to lose.

"Come on in. I've been expecting you," was all he

said. And so began our intense but sporadic relationship.

That first evening, I felt like I was in the presence of some holy man. He sat me down in his living room, and we talked while the sun set, the splinters of light that seeped through the mesh curtains giving way first to shadows, finally to darkness.

Cal hardly seemed to notice, and at first I thought he was partially blind. He chain-smoked while he listened to why I wanted to play jazz. For distraction he nuzzled the ear of his only companion, a tan Labrador named Milton, who remained at his master's feet and regarded me with little interest.

As if suddenly noticing the darkness engulfing us, Cal turned on the one lamp next to his chair. There was a small table, laden with stacks of books ranging from poetry to essays to the novels of James Joyce.

"Let's go outside," he said. From the street, the house appeared to be wedged against the side of the hill, crammed between two mansion-size homes. But on the tiny balcony, there were two chairs and something of a view of Hollywood below.

Between coughing fits, we spent another couple of hours talking about jazz piano before he abruptly told me I had to leave. I thanked him for his time. He scribbled his phone number on a piece of paper and handed it to me.

"Are you coming back?"

"Of course, if you'll take me as a student. I'd be very grateful."

"Maybe," Cal said. "We'll see."

Weeks of visits followed. Long talks, listening to records, me going to the store to bring back bottles of Scotch and cigarettes. Finally Cal asked me to play on the shabby, scarred spinet piano that lay soundless in one corner of the room, stacked high with music, some of it penciled in Cal's own hand. When I did finally play, Cal simply said, "Come back next week. We'll start then."

In all the time I knew Cal, I never once heard him play that or any other piano. I learned later he had heard me many times, right after I began asking around about him.

Once when I came across one of his old records, I brought it to him, thinking he would like it. "Get that out of here," he'd said, as if I'd brought him something repugnant. I was determined to gain his favor and learn why someone so obviously talented had simply quit. I never found out, no matter how subtly or obviously I pursued the subject.

"I prefer not to," was his only reply. "That's from a Herman Melville story, 'Bartleby the Scrivener,'" he'd said with an enigmatic smile. I dug out the story, read it many times, but Cal's answer remained as ambiguous as Bartleby's.

Cal was ruthless in his teaching, spare in his praise, but always inspirational. He saw something in me that I didn't see myself, and with his own eccentric method sought to expose, develop, and nurture what talent I possessed. "You have a gift, don't squander it." His words rang in my head for weeks.

Finally, at the end of one long, grueling session, he said, "Get out of here. I can't teach you anything else."

As my career progressed, we lost touch, mostly due to my neglect. The visits became fewer and were reduced to the occasional phone call, but I know he kept track of my minor successes. Over the years, our relationship went from student-teacher to friend-mentor.

He berated me, for example, for playing and conducting for Lonnie Cole. "Why waste your talent on some goddamned singer unless it's Ella or Sarah?" He critiqued my one album as a leader harshly but fairly and with a touch of praise: "Not bad, Evan, not bad."

Only once did he call me, and that was shortly after the accident that left my solo hand useless and my career in doubt. "I'm sending you something," he said. "Don't give up, Evan." Those three words became my motto.

A few days later, a package arrived. It was a Charles Mingus album—Cal had total disdain for CDs. There was a brief note attached that said, "If you don't know this piano player, you should. Three fingers on his right hand don't work." The pianist was Horace Parlan.

I nearly wore it out, playing it again and again, eventually replacing it when it was reissued on CD.

Now, as I pull up in front of Cal's house, I know he is the one person who will understand why I'm chasing Clifford Brown's phantom, why I can't let go of so many things. Information and reassurance is what I want, and hopefully what I will get from Cal.

He opens the door, Milton at his side, and ushers me in. As usual the room is lit only by the reading lamp. A book is open facedown on the table. He sees me glance at the title. It's a collection of essays by critic and essayist Stanley Crouch.

"Just reading about Miles's sellout," Cal says. "Crouch is right. Miles fucked up. Couldn't play anymore, so he became a rock star." He lights a cigarette from a still-burning butt, settles in his chair, and gazes across at me.

I don't have to ask how he's doing. The cough still

racks his body, and he seems to have shrunk. His hair, all white now, is long, straggling over his collar in thin strands, but his eyes are still clear and sharp, his voice hoarse. He watches me take in his appearance. He smiles, chuckles.

"What were you thinking of saying? 'Looking good, Cal'?"

"No, I wasn't. Have you seen a doctor?"

He shrugs, waves a hand in the air. "I'm dying. I don't need a doctor to tell me that. Put it out of your mind. I have."

We sit for a few moments, letting the stillness surround us while I wonder for the thousandth time why he quit playing.

"Drink?" he says, eyeing the paper sack I'm holding.

"Sure, why not?" I hand him the bag, and he pulls out the bottle.

"Oh my, Glenlivet. The detective business must be good." He winks and smiles, letting me know he knows all about what I've been doing. He goes to the kitchen. I hear the clatter of ice trays, cubes clinking in glasses. He returns, pours us both an ample drink.

"To you, Sherlock," he says, raising his glass. "Well, let's review for a moment. You put Lonnie Cole and his partner in jail, uncovered a record scam, and in Las Vegas you almost solved Wardell Gray's murder. You were right, that's what it was, a murder. Poor Wardell, just wanted to play his horn. And now you're chasing after Clifford Brown. You have good taste, I'll give you that." He looks again at his glass. "In Scotch and musicians."

When I called, I briefly ran down what I knew so far, told him about the tapes, and asked if he'd listen to the cassette. I was counting on Cal to dredge up some memories of the West Coast jazz scene, see if he could remember anyone who could play so much like Clifford Brown or if he knew about any recordings Brownie had done that nobody would have known about.

"Where's this trumpet?"

"In a pawn shop in Las Vegas."

Cal nods, sips his drink. "Smart—some irony to that as well. Let's hear the tape."

Cal's distrust of CDs is still unwavering. There's a turntable, a couple of hundred records—many of which would be interesting to collectors, I think now—and a cassette deck. I put the tape in and press the play button. We sit in the semidarkness for one whole side of the tape. Cal's only movement is to pour another drink. Milton occasionally cocks an ear at one of the trumpet's high notes. These are again some tunes I don't know, but the sound is there, the heartbreaking vibrato on the ballads, the total control on the fast tempos. Every time I hear the tape, I think something different. When it ends, there's a click as it shuts off.

For a few moments Cal says nothing. His face is totally in shadow. I can't read his expression. Finally, he puts his head back on the chair. "Jesus, that's impressive," he says. "The trumpet, I mean. The piano player's really scuffling though. Definitely not Richie Powell, nor is the drummer Max Roach."

"But is it Clifford Brown?" If anyone knows, it's Cal. Not from educated guesses, but from gut feeling. He won't be able to explain how or why he knows, but his answer will be enough.

He crumples a cigarette pack, opens another, and lights up. "I don't think so."

"The FBI have verified that the tape was vintage fifties stuff, so it wasn't made recently."

"The FBI—well then, we've nothing to worry about. I'm sure they did, but that doesn't matter. It's someone so close to Clifford but just missing, not by much, but enough. I'd stake what's left of my life on it."

Well, there it is. Proof—but from an eccentric, reclusive former jazz piano player who lives in the Hollywood hills with a dog named after a poet. He sees no one and wouldn't dream of entering a courtroom. A perfect witness. I might as well have Howard Hughes for my source. I try to imagine Cal accompanying me to Rick Markham's office.

"Somebody was killed over this tape."

"So you told me." Cal downs his drink. "Another?"

"Not for me. You go ahead."

"I planned to."

"Did you know Clifford Brown when he was out here?"

"No, heard him a couple of times at the Lighthouse, got the records. Phenomenal talent. Fucking car crash, and I'm sitting here still, drinking Scotch. What do you suppose God had in mind?"

"Do you know if he ever played with Duke Ellington, at the Ambassador Hotel, maybe just subbing for a few nights?"

"God, or Clifford Brown?" Cal smiles at the thought. "It's possible. Duke would have liked Brownie. Lionel Hampton did. What a trumpet section that was. Brownie and Art Farmer sitting side by side, and a very young Quincy Jones. You think anything like Michael Jackson was on Quincy's mind then? Jesus."

I let Cal's triggered memories rise to the surface of his mind. "Every radio station in America should play something of Duke's every day," he says. "This trumpet you have, what makes you think it's Brownie's?"

"His initials are engraved inside the horn."

"Do you know for sure he had that done? That sounds kind of vain for Brownie. He wasn't that way, despite his talent."

"Who then?"

Cal shrugs. "Someone with the same initials."

"Who also plays that much like Clifford Brown?"

"How much did you play like Bill Evans when you first came to me?"

"A lot, I guess, but no one would mistake me for Bill Evans."

"Somebody who didn't know—really know—might." Cal leans forward, peers at me through the shadows. "You really want it to be him, don't you?"

"Yeah, I guess I do."

"Do you know why?"

"I don't know. Because I want to know I've found something valuable to jazz, something that people can enjoy, appreciate." I look back at Cal. His gaze is steady.

"Listen to me," he says. "That's why you're the one."

"The one what?"

"To find the truth." I don't know if it's the Scotch talking or Cal's rambling mind. "What do the experts say about your hand?"

I tell him but leave out my fears about recovery. Cal knows about those.

"If it's supposed to, it'll work out. You may not play

piano again the way you want to, but until you can, this is what you're supposed to be doing."

"I don't understand."

"Of course you do. You already know." Cal's eyes burn with passion; his voice resonates with quiet feeling. "Wardell, Brownie, they're reaching out to you, somebody who understands them well enough, what they did, what they mean, what they represent. You have to prove that's not Clifford Brown on that tape so the public, a record company, isn't sold a bill of goods. But more importantly, so Clifford Brown's memory isn't tarnished. There's a lesson in this for you too, if you look for it."

"But what if it is Brownie, what if you're wrong?"

"If you believe that, then prove that it is Brownie. Don't give up, Evan, don't give up."

There are two messages on my machine. One from Natalie, telling me she's studying for a big exam and she'll see me tomorrow. The other is from a Roy Lewis of the Conn company in Elkhart, Indiana.

"I'm retired now, Mr. Horne, but I remember Clifford Brown's scheduled visit very well. I was looking forward to meeting him, but as you know, he never arrived. As for the trumpets, I'm afraid I have no idea what happened to them. Please call me if you'd like to talk about this further."

He leaves a number where I can reach him. Trumpets? More than one?

Cal is right. I already know. I know the lesson he was talking about as well.

Clifford Brown recovered from his first accident and played again.

CHAPTER
ELEVEN

I WAKE UP EARLY AND, WHILE THE COFFEE IS BREWING, get on the phone to Roy Lewis at Conn. Hazy sunshine filters in the window, but according to a local Willard Scott clone, the weather forecast is for light rain that will get heavier in the next few days. The annual Malibu mud slides can't be far off.

Roy Lewis is very pleasant and cooperative, doesn't even ask why I want to know about Clifford Brown's trumpets.

"As I said on the message I left, Mr. Brown, of course, never arrived at our factory. It was a terrible shock to learn of his death. Such a talent."

"And you don't know what happened to the trumpets?"

"No, I'm afraid not. That was so long ago. I assume they were put back in stock."

"Do you happen to know if the trumpets were engraved with his initials, inside the bell of the horn?"

Lewis pauses for a moment, thinking about it. "No, I don't remember that. Of course we could have done that if he wanted. I'm not sure if that was done here at the factory."

I listen to Lewis, trying to remember something else I want to ask him.

"Are you still there, Mr. Horne?"

"Yes, sorry. Is it possible that someone at the company might have, how shall I phrase this, kept the horns as a souvenir?"

Now it's Lewis's turn to think. "Yes, I see what you mean. I suppose it's possible, but very unlikely. They would have to be accounted for in the inventory."

"But it is possible." A trumpet or trumpets earmarked for a famous musician could easily get lost in the shuffle, misplaced, put away and forgotten over the years.

"Well, yes, but if you're suggesting some impropriety on the part of myself or one of our employees, well—"

"No, no, nothing like that, it's just that Clifford Brown was a very famous musician, and—"

"Yes, of course, I see what you mean. Well, I'm afraid there would be no way to determine that, unless of course you found one of the trumpets."

"Thank you, Mr. Lewis. You've been very helpful."

"Not at all. There is one thing you could do for me."

"Sure."

"If you should uncover something, discover what happened to the trumpets, I'd like to know."

There's no waiting at Rick Markham's office. His secretary ushers me right in, and Markham is already on his feet, coming around his desk, his hand outstretched.

"Evan, great to see you again." Markham is still not

totally L.A. yet. His dark Brooks Brothers suits and ties haven't been traded in for open silk shirts and gold chains. We shake hands, and he motions me toward another man seated on the small leather couch adjacent to his desk. "Evan, I want you to meet Barry Hastings. Barry heads up our reissue division, and I think you'll find he knows his jazz."

"How you doin', man," Barry says, bouncing to his feet. He's probably mid-thirties—deep tan, long blond hair, blue eyes, white duck pants, deck shoes, and a black T-shirt. All that's missing is his surfboard.

Hastings and I sit on opposite ends of the couch. Rick Markham moves a Grammy to one side and perches on the edge of his desk. "Now," Markham says, "I sketched in what you told me yesterday for Barry, and he's pretty excited."

"If the tape's real, this could be, like, deep," Hastings says. He's sizing me up, trying to figure me in with Markham. "You got a sample of the tapes, right?"

"Yeah, but as I told Rick, I'm representing someone else who asked me to see what I thought about the tapes and if possible determine their value. I just want to get an idea what something like this might be worth to a record company and how you would handle it. Then we'll play the tape."

"Barry?" Markham says. They've clearly discussed this before I arrived.

Hastings bounces up again and paces around the office. "If this is really Clifford Brown, this is, like, a major find. I don't have to tell you the reissue game is big and good for us—no recording costs, artist fees, that kind of thing. But I need some background on how you or your client—is that the right word?—came into the tapes. Frankly, we're behind some of the labels on reissue jazz series stuff. We bought some masters a few months ago and released a couple of things last year. What Mr. Markham tells me, you might have enough for a two-CD set or more. If there's more, we hold some back for later release."

Hastings spreads his hand in a gesture as if it's already a done deal. Markham nods his approval and looks at me.

"Does that mean you'd be interested in buying the tapes?"

"Well, yeah, of course," Hastings says. "Major promo, maybe even something like a tiny trumpet case to go with the set, some blurbs from Max Roach, Harold Land, Sonny Rollins, some heavy critics, that kind of thing. I've got a lot of ideas. This could be big, man, real big."

I have a hard time aligning Barry Hastings with someone like Teo Macero, who produced Miles Davis. Hastings throws out the names, but his affinity for jazz is not reassuring. Maybe it's the surfer image, the language quirks. They just don't jell with the forced seriousness. On the other hand, he might be just what I'm looking for. I decide to really bait the hook.

"What if there was a trumpet to go with the tapes? The actual horn Clifford Brown used on gigs and recordings?"

Markham and Hastings exchange glances. "You didn't mention that, Evan," Markham says, "but I think it's safe to say that would tie in with the promotion."

Hastings stares at me. "You actually have Clifford Brown's trumpet?" He looks around as if I'd brought it in with me and he'd missed seeing it.

"Possibly. The horn hasn't been definitely authenticated as yet."

There's a hissing sound as Hastings leans back on the couch. "Wow, this is way cool."

I look at Rick, who waves me off with his eyes. I already have reservations about anyone who refers to Clifford Brown as "way cool," but then, this is the business side of the record industry, and I've never been in tune with that.

"Can you give me some idea of value here, some kind of estimate I can pass on to my client?"

Again Markham and Hastings look at each other. "Have you talked to any other label yet?" Markham asks. "Does anyone else know about these tapes?"

"No, and I think you know me well enough to know that I wouldn't recommend the person I'm representing to try to play one against the other. He simply wants a fair price; I told him I'd prefer to go with a company I know."

"Yes, I do know you," Markham says. To Hastings he says, "Evan saved us considerable money a couple of years ago when he uncovered a record scam, and Charlie Crisp a good deal of embarrassment. I trust his judgment entirely."

Markham goes behind his desk and gets into his M.B.A. mode. He consults some papers, then looks up at me. "This is all very preliminary, you understand, and totally contingent upon the tapes being genuine and warranty that they're legal. We're thinking in terms of $50,000 with a royalty clause, and of course a percentage to the Brown estate, assuming there are survivors. We would also be willing to add a finder's bonus for you, which I think you will find most generous."

This is the second fee I've been offered in a week, but I probably won't collect this one either.

"Yeah," Hastings says. "Let's hear the tape."

I hand it over, and we all listen for about fifteen minutes. I watch Hastings's eyes get big, a smile spread across his face, as the sound of what I hope is Clifford Brown's trumpet bursts from the small bookshelf speakers. Neither Markham nor Hastings has any comment on the rest of the band. Like everyone who's listened so far, they're overwhelmed by the trumpet, and psychologically convinced before they hear anything. Haven't I told them this is Clifford Brown? I shut off the tape and wait for their reaction.

Hastings says, "Cool. You got to bid on this now, Mr. Markham." He claps his hands together. "Jesus, a guy walks in off the street with undiscovered Clifford Brown. Un-fucking-believable."

Markham is not quite so enthusiastic. "We have to have confirmation, Barry. It's not like we're buying bona fide masters from another label."

"Exactly," I say. "How would you go about authenticating the tapes?"

Hastings has his own answer. "Hey, man, trumpet is my thing. I know Miles, Art Farmer, Lee Morgan, Randy Brecker, and I *know* Clifford Brown."

"How do you know Clifford Brown?" I ask Hastings. Barry just doesn't strike me as a jazz buff.

Markham is already ahead of him. "The point is, it would be embarrassing for Pacific Records if it turned out these tapes are not genuine. We would certainly want to go ahead with this, but we need absolute confirmation."

"But Mr. Markham, we—"

"No, Evan is right, and I trust him." Hastings looks

crestfallen, but nods in agreement. "Would you excuse us, Barry? I'd like to speak with Evan in private."

"Sure. Later, man." Hastings leaves, looking like he can't wait to get to a phone.

"Where did you find him?" I ask Markham, once the door is closed.

Markham smiles. "I know what you're thinking, but Barry knows the business, and despite his demeanor, he's done some good projects for us."

Markham studies me for a few moments. "Evan, what are you really up to? Why do I have the feeling that you're holding something back?"

"Do you doubt the tape?"

"No. At least I think *you* believe that's Clifford Brown, and I understand your enthusiasm. I don't know how, with something like this, but we have to know the tapes are genuine and free of any copyright or ownership controversies."

"I will tell you this. The tape has been tested by the FBI crime lab, and there's no doubt it was manufactured sometime in the fifties."

"The FBI? How did they get involved?" When I don't answer for a moment or two, Markham says, "They're stolen, aren't they?"

I get up and take the cassette out of the machine. "There's a collector involved, and how he came into the tapes has still not been determined. You have my word they won't be offered for sale if they're not genuine and free of any illegality."

"Fair enough," Markham says. He swivels his chair toward the window, studies the smog layer of the valley for a minute, then turns back to me. "If this was a painting, a stamp, a book manuscript, authentication wouldn't be too difficult. But music? How can we know for sure?"

"That's the big question, but it's something I think I can find out. I'll pass your requirements on to my client."

I start for the door, then turn back. "One more thing. Keep a lid on Barry, okay? We need to keep this conversation in this room. No press leaks, right?"

"Absolutely," Markham says. "I'll handle Barry just the way you want."

I try several more music stores in Hollywood, but the results are all the same, including the Professional Drum Shop across from the Musicians Union. Ronnie, one of the owners, looks at the glass bottle, holds it up to the light, and frowns. His reaction is a replay of the clerk at the Santa Monica store.

"Glass. Haven't seen anything like this for years," he says. He thumbs at several larger plastic bottles lined up on a shelf behind him. "All the guys use that stuff now."

"Yeah, I know. Even Wynton Marsalis."

Ronnie gives me a look. "Where'd you get this?" He sets my bottle down on the counter and studies it.

"Just came across it, wondered when it was made."

"Can't even read the name. Ick Stu?"

"Any ideas?"

Ronnie shrugs. "Some of the old trumpet players might remember. Try the Union. You know Tommy James? He's a business agent now, but he played trumpet with some of the bands."

I walk across the street to the offices of Local 47 and wander around on the second floor. There's no one in the office with Tommy James's name on it. I stick my head into the one next door.

"You seen Tommy James?"

A husky man with dark hair and black-framed glasses perched on the end of his nose looks up from a magazine. "Yeah, he was around. Think he went for a sandwich. Anything I can help you with?"

"No, thanks. I'll just wait, if it's all right."

"Help yourself."

I take a seat in James's office, thumb through some old copies of *Downbeat*, and wonder if it's okay to smoke. I decide to try, and take out my cigarettes when a voice behind me says, "Don't even think about lighting that."

I stop, cigarette in one hand, lighter in the other. "Tommy James?"

"That's me." He's a thin, wiry man with a thick brush mustache and a bad hairpiece. He walks around me and sits down behind his desk. He glances at my cigarette. "What I meant was, don't think about lighting that unless you're going to offer me one too." He smiles and pulls an ashtray out of his desk drawer. "Shut the door. We're not supposed to smoke in the building." He reaches behind him and opens a window. Cool air drifts in the office and collides with the central heating.

James takes a long drag on the cigarette I light for him. "Man, it's still good, but what the hell are these?" He frowns and looks at the cigarette. "Diamond Plus Menthol?"

"I'm trying to quit."

James smiles. "I know that scene. I been trying for years, but somebody is always coming by my office offering me one. These things are worse than drugs." He takes another drag but doesn't put it out. "So how can I help you? You got troubles on your gig? What do you play?"

"Piano, but it's not about that." Theoretically, the Musicians Union business agents are supposed to oversee contracts with nightclubs and restaurants, but if a club owner wants to go nonunion, pay under scale, there's very little they can do except put him on the unfair list and publish his name in the Union newspaper. Nobody reads that. Most of the reps are like James, former full-time musicians.

"Ronnie over at the drum shop said you played trumpet and that you might help me." I take out the bottle of valve oil and set it on James's desk. "Would you know what brand this is?"

James leans forward, puts his cigarette in the ashtray, picks up the bottle, and examines it. He looks at the label, and a smile begins to form. He unscrews the cap and sniffs. The smile becomes a grin. "Damn! Slick Stuff in the old glass bottle. I got one of these at home somewhere."

"Slick Stuff?"

"Yeah, that's the name. See here." He runs his finger across the label. "This is Slick Stuff, no doubt." He sniffs again, then puts the top back on and sets the bottle down. "No mistaking that kerosene smell. Leaks out of the bottle, the valves, oil gets in your case, on your clothes. You can always tell a trumpet player by the smell of his tie. Where'd you get this, anyway? It's all plastic these days."

"It was in the case for a trumpet I bought at a garage sale. I was just curious how old it was. You've used this?"

"Hell yes, every trumpet player did. Let me see."

James takes a final drag on his cigarette and mashes it out. "I was on the road with bands in the late forties, early fifties. We all used it then. Wasn't nothing else."

I pick up the bottle and look at the label. Slick Stuff. Fifties tape, fifties valve oil, and a postcard written by Duke Ellington.

"Well, thanks for your time." We both stand up, and James reaches across his desk to shake hands.

"Anytime. Hey, I didn't catch your name."

"Evan Horne."

"Well, Evan Horne, if that bottle was in the trumpet case, you got yourself a real old horn. Might be valuable. Bring it by sometime, and I'll look at it."

"I just might do that."

"Thanks for the smoke."

"Thank you. You just saved me a call to Vanna White."

Three messages on my machine at home. Natalie wants to have dinner, John Trask wants me to check in, and Ace sounds exhausted. I try Ace first, but get his machine.

There's a few bars of Louis Armstrong doing "Basin Street Blues," then Ace's voice. "This is Charles Buffington. I can't come to the phone now, but if you leave a number and a short message, I'll get back to you as soon as possible."

There's a few more bars of Louie, then the beep. "Ace, it's Evan, I'm just returning your call, and—"

"I'm here," Ace says, picking up the phone. "I'm screening my calls. I'm so sick of talking to collectors about Ken's records."

"Bad, huh?"

"Unbelievable. I just got rid of the last of them. Ken

had over seventeen thousand records in his collection. They would have cleaned him out if I hadn't been there to watch over them. There have been bids on the entire collection, so I've advised his sister to wait it out and go with the highest offer."

"Seventeen thousand? How did you find the right records?"

"Oh, Ken kept very careful records, and they were all organized. Most of the big collectors do. One guy has a climate-controlled room in his house just for records. The whole collection was insured, of course, but money couldn't replace some of the records Ken had."

"How's Felicia?" I still have a vision of Ken Perkins's sister walking into Bally's, head down, her request still ringing in my mind.

"She's okay. Put the house on the market with a realtor, so at least I don't have to be involved with that. How are you doing?"

I fill Ace in on my news about the tape analysis, the valve oil, and my meeting with Rick Markham. It all adds up. "I can't believe I'm saying this, but I think the trumpet might be for real, Ace."

"Sounds like the tapes might be too. How else could they have been done? Listen, there's another guy you should talk to. He was a collector, but he's kind of a dealer now. He was here for the funeral, offered to help with the record auction. Seemed pretty straight. He goes by the name Blackbyrd; at least, that's what it says on his card. Let me give you the number."

I copy it down. "Thanks, Ace. I also had a message from Lieutenant Trask. You know what he wants?"

"Yeah, he called here, just kind of sniffing around, asking questions, said he'd be calling you, but I don't think they have any leads on Cross. That's how it sounded to me, like he was hoping you'd turn up something. I just don't understand how someone can disappear like that."

"Well, I'm trying. I'll stay in touch."

"Do that," Ace says. "And watch yourself."

I get Natalie's machine as well but tell her to come over, offering her dinner if she gets the message in time. Trask has already gone home, Dave Ochoa too, but I leave my number.

I get restless sitting around, looking at the packing I still have to do, but I'm not in the mood to work on that. I decide to go for a walk on the boardwalk. Who knows when I'll get another chance? I bundle up in a sweater and jacket and walk halfway to Santa Monica Pier, thinking about what I know and don't know, while the other more hearty folks walk or bike or glide by on skates despite the mistlike rain.

Maybe I have it all wrong. The tape is fifties, and so is the Slick Stuff valve oil, so maybe it follows that the trumpet is genuine as well. But Roy Lewis's call from Conn bothers me. He seemed unaware of any engraving of Brownie's initials on the horn or horns. Wouldn't he know, if he was one of the designers? On the other hand, some executive could have done it after the fact, kept the horn as something to show off to friends, embellish the story.

There's still the music. Is it possible I'm just dealing with a simple theft of genuine, original master tapes of Clifford Brown, truly recorded sometime before 1956? Pappy Dean seemed convinced; Jack Montrose said it was entirely possible that it was Brownie but admitted someone just might be able to imitate him convincingly enough. Cal's opinion carries a lot of weight with me, and he didn't think so, but maybe for once he's wrong.

If it wasn't Brownie, then how and when did this tape get made, and where did the trumpet, the valve oil, come from? And the postcard? I have no doubt it's from Duke Ellington, and it's addressed to someone with the initials C. B., but could it be faked as well? Was there someplace you could buy old postcards?

I turn back toward my apartment, dodging some joggers and a couple of bicyclists. The ocean and the sky are contrasting shades of gray. As darkness settles over the beach, I walk a little faster, then stop and sit on one of the benches spaced along the walk, facing the beach.

Meanwhile somebody named Cross, who committed a murder, is roaming around free and probably looking for the trumpet and me, unless he thinks he's really gotten away with it. And why shouldn't he? Ken Perkins is buried, and the police have no leads.

Maybe Cross will get complacent, let his guard down, go back to whatever it is he does for a living. I can't believe he'll give up the idea of the tapes, any more than I will. He's got one, and he probably assumes I have the trumpet, and maybe that's enough to bring him out.

I'm not sure Barry Hastings took my bait, but it shouldn't take long to find out. If that worked, I'll know very soon.

I feel two arms come around my shoulders, warm breath on the back of my neck. "Got it all figured out, Mr. Piano Man?"

I turn to look at Natalie. She's wearing a short skirt, sweater, makeup, earrings, and a light raincoat—the best-dressed woman on the beach. "You need to change. You're taking me to dinner. Exams are over!"

"How'd you do?"

"I don't even want to think about it."

We walked back to the apartment, arms around each other's waist. After much friendly haggling and indecision—Natalie wants Italian, I want a steak—we finally settle on a Mexican restaurant we both like in Santa Monica. The margaritas and food are good, the conversation better, and the promise of the rest of the evening better yet. We hardly talked about Clifford Brown, trumpets, tapes, or valve oil.

Everything is fine until I get my car from valet parking. As I pull out of the driveway, a white sedan parked across the street makes a U-turn and follows us down Wilshire. The driver stays a couple of cars back, but he's with us all the way to Ocean Avenue. I lose sight of him after that, and I wonder if I'm imagining things again.

Hello, Mr. Cross?

CHAPTER

TWELVE

COOP CALLS IN THE MORNING, JUST AFTER EIGHT. BEfore I tell him about the white car and that it's possibly Cross keeping tabs on me, Coop's already on to something new.

"How'd you like to go to court this morning, strictly as an observer?"

"Any particular reason?"

"All will become clear," Coop says. "An arraignment you might find interesting." I imagine him smiling to himself, knowing I'll be confused and puzzled. Is it Cross, some other lead?

I sigh into the phone. "I know you're not going to tell me why, so I won't ask. What time?"

"Nine. I know that's early for you, but I think you'll find it interesting."

Coop is standing outside Santa Monica Municipal Court, smoking one of his skinny cigars, drinking coffee out of a paper cup, when I arrive. "Full docket this morning," he says. "Lots of bad guys and gals being arraigned. Let's go. The wheels of justice are turning."

"There were other wheels turning last night." I tell

him about the car that followed us from the restaurant, and that it might be the same car I saw on the way back from Las Vegas.

"I suppose it's too much to ask if you got the license number."

"He stayed too far back, and I didn't want to spook Natalie."

"She was with you?" Coop drops the sarcasm and angrily shoves his cigar into a cement planter full of sand. "You should have told me before," he says. "This guy killed at least once. Detectives are supposed to remember things like that."

We go inside and sit in the back row of the small courtroom. A long line of prisoners handcuffed together is led in from a side door. They sit in a row up front, where an assortment of public defenders, defense attorneys, and assistant DAs are milling around the court tables, pulling out papers from overstuffed briefcases. A few minutes later, the bailiff announces the judge's arrival, and court is in session.

Coop leans over and whispers to me. "Fourth guy in line, Sammy Dell."

I still don't know what this is about, or why I'm here, but Coop likes surprises, especially when he's the instigator. The first three cases are dealt with in a matter of minutes. Drugs, car theft, and purse snatching start the day. The judge, a heavyset woman with a deep voice and short-cropped hair, goes through the drill, looking weary, as if she's heard it all before. The court reporter sits stoically, the machine between his knees, his fingers moving over the keyboard, as names are logged into the record, charges read off, pleas entered, and deals made.

Number four stands up, and the DA reads from a

file. "City of Santa Monica versus Samuel S. Dell." Dell's address is read into the record along with the charges: burglary of a recording studio in Santa Monica. That's when I sit up straight and peer at Dell.

"Thought that might get your attention," Coop says, glancing at me with a smile.

"That's not Cross, if that's what you're thinking," I say.

The case is briefly discussed. Dell was arrested leaving the premises of Two Dot Studios on Colorado Boulevard in the possession of two boxes of recording tape. The judge asks for a plea; Dell's attorney enters not guilty, which brings a smirk from the DA. The trial is set for thirty days from today. Dell will remain incarcerated until trial.

"Next case," the judge says, glancing at her watch.

I'm still staring at Dell when Coop gets up. "Let's go," he says. I follow him outside. Coop looks at his watch and lights a cigar. "You want to talk to him?"

"I don't know. Should I?"

Coop says, "I came across the arrest report yesterday. Thought there might be some connection. At least he's stealing the right kind of stuff. Dell was busted a few weeks ago by Hollywood Division, but it was thrown out over some Miranda shit, illegal search and such. All he had in his car were three stereo systems. Guess there wasn't probable cause. They thought he was connected to some burglaries at some recording studios. Numerous priors." Coop smiles again. "Making some sense now?"

"Yeah, I'd like to talk to him. Can we do that?"

"Hey, I'm a lieutenant, remember?"

Coop signs me into the jail, and Samuel Dell is

brought to one of the lawyer rooms. He looks scared but bored, as if he's been through all this before.

"Sit down, Sammy," Coop says. "This is my associate, Mr. Horne."

"Yeah, right," Dell says. "Got a smoke?" He clasps his hands together on the table in front of him. His fingernails are bitten to the quick.

Dell takes in the visitor's badge clipped to my shirt. He's rail-thin, with long, lanky hair, pasty complexion, and a prominent nose. His eyes dart everywhere. He's all but lost in the jail jumpsuit, a couple of sizes too big for him.

"Not in here," Coop says. "You know the rules by now."

"Fuck the rules, and it's Spinner."

"Spinner?"

"Yeah, you know, I like records and tapes." He smiles like he's said something profound.

"How symbolic," Coop says.

"What was on the tapes you took, Spinner?" I ask.

"Music. What do you think they were, the Nixon tapes?"

Coop leans over Dell, about three inches from his face. "Listen to me, Spinner. I don't care if you boosted *The Best of the Village People.* You cooperate with my friend here, and we might be able to cut you some slack."

Dell leans back away from Coop. He's wary, but not scared. "Okay, okay."

Coop nods at me and walks away a few steps. "What kind of music?" I ask him.

Spinner shrugs. "Any kind. I don't care, I just sell them."

"To whom?"

"Whoever's buying. What the fuck's this all about, anyway? You an attorney? I already got one."

"I'm looking for some missing tapes, Spinner. Music tapes. Jazz. You ever run across anything like that?"

Spinner seems suddenly relieved. "Oh, you mean like the other guy asked me about."

"What other guy?"

"The court reporter."

Coop and I look at each other for a moment, as if we've both missed something. "The court reporter? You mean, in court?" I guess Spinner means the reporter asked him to repeat something, but I'm way off.

"No, I mean like out of court." Spinner glances quickly at Coop. "Shit, I knew something was wrong. Guy came to my house, wanted to know about some tapes, offered to buy them."

"What guy?"

"I told you, the court reporter. Not the one today, another one."

I suddenly know exactly what he's talking about. "What was this guy's name?"

"Cross, at least that's what he said." Spinner looks from me to Coop. "What's going on, anyway?" He tries not to show it, but he's looking panicked.

I sit back in my chair and look at Coop, who for once is surprised himself. "I'll be right back." He goes out and leaves me to pass a few minutes with Spinner.

"Tell me about Cross, Spinner."

"Nothing to tell. Said he was a record collector. I told him I just had tapes, he said that was okay, he liked tapes as well. Wanted me to sell them."

"And did you?"

"That's the idea, ain't it? Gave me two hundred and

fifty. Safe too, like a court reporter is going to talk about receiving stolen goods."

Coop comes back with a guard, who takes Spinner back to his cell. Once we're alone, he sits down in Spinner's chair.

"You're going to love this. Raymond Cross is a court reporter, twelve years, perfect record, even the employee of the month once. I think I know who he is. Lives in Malibu. No wonder nobody could find him. We were looking in the wrong places."

Now it all made sense. Sitting in a courtroom day after day, Raymond Cross had his own special source for records and tapes, and it was he who typed out Sammy Dell—Spinner's—name and address.

"Can we talk to him?"

Coop says, "Cross went on vacation a week ago."

Blackbyrd is not black at all but has pale, almost white skin sprinkled with freckles, thinning, reddish blond hair, and thick wrists and forearms. He wears large, square, black-framed glasses on a turquoise neck chain. He continually takes them on and off as he swings back and forth from me to his computer screen.

"I know," he says. "I should have bifocals, right? Tried them. No good. Didn't like them at all, so I got this." He fingers the neck chain like a rosary, rolling it around in his hands when the glasses are not on. He spits out phrases in short staccato bursts that are countered by long monologues as we talk about record collectors.

I left Coop to check further on Raymond Cross and found the sixties ranch-style house in this older section of the San Fernando Valley. Greeted by Blackbyrd's wife, Marie, I was escorted through the house to the kitchen, where she pointed out the screen door to the small structure at the end of the yard that at first glance looked like a tool shed.

"He's out there," she says, "and don't worry about Buck. He sees you with me, so he knows you're all right."

"Thanks," I say, opening the screen door and going down the steps. I hope she's right. Buck is a huge rottweiler, already at attention, watching my approach. He ambles forward and gently nuzzles my hand. I scratch his ear, and he emits a pleasurable growl that's not at all threatening. He allows me to enter Blackbyrd's domain. Inside, it's anything but a tool shed.

The walls are wood paneling that reach down to meet the sand-colored carpet. Most of the room is taken up by a corner computer workstation and Blackbyrd's huge leather desk chair. It swivels, rocks, and rolls as he rotates between the computer, fax machine, and telephone. To the left of the computer layout are three glass-framed 45rpm records. I can't make out the titles. Blackbyrd catches me looking at them.

"My last finds," he says. "Those represent the end of my collecting days. You're a jazzer, right, a musician? You wouldn't recognize the groups if I told you. Black R&B, doo-wop guys from the fifties. When I got the third one, I played it once, put it back in its perfect sleeve, thought about it for a couple of days, then I had—what do you call it?" He snaps his fingers. "An epiphany. No rush. Nothing. The kick was gone." He takes the glasses off and spins around to the computer, checks something on the blue screen, then turns back to me.

"That's when I became a quasi-dealer, broker for

other collectors, people just looking for an old favorite. I get a finder's fee, but I don't collect anymore myself."

"And that's how you got the name Blackbyrd, because you collected black R&B groups."

"You got it. Most outsiders don't know it. When you called, I knew you had some contact. Who was it, Charles Buffington? Call me Willis. My wife and kids do."

"Okay, Willis, I think I like that better."

Willis punches a button on his intercom phone, which has several lines, and activates the speaker phone. "Marie, you there?" Marie answers quickly. "How about some iced tea?" He looks at me for approval, and I nod.

"Five minutes, Willis." He shuts off the phone, but before he can speak again he's interrupted by the fax machine, which begins spewing curls of flimsy paper. He watches, scanning the message, rips it off, and drops it in a tray.

"I'm running an auction for another guy. Closes today at five. Highest bidder gets the record," Willis says. "They come in day and night, and there's always one who calls fifteen minutes before we close. If he wants to top the highest bid by ten percent, he gets the prize."

"What's the highest anyone's paid for a record?"

"Most I can remember is twelve thousand."

"For one forty-five?"

"Hey, I told you these guys are nuts. The bids they come in with are for weird amounts like $150.27 or $66.43. They don't want to tie with anyone." Willis shakes his head. "Fax, computers; we'll be on the Internet eventually."

"You know another collector, guy named Mojo

Boneyard?" It was another of the names Ace had mentioned.

"Yeah. He's always out—garage sales, estate sales, Salvation Army thrift stores. Looking for grooving records in the boneyard of life, that's Mojo's motto. I heard he just made a big buy from a jukebox company. Figures to move the records for three or four bucks apiece, maybe find a gem in there somewhere. It's all changing now, but you watch. Vinyl will make a big comeback now that everything is on CD."

I glance around at all the equipment. I don't see any signs of an alarm system or heavy locks. "Don't you worry about break-ins?"

Willis smiles, shows me white but uneven teeth. He turns his head to the open window and shouts, "Buck, you there, boy?"

Buck responds with a couple of short, deep barks that bring another smile to Willis. "Good boy! Buck is better than any alarm system. How'd you like to jump over my back wall late at night and say hello to Buck?"

"I wouldn't."

"Exactly," says Willis. "Now how can I help you? I didn't know Ken Perkins well, but he was a straight-up collector. I hope they catch whoever did that to him. Except for that one prank—he paid everybody for the joke—Ken was okay. A collector, but okay." Willis shakes his head and smiles. "Ken really had them going."

"What joke?"

"Oh, you don't know about that, huh? Well, nobody wants to admit they were taken. A great story, one of the legends of this business. Got to be known as Vinylgate. Here's how it went, see.

"Collectors are nuts, man. What they want is to

have something nobody else has. You ever seen a big auction? People paying outrageous prices for dumb stuff. You watch when Jackie O's stuff gets sold. It'll bring millions for ordinary household items because they were JFK's or Jackie's."

"You mean like thousands for a chair or table?"

"You got it. Not worth it, but to a collector—coins, stamps, books, records, doesn't matter—it's something no one else has. Follow me?"

Willis doesn't wait for my answer now that he's launched into the story of Ken's joke. He clearly enjoys the telling.

"Okay, Ken knows better than anyone how obsessive collectors are because he's one himself, so here's what he does. He gets a friend of his, another collector, to go in on it with him. This friend's gig is, he's an exterminator, you know, like the Orkin Man. In people's houses all day. So they cook up this story. One of the houses on the friend's route belongs to a guy who was once in the record business. The friend says he comes across a box of records, offers to buy them. The guy says, 'Hey take them, I was going to throw them out anyway.' You with me here?"

"Okay, the friend makes up this story, right?"

"Right. Hang on."

We both look up as Marie arrives with two giant plastic tumblers of iced tea. Willis takes them both. "Thanks, babe." He hands me mine and sits back down.

Marie says, "Don't forget you have to pick up Bobby at three."

"No problem, babe. I'll be there."

As Marie leaves, another fax rumbles in. Willis scans

it and rips it off the machine, puts it with the other one in the tray. "Japan," he says, then continues his story.

"Ken Perkins has some old-time contacts in L.A. Takes a lot of research—you gotta understand the trouble he went to in pulling this off. He finds some fifties vinyl stock and record-label paper at a now-out-of-business company, finds some singers—two of them actually recorded at one time—and a small band, and even tracks down a saxophone player who made a lot of these dates in the fifties. Can't remember the guy's name, but he used to record with Charles Brown, the blues singer. Then he buys some time at one of those crap studios in Hollywood where they make demos, low-grade stuff, supervises the session himself, and lays down two tracks with this bogus doo-wop group."

"And it was that easy?" I could see several problems in something like this. Making the recording sound old, getting the musicians to emulate that style of playing. "How did he keep everybody quiet?"

Willis shakes his head. "Money. Not easy at all. This took months of planning to pull off, and at the session he got into a big argument with the sax man, who couldn't remember how he played in those days, playing too modern for what Ken had in mind. Anyway, they finally get it done, and Ken has seven copies made."

"Why seven?"

Willis shrugs. "Who knows? Ken was living in Las Vegas by then, so maybe that was why. Lucky seven? Anyway once they have the copies, they leak the word out about this great find. Ken runs an auction and sells six of them for top money, keeps one himself. I tell you, it was the talk of the trade."

"So what's the punch line?"

Willis says, "This is the part I love. Ken lets every-body wallow in their glory, thinking they have one of only six copies of this bogus group, for three years. Three years. Think of it. Then at one of the conventions, he takes all six buyers out to dinner and spills the beans, tells the whole story of how he did it, made the whole thing up."

What Willis is telling me immediately makes for six murder suspects, but as if he's reading my mind, he points a finger at me.

"No, I know what you're thinking. You can elimi-nate all six of these guys."

"Why?"

"As soon as Ken told the story, he gave them all their money back plus ten percent, called that the joke interest. Told the buyers to keep the record as a souve-nir of their obsession."

It's a good story; I wonder how much it has been embellished over the years of telling and retelling. Like the musician Joe Venuti, who hired fifty bass players and told them to meet him at Hollywood and Vine on Saturday night in a tux just to see what it would look like. Venuti also paid all the musicians scale.

"And you're sure that's exactly the way it hap-pened."

Willis gives me a strange look. "Absolutely." He smiles and holds out his hands in a gesture that says it all. "I was one of the buyers."

Maybe one of the six learned from Ken Perkins, gets some fifties recording tape, brings in a group, and—no, it is too much of a stretch, and Cross would still have to find the perfect Clifford Brown imitator.

Between faxes, phone calls, and checking his com-puter for e-mail, Willis gives me a lot more information about collectors, some of it very interesting, especially when it comes to evaluating records.

The original Miles Davis Prestige LPs, *Relaxin'*, *Cookin'*, *Workin'*, for example, provided you had the whole set and they were yellow-label copies, the right serial numbers, would bring somewhere in the neighborhood of $15,000.

"They'd have to be in mint-minus condition. Notice I said mint-minus. Mint only applies to untouched, unplayed from the factory. Then there's VG, very good; VG-minus, and so on."

If early Miles was worth that much, then Rick Markham's offer was not only fair but generous. Clifford Brown's worldwide reputation, coupled with his relatively meager output of recordings, even after the initial hoopla over the discoveries, would ensure that a new compact disc set would sell for years. Then there was the trumpet.

"I'll tell you what," says Willis, "you have to keep in mind this concept of having something nobody else has. That's the key. Let's say a collector came across a box of perfect Miles LPs, say, twenty-five of them. Know what he'd do?"

I shrug. "I guess keep one for himself, sell the rest."

"Wrong," Willis says. "Half wrong. Sure, he'd keep one for himself, but the other copies? He'd destroy, break them into little pieces. Only way he'd be sure he had the only copy. Want a worse scenario?"

"It's hard to imagine one, but go ahead."

"Okay, try this on for size, and no, it wasn't me.

"A collector wants a copy of this awful doo-wop group, really wants it, determined to get a copy somewhere. He hires a private detective to track down the members of the group. This was a real group, remember. Okay, the PI checks out all the guys, flies all over the country. None of them have a copy of their own record, but one of them thinks his grandmother might have one and agrees to let the PI talk to her. She's like ninety-three years old at the time.

"The PI finds her, and guess what? What do you think he tells her?"

"I don't know—he offers her money for the record, providing she has one."

"He tries," Willis says, becoming more animated now. "He offers her a fair price and then some. She wavers, but she's not entirely convinced. See, it's her grandson's record, sentimental value, all that. The PI picks right up on this, tells her the collector's wife is dying of leukemia and her last wish is to hear this song one more time. It was their song."

Willis rolls his eyes and almost stops as another fax comes reeling in. He glances at the fax and continues. "Well, the grandmother is touched by this story but not stupid. She relents, lets him have it for twelve hundred. Of course the whole story was bull, the wife never heard of this song or the group. The PI goes back to the collector, gets his bonus for finding the record, plus his fee and all expenses. Cost the collector somewhere around five grand for the whole deal."

"And was it worth it?"

"To the collector, yeah. He had something that nobody else had. The music was nothing, never even a minor hit, terrible sound quality." Willis shrugs. "That's collectors for you. That's the kind of guys you're asking about. It's a fucking treasure hunt."

While Willis busies himself with logging in faxes

and checking his e-mail again, I digest what he's told me. For people that obsessive, a murder could easily be the next step, and I'm beginning to see some additional motive for killing Perkins, but I'll have to prove it.

"Do you know all the people who were taken in by Ken's practical joke? Besides yourself, I mean."

"Oh yeah, everybody in the business knows."

"Was Raymond Cross one of them?"

"You betcha. Ray went down like the rest of us. Mojo too."

I only have one more question for Willis. "You were talking about the value of records, tapes. Could you put a ballpark figure on two master tapes of Clifford Brown to a record company?"

"Are they stolen?"

"Probably, if they're genuine."

Willis thinks a moment. "If they're genuine, their value would be to a record company. Auction, take the offer of the highest bidder, but they'd have to be authenticated, record company would be very careful about that. I'd say thirty-five, forty grand wouldn't be out of line if they were sold to a company like Blue Note, Verve. They'd be drooling over those."

"What if there was a trumpet also?"

"Clifford Brown's trumpet, the one he actually played on?" Willis leans forward on the desk. "Whoa, I wouldn't even venture a guess like that. Big, very big bucks. Didn't Charlie Parker's horn go big at an auction in Paris sometime back?"

Before I leave Blackbyrd to his faxes, phone calls, and e-mails, I give him the title of my own album to put out on the network. He takes down the information about the title, label, print run. I watch him type in the information on his computer. If Blackbyrd can't find a copy, nobody can.

"Maybe we'll get lucky," he says.

"Yeah, maybe we will."

CHAPTER
THIRTEEN

BLACKBYRD'S MENTION OF THE RECORDING SESSION Ken Perkins organized triggers another idea I've already been working on. If that isn't Clifford Brown on those tapes, it's some other trumpet player, and it was recorded in the fifties. All I have to do is find where these recordings were done.

I spend an hour on the phone in Hollywood, calling recording studios. I go through nearly fifteen listings in the yellow pages till I find what I'm looking for. Only two even remotely know what I'm talking about. The rest were not in business at the time, and none have reported any recent burglaries.

The last guy is the most helpful. "Try Gladys Cowen at Cosmos Recorders," he says. "Her husband ran an operation like you're describing."

Even the name sounds right. Cosmos Recorders, and if I remember, it's near the site of what was once one of the premier jazz clubs in Hollywood—Shelly's Manne Hole.

A woman's voice answers when I finally get through. "What?"

"Hello, is this Cosmos Recorders? Gladys Cowen?"

"Well, of course it is."

"Okay, well, I'm doing some research on some lost recordings that were done in the fifties, and I wonder if—"

"Not now, I'm having lunch. Call back," she says and hangs up.

I stand for a moment staring at the pay phone, listening to the dial tone. Okay, I'll call back. I'm not far from the Musicians Union on Vine Street, so I decide to run down there and talk to Tommy James again, see if he remembers anything about cowboy studios.

It's a wasted trip. James is out and won't be back till later in the afternoon. I'm still waiting to see someone else when I try Cosmos again from a phone outside a rehearsal studio evidently occupied by an ear-splitting rock group.

"Hello, I called a little while ago about the missing tapes?"

"I know you did," the woman's voice says.

Her voice has a brittle quality to it. Hopefully she's old enough to have some memories. I explain what I'm looking for, but before I can finish she cuts in again.

"Oh, you want to know about the robbery. Well, come on over. I want to talk to someone about it."

I pause for just a moment and say, "Yeah, it's about the robbery, I'm working for—"

"You can tell me about it when you get here, but hurry up. I'm going home soon."

I hang up the phone and sprint for my car. This I want to hear about.

I squeeze into a parking spot just off Cosmos Alley that I hope is enough out of the way to avoid a parking ticket and walk up the narrow street—really just a passageway—checking the doors of a low pink stucco building. They're all white with faded and peeling gold lettering. The third one is Cosmos Recorders. I press the buzzer.

While I wait for an answer, I look around. Across the narrow alley is the back door of what was once Shelly's Manne Hole. I've heard stories about the great drummer's club that flourished in the sixties, then finally closed down, ironically, when the recording studio next door complained that noise from the club was leaking into the studio. Shelly reopened the club in Beverly Hills, but it was never the same. Another example of recording technology ending live music. For me, the supreme irony was that I had once recorded at that very studio.

I turn as the door opens and Gladys Cowen stares at me. "Well, come on in, young man." She steps aside to let me into a tiny office with a desk, phone, and a TV across the room, on which the credits for a show that's just ended are rolling.

Gladys shuts the door, turns off the TV, and sits down at the desk.

"You caught me during lunch and my soap," she says, nodding at the TV. "Anybody that knows me knows not to call between noon and one."

I sit down opposite her in the only other chair. "Sorry, I didn't know," I say. Gladys must be in her seventies: snow-white hair pulled back in a bun, wrinkled face, clear blue eyes. On the desk is a large black plastic ashtray, the kind with slots to hold burning cigarettes. A package of Menthol 100s and a Bic lighter rest nearby.

"Yeah, that's right, I smoke," she says with more than a trace of defiance. She takes it a step further and after wrestling with the childproof catch, lights up. Gladys and I are going to get along fine.

"My name is Evan Horne. I'll join you, if I can try one of yours?"

She smiles for the first time. "Thank God. I'm so sick of this California health thing." She takes a drag off her cigarette and blows a cloud of smoke over my head. "People see you from across the street with a cigarette, and they start waving their hands in the air. Don't they see the smog? L.A. is one big smoke bowl. A little cigarette isn't going to dent that. Now what about this robbery?"

I feel like I'm talking to a hip grandmother as I try to explain the misunderstanding, what I'm looking for, and how I've ended up here. Gladys doesn't seem disappointed or surprised.

"Well I knew you weren't a cop. What are you anyway, a private dick?"

Good question; that's something I've been thinking a lot about lately. I explain about my accident, tell her some of the people I've played with, and eventually get to the Clifford Brown tapes. Gladys listens attentively, genuinely sympathetic.

"I'm so sorry, son. I know how much you boys like to play. It must be awful." She smiles and pats my hand. "Clifford Brown, huh? Yeah, he was out there then. I think he played at the Lighthouse."

I can't help smiling. "Excuse me, but how is it you know so much about jazz?"

"Tom, my husband. He ran this studio for years. I helped him out with the office, but I was around for a lot of the sessions. They used to walk right through that door you came in. Sometimes at three or four in the morning. Chet Baker came by one night."

"Chet Baker recorded here?"

"No, I don't think so." Gladys searches her memory. "He was such a beautiful boy. Sent me a postcard from somewhere in Europe. But Tom used to round up musicians and bring them over here after their jobs. That went on for years."

"What happened?"

Gladys shrugs and stubs out her cigarette. "The business changed. The only way Tom could make a go of it was to do demos, some masters for rock groups, lots of vocals. He sold some of them to the majors, but jazz was his passion. He used to tell me, 'Honey'—that's what he called me—'someday these tapes are going to be worth a lot of money, and these musicians are going to be famous.'"

"What happened to those tapes?"

"When we stopped doing jazz, Tom put them in storage. Airtight, waterproof boxes, thought they'd be safer here than at home." Gladys sighs, lost for a moment in some distant memory. "Hollywood has changed a lot since those days. Hookers, drug dealers, looks like Times Square out there on Hollywood Boulevard. That's what I meant about the robbery. Somebody broke in here a few weeks ago."

"And those tapes were the only thing stolen?"

"Yeah," Gladys says, "like they knew what they were looking for. I haven't talked about them to anyone, so I don't know how anyone would have known."

I think I do, but I decide to let Gladys in on that later. "Do you have any idea who was on those tapes or when they were done?"

Gladys gives me a sad look. "I knew you were going to ask me that. Tom kept pretty good records, wrote everything down on three-by-five cards, but they—"

"They were in the boxes."

Gladys nods. Well, that's that. Somehow Raymond Cross stole the tapes or had someone steal them for him—maybe Spinner—because he knew about the recordings or just got lucky. Through the collectors' network? Musicians? It's impossible to tell.

"Wait," Gladys says. "There is this." She opens a desk drawer and takes out a torn white three-by-five index card. "They must have torn it when they looked into the boxes and dropped it on the way out." She hands it across to me.

It's not quite half the card. There's a piece of cellophane tape still attached to one edge. The writing is neat printing in pencil, and two names are still visible.

Piano—Nolan Thomas. Trumpet—Conrad Beale. C.B. I look up at Gladys, feel like my body is drenched with adrenaline.

"Do these names mean anything to you?" Come on, Gladys, show me just how hip you are.

"Sorry." She shakes her head. "That was so long ago." Then she sits up straight and places both hands on the desk. "Wait a minute."

She disappears into the back, where I guess the studio is. Five minutes later she's back with a metal file box. She sets it down on the desk and opens it. "I'd almost forgotten about this. Tom's filing system."

There are divider tabs with the letters of the alphabet, and the box is stuffed with cards. "What's that first name?"

"Nolan Thomas."

Gladys flips through T's and pulls out a card. "Here you go."

There's not much on it. Thomas's name, piano, and several dates—listing, I assume, the times he recorded—and an address and phone number. The last date is 1955. The address and phone will likely not be good. What am I thinking of? Thomas could also be dead. Still, he was probably a union member, and they might have an address.

The same information is on the card for Conrad Beale, except there's no address listed at all. "Could I look through that box?"

Gladys looks at her watch. "Suit yourself," she says. "I've got to do some writing. You can look all you want, make notes, but right here. You can't take it with you."

She moves some papers aside to reveal a laptop computer. She opens it up and smiles at me. "I'm on the information highway."

I spend the next thirty minutes going through the box while Gladys clicks away on her computer. Most of the names mean nothing to me, and the cards vary from entry to entry. Some are done in different hands, maybe by the musicians themselves. A few names, however, catch my eye. Art Pepper, Al Haig, Zoot Sims, Jack Montrose, Frank Butler—all prominent on the jazz scene in Los Angeles in the fifties. How many of these musicians would even remember dates in a place like Cosmos? With the passage of time, the drug haze, memory lapses, it was definitely a long shot.

I put all the cards back in the box and turn to Gladys. She nods at me and clicks on the mouse a couple of times, and the screen goes blank. She shuts the case and turns to me.

"What did the police say about the robbery? You reported it, right?"

"Of course, but they didn't offer much hope. I showed them the torn card, but what would they do with that? If I had a card with Miles Davis's name on it, they wouldn't recognize it."

I start to hand back the torn card, but Gladys stops me. "You keep that if you want, if it will help. And I'll tell you something else. If you get those tapes back, I'll make it worth your while."

I pocket the card. Fee number three. "Gladys, if I find these tapes, it'll be my pleasure to return them to you for nothing."

She blinks at me. "You're a good boy, Evan Horne."

"Thanks. One more thing. Now that you're a nineties gal, Gladys, why don't you enter all those cards on your computer?"

"Good idea," Gladys says. "Good idea."

There's no ticket on my car and still time to get back to the Musicians Union and check again with Tommy James. This time he's in.

"Hey," he says, "got that trumpet for me to see?"

"Not this time, but there's something else."

"Shoot," James says. He leans back in his chair.

Where to begin? I give him an edited explanation about the tapes and what I'm trying to find out. He listens, frowns occasionally, but doesn't interrupt until I'm through.

"Yeah, I can help you with the names, see if they're still members," he says. "You said Nolan Thomas and Conrad Beale. Piano and trumpet, right?" He writes down the names on a pad. "Hang on a minute and I'll check."

I wait, but not patiently. I wander around James's office, looking at the souvenir photos on the wall. There's one PR photo of Benny Goodman inscribed to James, one of a very young Tommy James posing with his trumpet. The others are group shots, James smiling with a lot of people I don't recognize.

I open the window, light a cigarette, and gaze out at Vine Street. A light rain begins to fall, but the cool air feels good. I can't believe I could get this close and strike out. There has to be some connection between the tapes stolen from Gladys Cowen and the ones bought by Raymond Cross from Spinner.

James comes back in a few minutes. "Found one of them. Nolan Thomas." He hands me a slip of paper with an address and phone number. "Thomas is still a member. No listing for the other guy. Hell, man, these guys got to be late sixties, early seventies now."

"I know, it's a long shot."

James sits down behind his desk again, studies me a few moments. "Even if these are the guys you're looking for, they might not remember. And finding somebody who used to imitate Clifford Brown, well, that's something else again."

"I know. Well, thanks, Tommy."

"Don't mention it. I still want to see that trumpet, and if you find a guy who can play that much like Clifford Brown, I want to see him too."

A radio interview I'd once heard with Stan Getz right after the saxophonist's death is much on my mind. The interviewer was academic sounding, a jazz historian, much like Ace Buffington. I could tell from the sound of his voice that he was intimidated to be sitting across from one of the greatest saxophonists of all time. For Getz's part, he sounded bored and a little wary of the interviewer, who began by asking Getz about a recording he'd made with Lionel Hampton. He hoped Getz could identify the trombonist. Getz sounded genuinely puzzled.

"I never recorded with Hamp," Getz said.

"Well," the interviewer said, nervously contradicting. "Maybe this will refresh your memory." He played the cut and must have been watching Getz's expression closely. The saxophone solo was clearly Getz—the elegant sound, even at that stage of his career, unmistakable. The trombone solo followed, then the record ended.

"Well," the interviewer said. "Wasn't that you?"

There were a few moments of dead air before Getz said, "I'll be damned. . . . I have no recollection of that, and I'm . . . I'm sorry, I have no idea who the trombone is. Could we hear that again?"

This is what I hope Nolan Thomas is going to tell me now.

I find him with a student at his home studio. The student is a tall gangly kid of about sixteen and he's clearly intimidated by Nolan Thomas.

Thomas is a short wiry man with coffee-colored skin. His hair and his pencil mustache have gone snow-white. A bulky sweater hangs well over his waist. His tiny feet are encased in worn terry cloth slippers.

"Be with you in a minute," he says, motioning me to a chair to the left of the baby grand piano.

The room is dominated by the piano. On the wall are photos of Thomas on various gigs or smiling with people, some I didn't recognize. In one he's being hugged by a young Charlie Parker. There are shelves of record albums, books, a mini–sound system for CDs and cassettes, and in one corner a red Naugahyde recliner chair and a small television.

I'd called him earlier and explained what I wanted,

and he reluctantly agreed to give me thirty minutes. "I've had students all day," he said. "One to go." Now he was almost finished.

"Play that part again," Thomas says to the student, pointing to the music. "You still don't have it right. Your mama told me you ain't been practicing like I told you, have you, Ronnie?"

Ronnie is silent, staring at the keyboard. I feel for him. He reminds me of my own bouts with teachers, especially Cal Hughes.

"Well?" Thomas says. "All right, play it again." Thomas turns to me and winks, and turns on his impish smile.

Ronnie struggles through the cycle of fifths once again, this time to Thomas's satisfaction. "Yeah that's it. Now let me hear them blues scales."

Ronnie complies and looks up at Thomas for approval.

"All right, now get out of here, and next week I want to hear some improvement."

"Yes, sir," Ronnie says. He stands, gathers up his music, and makes a quick retreat.

"Boy's got some talent," Thomas says. He drops into the recliner and turns on the TV. "Gotta check on my Lakers," he says. "You follow basketball?"

"A little, used to go to some games once in a while."

Thomas grunts and then moans as Magic misses an easy layup. "Now what's this about Clifford Brown?"

I take a deep breath and look at Thomas. Is he going to think I'm crazy? He watches me expectantly, waiting for my question.

"Do you remember recording with Clifford Brown?"

Nolan looks as if I had just asked him if he'd ever had dinner with Donald Trump. "Clifford Brown? I told you on the phone you got the wrong guy, son. I never recorded with Brownie. You think I wouldn't remember that?"

The cassette in my pocket feels heavier than usual when I take it out. "This is the cassette I told you about over the phone. Okay if we just listen to a little of it?" I nod toward Thomas's tape player.

"Be my guest." He turns the sound on the TV down. I put the tape in and press the play button. The first eight bars are a piano solo. Nolan cocks his head, and moves closer to the speaker as the band comes in. I reach for the player but he holds up his hand, signaling me that he wants to listen to more. After the trumpet solo, he listens to the two piano choruses and smiles, nods his head.

I press the stop button as the tune ends and ask the same question the radio interviewer asked Stan Getz. "Well? Isn't that you?"

Nolan is laughing now, nodding his head. "Yeah, baby, you got that right, that sure is me."

All I can feel is relief at his admission. Finally I've got what I came for. But the relief is short-lived. Thomas continues to laugh. Finally he gets control and lights a cigarette.

"Oh, man," he says. "I'm sorry, man, I know you think you found something big, some lost tape in somebody's attic or something like that."

"What do you mean?"

"I mean that's me playing piano, but that ain't Clifford Brown."

"Are you sure?"

"Oh yeah, I'm sure. I know who it is, too."

"Who?" There's so much more I want to ask.

"That's a guy called Connie—Conrad Beale, but they called him Connie. Lotta talent, but he got too into Clifford Brown, never could get his own voice, you know?"

"Do you know if this Conrad Beale ever played with Duke Ellington, even for a short time?"

"Oh yeah," Nolan says nodding his head. "That part you got right too. Connie never let anyone forget that. But he was only there a minute—three nights at the Coconut Grove. Somebody got sick or something, I don't remember how, but Connie got the call."

"Tell me about the recording session. Do you remember doing it? Cosmos Records. Tom and Gladys Cowen ran it."

Thomas runs a hand through his hair and stares at a spot on the floor. "If you say so. I remember some couple had a studio, record a lot of people. Damn, they still in business?"

"Gladys is. Her husband died several years ago. The studio was across from Shelly's Manne Hole, in that little alleyway."

"Okay, okay, yeah I remember," Thomas says, his head bobbing to his own words. "We used to get fifty bucks a pop, I think. Never heard what happened to any of those things."

"Tell me about this recording."

"We were working for some little joint in Hollywood. Connie, me, bass, and drums. I don't even remember who they were now. This guy—Cowen, you say his name was—came by and asked if we wanted to make some quick bread, cut a few tunes. We said, hey, why not. A gig's a gig. We got over there, set up, and were just messin' around, waiting for him to get set up. Connie went into his Brownie bag, playing 'Joy Spring,' 'Jordu,' one of them tunes. Well, the recording guy, Cowen, just flipped out when he heard Connie do that." Thomas looks away, remembering more. "Yeah, that music is bringing it back now.

"He said, 'My God, you're Clifford Brown.' Connie could do it, sound just like Brownie. Knew all the tunes, most of Brownie's solos. Well hell, you got the tape, you know. Anyway, the guy said he'd up the money to seventy-five bucks if we laid down some tracks with Connie doin' his Brownie thing. We said sure."

"What happened after that?"

"Nothing. Never heard of his tape till you played it just now. I did some other stuff for this guy. Always paid up front. It was cool."

Now for the big question. I'm almost afraid to ask. "Do you know if Connie Beale is still around?"

"He was about five years ago. I ran into him once. Said he was about retired from the post office."

"Was he still playing?"

"Just casuals, weddings, dances, that kind of thing. Musicians never quit playing 'less they have to."

"Do you know how to get in touch with him?"

"Naw, it was just one of those chance meetings. I hadn't seen him for years." Nolan Thomas watches my reaction, sees my disappointment. "I know you thought you found you some Clifford Brown nobody knew about, right?"

I feel a disappointment that goes deeper than Nolan Thomas could possibly fathom. There was always that sliver of hope that I might be wrong, but now Nolan

Thomas has just confirmed what I suspected all along. It still comes as a jolt, hearing the truth. It always does.

"Yeah, but believe it or not, I'd rather know it's not Clifford Brown. Thanks, Nolan, you just helped me figure something out."

CHAPTER
FOURTEEN

I GET BACK TO MY PLACE FEELING PRETTY SATISFIED with myself. Part of the mystery at least is solved, but I still have to find Conrad Beale and check with Coop to see if anything has turned up on Raymond Cross's disappearance.

I get a beer out of the refrigerator and call Natalie. We have an arrangement. Sometimes she stays at my place, sometimes I stay at her apartment in Santa Monica. If either of us feels like just being alone, we do that too, no questions asked. So far it's working.

"Hi, what are you doing?"

"What every student does after exams. Lounging around, drinking wine, watching trash TV, and—oh my God. Is your TV on?"

"No, I just got in. Why?"

"Turn it on, quick, Channel 36."

I walk over and switch on the television. It's one of those tabloid entertainment-type things. I see a backdrop photo of Clifford Brown behind the boy-girl anchor team. I recognize the photo from a lot of old jazz histories.

"You see it?" Natalie says.

"Yeah, jazz on E.T., and it's not Kenny G." I usually keep a tape on standby, for anything interesting that comes up I might want to see again. I press the record button and lean back on the couch.

"Well, Rick," the woman says, "here's a story for John Tesh." She has a blinding, Chiclets-like smile, and of course, perfect blond hair.

"Legendary jazz trumpet man Clifford Brown left a small legacy of recordings before his tragic death in an automobile accident in 1956. But now it seems there's more to come. Our own Steve Dunning has this exclusive inside look on the story."

I'm always amazed at how quickly television can get things together. A politician or movie star dies in the morning, and by the evening news, they've put together a mini-documentary complete with clips and interviews.

There's some real Clifford Brown playing in the background while the camera zooms in on the reporter, who stands in front of a white building with the Pacific Records logo behind him. I would have chosen the Lighthouse in Hermosa Beach.

"He was known as Brownie to his fellow jazz men, but it seems there was at least one wild jam Clifford Brown made that no one knew about until now. We spoke to Pacific Records executive Barry Hastings earlier this afternoon."

"Wild jam?" Natalie says into the phone. "Please."

The camera pulls back to reveal Hastings, still in his surfer uniform, Ray-Bans on top of his head, smiling at the reporter.

"Tell me, Barry, how did you come into these recordings?"

"Well," Hastings says, gazing into the camera. "I can't reveal the source, but I've been assured by a prominent musician these are genuine Clifford Brown recordings, made some time just before his tragic accident."

"And what happens to the tapes now, Barry?"

"They'll be remastered and issued on CD." Barry pauses for a moment and assumes an air of solemnity before continuing. "Clifford Brown was one of the jazz greats, and Pacific Records is proud to be a part of jazz history."

There's a few more seconds of Brownie, then they're back to the studio. "No release date has been set for these lost recordings," the anchor says, "and Pacific's head honcho, Rick Markham, had no comment."

The woman anchor turns to her partner and flashes her smile once again. "How about that, Rick?"

"Sounds like a swinging deal to me," Rick says. "When we come back—"

I push the mute button. This is better than I expected, and a lot faster. I haven't played in over a year, and I'm a prominent musician.

Natalie says, "Is he talking about you?"

"Could be, or it could be Quincy Jones, Max Roach."

"They don't know about the tapes, do they?"

"They do now, or somebody will call them."

Barry bought in all the way. His little performance will set a lot of things in motion.

"Listen," I say to Natalie. "I've got to make a couple of calls. Talk to you in a few minutes, okay?"

"Sure. I'll do a little channel surfing, see if anybody else picked it up."

I dig through my book and call Rick Markham's private cell phone number.

"Rick? Evan Horne."

"The prominent musician? Barry's been fired," Markham says. There's a pause from both of us that lasts several moments before Markham speaks again. "I think—no, I know—you set us up, Evan. At least Barry."

"And I think you knew I was doing it." What had Markham said? *I'll handle Barry just the way you want me to.* "I didn't tell either of you the tapes were genuine."

"No, you didn't, but this is going to cause Pacific some slight embarrassment, you know."

"You'll survive. Trust me, Rick, you'll come out a hero on this."

"I'd better. I'd like to talk more about this. I'm having a few people over Friday night. Maybe you could come, bring a friend?"

"We'll see. I'll call you."

"Bye, Evan."

I hang up and sit for a minute, a million thoughts racing through my mind before I call Natalie back.

"Rick Markham. Isn't he the guy you told me about that was involved in the Lonnie Cole thing?" When I don't answer she says, "You going to tell me about this, and the car that was following us last night?"

"You will be a good lawyer. Okay, I wasn't sure it would work, but I was going to ask Markham to help. With this Hastings character, I didn't need to. Hastings was too eager to make a name for himself. I played the tape for both of them, said I was representing someone who had the originals, and wanted to know what they would be worth to a record company."

"And since nobody can find this Raymond Cross,

who you think is the killer, publicity like this might draw him out."

"My, but you're clever. It's a possibility."

Natalie ignores that. "It might also make you a target."

"No, I don't think so. Cross knows I can't identify him, or I would have already. He wants the tape, which the Las Vegas police have and he'll never get, and the trumpet, which I have, is in a safe place. I think he'll just wait till I lead him to one or the other."

Natalie is silent for a moment.

"God, I wish your hand would get better so you could go back to just playing piano. Evan, this is—" There's a long pause. I know Natalie is trying to decide whether to talk me out of things or not. *Not* evidently wins.

"What's next?" she asks, the resignation heavy in her voice.

"Believe it or not, I've got to try and find a guy known as Mojo Boneyard."

"Good night," Natalie says.

I get the numbers from Blackbyrd. Mojo has a home phone with an answering machine, a fax, two beepers, and a cellular phone.

"Despite all the numbers, he's sometimes hard to track down," Blackbyrd says. "Mojo is always on the move."

"Any luck on finding *Arrival*?" I'm still hoping a copy of my own album will turn up somewhere in the collector's world.

"Not yet, but I've got the word out. If there's one out there, it'll turn up. Good luck with Mojo."

"Thanks, I'll probably need it."

"One other thing," Blackbyrd says.

"Yeah."

"The story I told you about the collector who hired a PI."

"Sure, I remember. What about it?"

"The collector was Ray Cross."

I leave messages on both beepers and the answering machine, then try the cell phone number. What do I call him? Mojo? Mr. Boneyard? While I'm deciding, he answers.

"Yo, Mojo. Talk to me."

"Mojo Boneyard?"

"No, it's American Express. Who's this?"

"My name is Evan Horne, Mojo. I'm trying to locate something."

"We all are, man, that's the name of the game. Do I know you?"

"Blackbyrd told me you might be able to help me. He gave me your numbers."

"Blackbyrd, huh. You a collector?"

"No, I'm trying to track down the source of a tape and locate a trumpet. I think both might be valuable."

"I'm only talking to you because you mentioned Blackbyrd, but I got to check that out. Give me your number." He seems surprised that I have only one to give him.

He calls back in five minutes. "Blackbyrd says you're okay, and I don't mind helping if this has something to do with Ken Perkins's murder."

"It does."

"Okay, I don't know what I know until you ask me. There's a coffee shop in Brentwood, on San Vicente. I'll be there in thirty minutes. Look for a blue van."

Mojo is gone before I can agree, but when I get to

Brentwood, he's right where he said, parked on the street near a Starbucks. The van's sliding side door is open and Mojo is sitting on the runner, drinking coffee from a paper cup, when I walk up.

"Mojo? Evan Horne."

He nods, stands up, and reaches in the van, comes out with a coffee for me.

"Thanks," I say, taking the coffee. Mojo is dressed in running shoes, a light sweater, a windbreaker, and jeans held up with a wide black web belt to which are clipped two beepers and a holster that holds a small cell phone. Even though it's overcast, he wears mirrored sunglasses. His face is weathered, tanned dark, like he spends a good deal of time on a boat. His hair closely resembles a style I've seen in pictures of Albert Einstein.

I glance inside the van as I join him on the runner, but he's up, pacing back and forth, pausing only to drink from his coffee cup.

"Looks like you collect lots of things." Inside the van, there are boxes of records, books, magazines, a snare drum, and a tuba.

"Records are my serious thing, but old instruments are fun. I run across a lot of interesting stuff." He tells me this almost reluctantly, regarding me warily, as if I'm going to try and talk him out of something.

"I'm waiting for a call now on an estate sale. Might be some heavy stuff there, and I just made a deal with a jukebox company. Sixty thousand records sitting around a warehouse that need a home."

"Sixty thousand?"

"Yeah." Mojo shrugs as if this were a minor purchase. "I can turn them over for two or three bucks apiece and maybe find something really fine and rare that will make the whole deal worthwhile." He smiles as if he knows something I don't. "Mojo is always lucky."

"Just out of curiosity, what's your real name?"

He takes out a large wallet from a zippered pocket in his jacket. It's stuffed with credit cards. He shuffles through one thick stack, pulls out an American Express corporate card, and points at the name: Mojo Boneyard.

"That gets a lot of laughs at the airlines, but it's not my real name." He takes off the glasses and rubs his eyes. They're dark brown and bloodshot. "Arthur Klein," he says softly, "but legends aren't made on a name like that. On Mojo Boneyard they are."

I think back to when Ace first told me about collectors and how different they are. "I'm trying to locate the source of a trumpet I've come into. Seems old, might be worth something. Actually, I'm trying to prove it's not worth something, at least to a collector."

Mojo studies me for a moment, I guess to see if I'm serious or if he's heard right.

"Let me get this straight. You have this trumpet. You want to know where it came from. You think it might be valuable, but you don't want it to be."

"Yeah, that's right."

"That's a strange concept, one that's alien to collectors. Well, that's what I do. Buy and sell, collect until someone else who collects wants to buy and pay more than I did. Then I sell. Hey, it's just like the stock market."

He reaches in the van and taps his fingers on the snare drum. It's a metal shell, the top head smudged with black marks from endless playing with wire brushes. He nods at the tuba.

"I bought that from John Philip Sousa's great-grandson. That'll be big."

I look at the tuba, then at Mojo, see that he enjoys the surprised expression on my face.

"I bought a trumpet a while back. It was old. Beat-up case and horn. Hadn't even decided what to do with it—strictly an impulse buy, but you never know. Guess what? Guy comes along, pays me four times what I paid. You see, Mojo is always lucky."

"Did you look in the case?"

"Yeah, saw a trumpet. What else was there to see?"

I take the bottle of Slick Stuff out of my pocket. "This was inside, in that little compartment where the mouthpiece is kept."

Mojo takes the bottle, turns it over in his hand, holds it up to the light, then hands it back to me. "You're not going to tell me what's in that bottle is worth more than the trumpet."

"No, but they go together to help establish some other things. Do you remember who you sold the trumpet to?"

"Yeah." Mojo suddenly looks thoughtful.

"What?"

"Nothing, I just thought it was funny at the time, and now with Ken Perkins getting whacked, I don't know. I sold it to Bernie Dalton, small-time collector, but he deals a lot for Ray Cross. I wondered why Ray wanted a trumpet. Now Ray is really plugged in, but he never deals in anything but records."

I can't see his eyes behind the mirrored shades, but Mojo looks over my shoulder, somewhere in the distance.

"Blackbyrd tell you about the scam Ken Perkins pulled off, the bogus record?"

"Yeah, he did. Pretty elaborate for a practical joke."

"Ray took it pretty bad when Ken took the wool away. Didn't think it was funny at all. Still"—Mojo shrugs—"murder is something else, man, and besides, Ray Cross has one of the best collections. When he goes, Mojo will be right there with the best offer."

"Did Dalton say he was buying the trumpet for Cross?"

"In a roundabout way."

"But you didn't ask about it?"

Mojo looks at me. "Doesn't matter where it comes from and who it goes to as long as the deal is cool. That trumpet you're talking about, I bought that at a garage sale for twenty-five bucks."

I finish my coffee without looking at Mojo. I don't have the heart to tell him that it might have been worth $25,000.

Back home, my answering machine has been getting a workout. I don't know how these people got my number, but there are messages from Max Roach, Quincy Jones, two entertainment news shows reporters, a very furious Tim Shaw from *Blue Note* magazine, and John Trask. Nothing from Raymond Cross. I listen first to Max Roach. I had tried him earlier, but he had never returned my call.

"Clifford Brown never recorded anything I didn't know about. These tapes, if they exist, are fraudulent." No greeting, no good-bye, end of story. Thank you, Max.

Quincy Jones says, "Please call me in regard to the Clifford Brown tapes." He at least leaves his agent's number. I'll just let that one go.

Tim Shaw doesn't even say please. "Goddamnit,

Horne, you promised me you'd keep me up to date, and I had exclusive rights to this story. Call me now." I do.

"Tim? Evan Horne."

"Listen, you promised me. If you think—"

"Wait a minute. You are talking about the TV story, I take it. I didn't give them anything. They, Barry Hastings at least, presumed, as it turned out, way too much. I was trying to get an idea of the tapes' value if they were genuine." That silences Tim for the moment.

"You mean there are no tapes?"

"I mean there are tapes, but they are not, at least I'm pretty sure, Clifford Brown."

"Pretty sure? When will you know?"

"Very soon. Look, Tim, this is part of a murder investigation, and we are definitely off the record here, but I promise I'll give you the whole story when it all goes down."

"Murder? Jesus, I thought it was just about undiscovered recordings."

"Yeah, me too. I'll be in touch."

There's nothing for me to tell Quincy Jones or the TV reporters. I hesitate before calling Trask. I want to talk to Coop first, but in person.

I drive down to Santa Monica Police Headquarters and find him in his usual position at his desk: feet up, ankles crossed, telephone to his ear, drinking out of a bottle of Gatorade. He waves me in, motions me to the chair in front of his desk.

He says "Right" two or three times into the phone, scribbles something down on a pad, and finally says, "Got it." He looks at me expectantly, as if I'm about to tell him something.

"What?"

"I hear you were mentioned on TV last night."

"Not by name. I'm so well known, all they have to say is 'prominent musician' and everybody knows it's me."

Coop snorts, gets to his feet, and stretches. "Nothing on Raymond Cross. No priors, no record, not even a parking ticket. A model employee of the city of Santa Monica."

"I'm not surprised. I think he just went over the edge on this deal. Some people don't take much pushing."

I tell Coop about my revenge theory, how Cross was one of the victims of Ken Perkins's practical joke.

"Add to that the standard collectors' obsession, and well, isn't it possible Cross just acted impulsively?"

"Sure," Coop says. "I never said it was premeditated. It's also possible he might act impulsively again—if it was him."

"If? What do you mean?"

"I mean we've got a solid citizen here with nothing to indicate he'd be capable of something like this."

"But how can somebody just disappear like this? Can't you check him out, bring him in?"

"People disappear every day. It's not that hard to do. You think he's just sitting out at his condo in Malibu? All we have is the theory of a piano player who thinks Cross might be responsible. We have to have some probable cause for a warrant, we have nothing concrete to charge him with, and you can't positively identify him. No go, sport."

Before I can come up with a counterargument, Coop's phone rings again. "Hi, John. As a matter of fact, he's sitting right here. Hold on." Coop hands me the phone. "Lieutenant Trask."

"Hello."

"Guess what my wife saw on TV last night? She never misses those shows, watches them all. Somebody talking about some Clifford Brown tapes. I wonder who that could be? Are you thinking about selling the tapes on your own? Don't forget, we have the other one."

"No, nothing like that. That was just some digging on my part that got out of hand, blown out of proportion by the record company."

"Cooper gave me everything on Cross. A court reporter. Who would have guessed that? He hasn't tried to contact you?"

"Not yet."

"Well, he might. If he comes back to Las Vegas, we can at least bring him in for questioning. Anything more on the tape?"

"I'm pretty sure they're not genuine, at least I don't think it's Clifford Brown, so they have no value to a collector. This was all a deal to scam a record company. I've found one of the musicians, and I'm still looking for another, the trumpet player. That'll cinch it."

"Okay," Trask says. "That's no more than we could have done. Let me know when you're sure. Put Cooper back on."

I hand the phone back to Coop. He listens, nods his head. "Right, we've got his license, address. We'll check it out here. Okay." He glances at me and says good-bye.

"You got a name for this other musician? I have a request from the Las Vegas police to run him for an address and phone. And that makes it official police business, so I can help."

"Conrad Beale."

"Hang on," Coop says as he gets up and walks out of the office. While he's gone, I get a look at his pad and try to read upside down. Coop comes back in a few minutes and hands me a slip of paper.

"DMV says this is current."

It's an address in the Valley, not too far from Blackbyrd's house.

"Thanks, Coop. This helps a lot."

Once in my car, I jot down the other name and address I saw on Coop's desk.

Now I know where Raymond Cross lives.

INTERLUDE
June 25, 1956

Brownie had been awake for a while, when they pulled into Philadelphia, long before Richie called to him. His body became aware of the change in the rhythm of the big car's movement from the steady hum of the highway to the stop-and-start jerkiness as they eased into city traffic. Eyes still closed, he lay there listening to the comforting city noises—horns honking, the piercing whistle of traffic cops, snatches of conversation, bus engines. The highway was a memory.

He'd dreamed again about the accident, the hospital, Dizzy and Miles and Fats Navarro standing over his bed with their trumpets, the three of them playing dirgelike blues. Then Brownie, sitting up in bed, waving them away.

"Hey, man, I'm not through yet. Get out of here with that sad blues." Then all of them smiling, Dizzy handing him a trumpet.

"Brownie, wake up. We're here," Richie Powell said, pulling the car into the parking lot at Music City. As soon as Richie turned the engine off, Brownie began to relax, think about what he was going to play.

They all got out of the car, Nancy yawning, still
with sleep-laden eyes, Richie stretching, Brownie tun-
ing in to the sounds of Philadelphia. It wasn't the first
Music City gig for Brownie. It was like a homecoming.
He had been born in Delaware, but Philly was his musical hometown, and these Monday jams at the music
store were getting famous now.

Drummer-owner Ellis Tollin and his friend Bill
Welch brought in some big names—Brownie realized
suddenly he was one of them—put them with local
cats, and somebody always had a tape recorder handy.
While Nancy and Richie took off, Brownie walked in
the store's back door, took Ellis by surprise.

"Brownie!" Ellis said, hugging him. "You made it,
man. And lookin' good."

"Of course I made it," Brownie said. "Everything
cool?"

"Oh yeah," Ellis said. "I got Billy Root and Ziggy
Vines on tenors, Sam Dockery on piano, Ace Tisone on
bass, and you know I'll be playing some drums for
you."

"Guess we'll have to play all ballads then," Brownie
said, laughing. This was going to be fun, he thought,
and it was.

The crowd spilled out to the doorway as he played
so sharp and clear, but he let everyone else stretch out
too. No pressure, just a blowing session. By the time he
finished his solo on "Blues Walk," he had them. He
glanced at the crowd and nodded at Art Blakey, Sonny
Stitt, Bud Powell, even Buddy Rich, over the bell of his
horn. They were all there, smiling back at him. That
young kid, Lee Morgan, a big fan of Brownie's, was
there too, just a teenager.

Brownie made a short speech after the gig, shook

hands with everyone, laughed and joked with his friends and fans. He signed a photo for Ellis, who was touched and promised it would go in a new frame in front of the store and stay there forever. Brownie liked that.

He ducked away for a few minutes then and called LaRue. "I miss you, baby. Happy birthday."

"You stay down there at your mom's and get some rest," LaRue said, "and don't you let Nancy Powell drive my car."

Brownie hung up the phone. Time to go. He was too tired to hang out more, just grateful to see Richie and Nancy arrive with the car. He glanced at the dark sheet of sky. Looked like rain. Once again, he climbed into the Buick's glorious backseat, where he would stay until they arrived at the Conn factory in Elkhart. He had a lot to tell Max, who would be waiting for him in Chicago.

He had a lot of music to play.

CHAPTER

FIFTEEN

WHEN I TRY CONNIE BEALE'S NUMBER, A YOUNG girl's voice answers. "Connie isn't here," she says. "He's working tonight." She sounds like a teenager.

"Do you know where? It's very important that I talk to him."

"Just a minute."

I hear a clunk as she puts down the phone. For a couple of minutes, I watch traffic drift by on Sunset near the Tower Records store. Cruising teens checking out the strip clubs, residents dropping down for dinner out of the Hollywood hills. Near a traffic light, a man in a suit holds up a hand-lettered cardboard sign that reads, Will Work for 40K.

"Mom says he's playing at a restaurant off LaBrea called the Peacock. I don't know the address."

"That's okay, I'll find it. Thank you very much." I hang up and flip through the yellow pages for the Peacock's address. It's not far from where I'm standing. Fifteen minutes later I pull into the parking lot and drive around back.

The Peacock has seen better days. It's one of those

small restaurant bars that occasionally gives jazz a try. I hear the music as soon as I open the door, a Miles-like muted trumpet working its way through "All of You."

A bar and dining area take up most of the room. The tiny bandstand is wedged in a corner between the bar and a few tables that cover what was once a good-sized dance floor and look like they were added and arranged as an afterthought.

Two couples—the guys both ruining the effect of their dark suits with white shoes and belts—sway in place with two women trying to look ten years younger in too-tight, too-short dresses, just in front of Connie Beale's trumpet. They're seemingly oblivious to the beat or tempo.

At first glance, the piano and bass look young enough to be teenagers; the drummer looks to be about Connie's age, which would put him somewhere near mid-sixties. Connie is stout and wears a suit that no longer fits him quite right. There's a bald patch on top of his head, and what's left of his hair has gone to gray. I take a seat at the bar, order a beer, wait for them to take a break to meet the man who played like Clifford Brown.

Somebody once said playing in a small jazz group is like a panel discussion. Playing solo is giving a speech; a duet is a debate; a big band, a rally. Connie is the moderator of this panel discussion, but nobody is making any points.

He looks over the bell of his horn, his eyebrows moving up and down as he stretches for a note here and there. He finishes his solo with an obvious nod to Miles, steps away from the mike, and watches the pianist. He holds the trumpet in his left hand and beats out the time on his leg with his right, some inner tempo that contradicts the piano player. He gives the drummer a look of concern.

The pianist, an eager-looking kid, takes three choruses. Nice touch, technique, but he flubs a couple of the changes before giving way to the bassist, who gets his say, even though he has to compete with the whir of the blender at the bar.

There's a brief exchange of fours with the drummer, who gets even with the blender. Connie, looking weary and resigned, brings them all home. It's for the most part uninspired, but the two couples on the dance floor stop and applaud before returning to their table, which is cluttered with the kind of drinks that have small umbrellas hanging over the edge of the glasses.

Connie looks at his watch, glances around the room, says something to the piano player, and they go into "Take the A Train," with the piano getting eight bars up front. Connie plays the melody chorus, this time without a mute. The tone is big, and he makes some high notes that make me think he was once a lead player. I wonder if he always thinks about those three nights with Duke. His two choruses are adequate, but none of them have their hearts in it. It's just a gig, a night to finish up, get paid, and file away as a cloudy memory.

They play two more tunes, then Connie speaks softly into the microphone. "Thank you for your kind attention, ladies and gentlemen. We're going to take a short break, but stick around. We'll be back."

No one takes any notice as they leave the stand. The two young guys head for the restaurant area. Connie and the drummer talk quietly for a moment, then walk outside the back door I came in.

I put a couple of dollars on the bar and follow them

out. They start to step aside when I say, "Are you Connie Beale?" Connie's eyes narrow as he tries to place me, figure what I want. "Your daughter told me I could find you here. I got your number from a guy at the union. Tommy James."

"My daughter? My granddaughter, you mean. Yeah, I'm Connie." He offers his hand while the drummer looks on.

"Evan Horne. I play piano." Both men visibly relax.

Connie says, "You know the changes to 'All the Things'? These young cats think it's all McCoy Tyner and that modal shit."

"Thanks, not tonight. I need to talk to you for a few minutes though, or we could meet later."

Connie looks at the other drummer. "How much time we got, Jimmy?"

"Plenty," the one called Jimmy says. "Shit, we could quit now and no one would care. I'll let you know."

Connie nods, and then says to me, "Come on. Let's go to your car."

We get in the car, and Connie takes out a small silver flask. "You mind?" he asks, then takes a drink and passes it to me.

"No thanks."

Connie shrugs and licks his lips. He unbuttons his suit coat and straightens his tie. "So, what's this about? You're not from the union, are you?"

I laugh. "No, not hardly."

"I didn't think so. Union guys wear suits."

"I'm doing some research on some old recordings. Ran across a tape we think was made in the fifties. Maybe you can help me out. I just saw an old friend of yours yesterday. Nolan Thomas, a piano player."

Connie tilts his head back and smiles, says the name

slowly. "Nolan Thomas. Nobody called that name for twenty years. He still teaching? I ran into him a while back. What's he doing?"

"Still teaching, at a studio in his house. Were you pretty good friends?"

Connie shrugs. "Not really, we played together a lot for a while back there, then just kind of drifted apart."

I shift in the seat, light a cigarette. "Well, look, I've got this tape I'd like you to listen to. We don't know who all the players are. Maybe you could help."

"Yeah, okay, sure."

I hesitate a moment. "I think one of them, the trumpet player, is you," I say.

I watch Connie for some reaction. He turns and looks at me, his eyes questioning. "Me?"

"Yeah."

I turn on the key and push the tape into the player. I watch Connie as the music begins, his eyes on the lighted arrow of the tape player. After the first few bars, he gives me a look I can't read, then leans back, rests his head on the seat. His eyes close. He listens for a few minutes, not saying anything.

After the trumpet solo he says, "I sound pretty good, huh?" He listens a few moments more, sighs, and seems to sink deeper into the seat, pushed down by the weight of his confession. "Yeah, that's me. I always knew someday, somebody would find that tape."

Well, there it is, the final note of truth torn from the past and brought up to the present. I've found the man who would be Clifford Brown.

I turn down the volume and wait for Connie to continue. He seems to gather strength from the music. "Where was this tape?"

"For nearly forty years, sealed up in a box in a recording studio in Hollywood. Cosmos Recorders? Got stolen a while back."

"Yeah, Cosmos Recorders," Connie says. " 'Just like Brownie,' that's what that guy at the studio said, thought it would be cool to do a whole bunch of Brownie's tunes."

Connie listens to himself again at low volume. I reach for the knob to turn it up, but he shakes his head. "I idolized him, man. I was twenty-two, studied the records, learned all his solos, figured it was fate, since we had the same initials." He sighs again and looks out the window. "Then the motherfucker went and got himself killed."

"What happened, did you stop playing?"

He looks at me as if I'd asked him if he stopped breathing. "What happened? Shit, man, Lee Morgan, Freddie Hubbard, Woody Shaw, even this young dude Wynton Marsalis, that's what happened. They learned from Brownie like he learned from Fats Navarro. But they made their own sound, their own identity. I was *too* much like Brownie." He looks at me with sad eyes. "You want imitation when the real thing is around? And anyway, after he died, I just couldn't do it anymore. I put down my horn for a year. People thought I was crazy, 'specially my old lady. She said, 'You ain't gonna play this horn, I'm going to sell it.'

"Eventually I started playing again, tried to forget about Brownie, but it was like I couldn't play any other way. He kept creeping into my solos, like he was looking over my shoulder. I did okay, some road work, big bands, a few shows in Las Vegas with singers, a little recording, made a living, then finally got on with the post office."

I push the stop button, and there's silence in the car

except for the ticking sound of the engine cooling down. "I never heard this tape after the night we did it. Where did you get it?"

"Through a friend. He thought this was Clifford Brown."

Connie looks at me, frowning. "You some kind of music detective or something, trying to find guys so they can get their lost royalties?"

I laugh. "No, nothing like that."

"Well, if you were, I could save you time. We got paid, but that was never released far as I know. Cat paid us seventy-five bucks, did it right here in Hollywood while Brownie was playing down at the Lighthouse."

Connie takes another drink from his flask and looks at his watch. "Well, I got to get back inside, finish this gig." He gets out of the car, starts to walk away, then turns around, leans back in, his dark face filling the window.

"You find the trumpet too?"

"The trumpet?"

"My old trumpet, raggedy case and all. Got *C.B.* engraved inside the bell. Got stolen a few months ago along with a lot of other worthless shit. I figured these was some dumb robbers to break into my house." He shakes his head, puzzled still. "Don't know why anyone would want it. Ain't worth nothing."

He turns away then, and I watch Connie Beale amble to the back door. He turns once to look at the car, then disappears inside.

"Oh, you're wrong, Connie, it's worth a lot."

"Pappy Dean, it's Evan. I need you to do me a favor."

"Long as it don't have nothin' to do with murder, police, any of that shit."

"No, nothing like that. This is easy. I left something in Las Vegas, and I'm too tied up here to come back for it."

"You still chasin' that trumpet player, sounds like Brownie?"

"I found him."

"Oh yeah?"

"Guy's name is Connie Beale. Ever heard of him?"

"Naw, I don't think so. He's in L.A., huh?"

"Yeah, just saw him on a gig."

"He need a bass player? Ain't nothin' happening around here. Trouble needs some work."

"I'll ask him. Look, I'm going to mail you a pawn ticket. I need to have you pick it up and bring it to me here. I'll pay for your flight."

"The trumpet? Oh Lord. This better not be Clifford Brown's trumpet."

"No, I thought it was for a while, but I still need it. Can you do that?"

"Well." Pappy hesitates and I don't understand why. "Look, man, I'd like to do this, but—"

"What?"

"Oh shit, man, I might as well just tell you. I don't fly. I don't get on no planes. I'm sorry, man."

I hadn't even thought of that. "Hey, it's okay. I've got another idea. You get the trumpet out of hock and meet Natalie at the airport. I'll have her fly up, okay?"

"Cool," Pappy says. "I like that a whole lot better."

"All right, I'll call you with her flight number, and I'll send the pawn ticket. Thanks, Pappy."

I press down on the receiver button with my finger and speed-dial Natalie, explain what I want her to do.

"Can't you go with me?" she asks.

"I wouldn't need you to pick it up if I could. I have some more things I want to run down here."

"Okay but leave enough time before the return flight so I can get in a little time on the poker machines. When do you want me to do this?"

"Tomorrow, if I can get a flight for you. I'll drive you to LAX. Want me to come over?"

"That would be nice. I've had enough down time, I think."

"Okay, see you in about an hour."

I grab my keys and go back out of the carport. I reach under the seat, feel around for the envelope with the pawn ticket I'd taped there earlier. I come away empty. I try again, running my hand under the entire seat. I get the flashlight out of the glove box and shine it all over the floor, under both seats, but I know it's not there.

I get out of the car and stand in the carport a few minutes, smoking, trying to remember where I've left the car, if I ever left it unlocked. With valet parking at a couple of restaurants, but I can't come up with anything else. I can't believe this.

Back in the house, I go over it all again, trying to figure it out, when the phone jars the silence.

"Hello."

"That was very clever, Mr. Horne. A good hiding place for the tape. Who would have thought of a pawn shop?"

I know the voice. Raymond Cross.

"How did you—"

"Get the pawn ticket? I searched your car twice. Missed it the first time. Valet parking is not very reliable. They get busy, don't notice things, and often don't lock the cars. It was quite easy. I was looking for the tape, but then I found the ticket, and now I'll have both tapes."

"But it's not for the tape. The police still have the tape."

Cross pauses, says nothing for a few moments, while my mind races with possibilities. "Really? What, then? Oh, of course, the trumpet. Even better. It was you who took it from Perkins's house. I wondered about that. You must have beaten me to it by minutes."

"Cross, you know that's not Clifford Brown on those tapes. They're not worth anything to you or anyone now. Neither is the trumpet."

"Aren't they? I saw the little scenario you must have created on television the other night. How much did the record company offer?"

"What difference does it make? Their offer was for genuine Clifford Brown. These tapes are bogus."

"Really? Can Pacific or any record company afford not to make an offer? They can't be sure they're not genuine. There's no foolproof way to tell, Horne, you know that yourself. We fooled you."

"Why did you kill Ken Perkins?"

"Not now, Horne. There isn't time for this."

"No, there isn't. The police are looking for you."

"Of course they are, but what are they going to charge me with? They have no witness, no weapon. Do you think that after twelve years of typing trial transcripts I don't know about procedure, evidence? I've simply been on vacation, and I'll return to work totally unaware of any police search."

For once I wish I had caller ID, to see where Cross is calling from. I wonder now if Cross is right. I can't positively identify him. Can he just do that, reappear with no consequences?

"Please do not try and tell me, even if the tapes are not genuine, that the trumpet isn't either. Why else would you hide it?"

"The trumpet belonged to the same musician who made the tapes. It just happens his initials are the same." Even as I say the words, I imagine how Cross must be taking them. Of course I would deny the trumpet is genuine, and who but Connie Beale could prove otherwise? "Meet me, let's talk about this some more."

"Why, so you can arrange with the police to tape my confession? Please, Horne, give me more credit than that. I'll decide when to do that. I will be in touch again."

"Wait—" But it's already too late. Raymond Cross is gone.

Now what? Cross could have been calling from Las Vegas, but if he was, he could already have redeemed the pawn ticket, so that leaves L.A. For all I know, he was calling from his house or LAX.

Even if the call came from LAX, the pawn shop in Las Vegas wouldn't open until tomorrow morning. There is a way to do this, identify Cross and get him at the same time.

I call Pappy back, explain the change in plans, tell him about Raymond Cross.

"You want me to what?"

"Stake out the pawn shop. Don't do anything, even let him see you, just follow whoever comes out with the trumpet case. Cross doesn't know you. He'll probably go to the airport. Soon as you see him get on the plane, call me and let me know the flight number and airline."

"Why I got to do this?" Pappy doesn't sound happy.

"C'mon, Pappy. I don't have time to get there and do it myself."

"Shit, you done made me a detective too. All right. I must be crazy. What's the name of the pawn shop?"

"Silver State Pawn on Fremont Street. Thanks, Pappy."

"We're even now."

"It may be over tomorrow," I tell Natalie. I tried Coop at home and at police headquarters, but no go.

Natalie pours me a glass of wine and brings a plate of cheese and crackers to the coffee table.

"Have you told Trask in Las Vegas about this?" She doesn't approve of my plan at all.

"Not yet. I will, in the morning."

"That's not going to give him much time. He's not going to like it that you've gone ahead with this."

"I know, but what else could I do?"

"You could leave it to them."

"Yeah, and nothing would happen."

"Nothing may happen anyway. You said you can't positively identify Cross. You're going up against a solid citizen who works in the system, for God's sake. He will have covered himself."

Natalie was right about that; and Trask for sure, Coop maybe, didn't buy Cross as Perkins's killer for exactly those reasons.

"I want to be there when he gets off that plane. I want that trumpet back. I want to see Connie Beale get it back."

Natalie looks away and is silent. She knows there's no point in trying to talk me out of it.

"Well, at least you proved it's not Clifford Brown on that tape. That's something."

"Yes, it is."

She sets her glass down on the table, puts her head on my chest, I put my arm around her, and we sit for a few minutes, neither of us speaking.

CHAPTER
SIXTEEN

I'M UP EARLY, GRINDING COFFEE, PACING AROUND waiting for Danny Cooper to call back and Silver State Pawn to open. I'd left a message with him to call as soon as he gets in, and I want to time the call to Trask so he won't be able to intercept Cross if he shows. I want that trumpet back, but it's all up to Pappy Dean now.

Just as I check my watch, the phone rings.

"My, we're up early today, aren't we?" Coop says.

"Coop, listen to me, then you can tell Trask if you need to."

"This doesn't sound good, sport."

Coop listens without interrupting while I tell him what's supposed to happen, about the pawn ticket, the trumpet. There's a long silence when I finish before Coop finally speaks.

"There's some holes in this. First, I've got to let Trask know."

"I understand."

"No, I don't think you do. Let's suppose Cross actu-ally does get off that plane and has the trumpet. We still have nothing, since you can't positively put him in Perkins's house the night of the murder. All you've got is a guy getting off a plane carrying a trumpet."

"But I can confront him. Maybe that will be enough."

"If it's him, at least we'll know who and where he is," Coop concedes. "Call me back as soon as you hear from Pappy. I've got to talk to Las Vegas. If the pawn shop opens at nine, the earliest flight he could get would be ten, which would put him here at eleven, if Trask doesn't pick him up first."

"Why would he? You just said they've got nothing."

"You don't know how much Trask wants a break on this."

"That's what I'm giving him."

"We'll see."

I hang up. Seconds later, the phone rings again.

"Pappy?"

"Yeah." I know he's talking on a pay phone. I can hear snatches of other conversations in the background, and I think, public address announcements.

"Are you at the airport?"

"Yeah, he came just like you said, waiting for the door to open, had a taxi waiting."

"Did he get the trumpet?"

"Oh yeah, little weasel dude, he got it, jumped back in the cab, went right to the airport."

"And?"

"I had to park, man, he didn't." Even before the silence I know what's coming. "I lost him."

"What?"

"I caught up inside the terminal but I got hung up at the security thing. That red light kept coming on. I had to walk through three times before they let me by. I told them I wasn't flyin' anyway, just looking for somebody. Lookin' for who? they wanted to know. I told 'em it was none of their damn business. They finally let me pass, but when I got to the gates there was so many airlines."

Pappy pauses like he's out of breath. I hadn't even considered he wouldn't know his way around an airport.

"I looked everywhere, man, but I couldn't find him. I'm sorry, man, I really am."

I don't know what to say. Cross is on a flight headed for L.A., and we don't know which one.

"It's all right, Pappy. You couldn't help it. At least we know he got the trumpet, and that's important."

"No, it ain't all right," Pappy says. "I'll do something to fix it. You let me know what, and I'll do it."

"Don't worry about it, Pappy. I'll get back to you."

I hang up and pound my fist on the counter loud enough to wake up Natalie. She comes out of the bedroom, belting a robe around her.

"What happened?"

"Cross was there, but Pappy lost him."

"Did he get the trumpet?"

"Yeah, he got it." I reach for the phone again and call Coop, relay the news to him.

"That was one of the holes I mentioned," he says. "I'll have somebody cover Burbank. Jesus, what do I tell them, look for a guy with a trumpet? I hope there are no bands coming in this morning. You and I are going to LAX. Pick you up in ten minutes."

"Okay, I'll be outside." I hang up and turn to Natalie.

"Can I do anything?"

"I don't know what. Stay here and cover the phone in case Pappy calls back."

"Call me," she says. She gives me a hug. "There wasn't anything else you could do."

"Yes, there was."

Coop has his red light on but still has to dodge cars as we careen down Lincoln toward LAX. He keeps both hands on the wheel, his eyes on the road, but manages to talk over the whine of the engine.

"Trask, as you might imagine, is furious with you, but if your friend is right Cross would have already been gone. You better hope we get lucky."

Coop changes lanes again and skirts a bus. I put one hand on the dash to steady myself as the airport exit at Century comes into view. We take the ramp almost on two wheels.

"Southwest is our best bet," I say to Coop over the roar of the engine and the squealing tires. He nods and cuts off two taxis to head for the terminal area.

We skid to a stop in front of Southwest and almost take off the toes of a wide-eyed skycap who jumps back on the curb. Coop whips out his badge case and flashes it to the skycap.

"Police business," he says, brushing by. "Keep an eye on the car."

"You got it," the skycap says, straightening his hat.

We run in the terminal and stop at the arrivals board to scan the listings, watching the cities and times change before our eyes. There are two flights on Southwest, one on United, due in from Las Vegas within the next fifteen minutes.

"I'll take United," Coop says. "You take Southwest." Coop gets us through security in record time, and we split off in different directions.

As always, the gate area is noisy and busy with travelers. Businessmen, families with small children, and the usual collection of friends and relatives waiting for arrivals. At Southwest I check the gates of the two arrivals. Still time. Both are due within minutes of each other.

While I'm waiting I check the other gates for any flights I might have missed. Cross could have got something that went via Phoenix or San Diego. For that matter, he could already have landed in San Diego and be at this very moment lining up at a car rental counter.

I watch the desk at Gate 17, finally see the attendant pick up the microphone and announce the flight's arrival. Outside, the plane taxis to the gate and locks on to the jetway.

I fight a crowd, all pushing toward the roped-off area, desperate for their first glimpse of a friend or loved one. The attendant gives instructions to boarding passengers to line up by boarding pass colors, and the first passengers file up the jetway and into the terminal.

I stand there for ten minutes, looking over heads and shoulders as the plane empties. There's a short break when I think they're all off, then a half dozen more people file past, eyes on the crowd, looking for the people meeting them. No Cross.

Across the way, the second Las Vegas flight is deplaning, and the entire process is repeated. All I can look for is a man with a trumpet, which I assume he'll be carrying. About half the plane is off when Coop comes up beside me.

"Nothing at United," he says. "Next flight from Vegas is due at noon."

"Same here so far."

We both watch, straining to look at each passenger. I curse myself for not asking Pappy what Cross was wearing. I'm just about to give up on this one when I see him.

"There, the guy in the dark suit," I say, pointing for Coop to see.

Raymond Cross, carrying an overnight bag in one hand and a battered trumpet case in the other, walks with the air of a man just back from a business trip whose only care is where he's going to have lunch.

I search my memory for images from the night at Ken Perkins's house. The build is right, the dark wavy hair, the thick glasses. It's Cross.

"Okay," Coop says. "Let me handle this."

We circle the crowd and intercept Cross as he starts for the main terminal and baggage area.

"Raymond Cross?" Coop says. He holds up his badge for Cross to see. "I'm Lieutenant Dan Cooper."

"Yes?" Cross says. He stops, looks at Coop, then catches sight of me. It's not much, but he registers slight indecision.

"A few questions, please," Coop says. "Could you step over here?" He guides Cross with his hand on his elbow. We walk to one of the gates that's not in service, and Cross sits down in one of the plastic chairs. I stare at the bag and trumpet case at his feet.

"What's this about?" Cross says, looking at Coop. "I know you, I think. I've seen you in court, haven't I?" He takes out a roll of antacid tablets and pops one in his mouth.

"That you have," Coop says. "We'd like to know about the trumpet."

Cross looks down at it as if he's just become aware of its presence.

"The trumpet? I hardly think the police would be interested in this old thing."

Coop has to go carefully here. He has no warrant, no probable cause for a search, no jurisdiction really. Cross will have to cooperate, and he knows how all this works.

"Am I under arrest, Lieutenant?"

"I didn't say that. We'd like to look at the trumpet."

Cross looks over at me. It's the first he's acknowledged my presence. He sets the case on one of the plastic chairs and flips open the catches, lifts up the lid of the case.

All three of us look inside. I try not to show my shock, but Coop sees it on my face when his eyes meet mine.

The case is empty.

Coop touches the inside of the case as if the trumpet is hidden somewhere under the lining. He straightens up and looks at me. "Well, isn't this interesting?"

I look from the case to Coop. "When I pawned this," I say, pointing at the case, "the trumpet was in there."

"Well, we seem to have a slight problem," Coop says.

Cross glances at me, smiles, and addresses Coop. "No, Lieutenant, *you* have a problem. This case is my property, as was the trumpet. A gentleman bought it at a garage sale. I subsequently purchased it from him, and I have a receipt. If you'll allow me?"

His hand goes to the inside pocket of his jacket. He

takes out his wallet, removes a folded slip of paper, and hands it to Coop.

"Who the hell is Mojo Boneyard?" Coop says, turning to me.

"Yes," Cross says. "A colorful name, but a bona fide dealer in collectibles nonetheless, as I am myself."

Coop hands back the receipt. Cross returns it to his wallet, puts the wallet in his pocket. He looks from me to Coop.

"I think a question you should ask Mr. Horne is how he came into the possession of the trumpet."

"Where is the trumpet, Cross?" I ask.

Cross ignores me. "That, Lieutenant, is something you should ask Mr. Horne."

The color is rising to Coop's face as he tries to maintain control. "The Las Vegas police have some questions for you, Cross, regarding the murder of one Kenneth Perkins."

"Then the Las Vegas police should contact me. As you know, I just came from Las Vegas, and I certainly was not detained in any way."

Coop looks at me again. His expression says, That's thanks to you. Cross straightens his coat, stands up, and looks at both of us.

"Now, if there are no more questions and I am not being detained, I would like to be on my way. Otherwise, I'll need to contact my attorney."

Coop shrugs and looks around the terminal but avoids my eyes, which are screaming at him to do something.

"Calling your attorney might be a good idea, but that'll be all for now, Mr. Cross. Sorry for the inconvenience."

"Not at all," Cross says. He picks up the trumpet

case and his bag and walks away, cool, confident, not a care in the world.

"Coop."

Coop holds up his hand. "Don't say a word."

We're halfway back to the street before Coop finally speaks. He takes out one of his cigars as we step on the moving walkway and lights up. Two business types in suits and carrying briefcases next to us give Coop a look and mumble something about smoking.

Coop glares back at them and holds up his badge. "I'll be happy to take your complaint." The two men move farther down the walkway.

Coop blows a cloud of smoke toward the ceiling. "Cross is one cool sonofabitch. You see his eyes? I don't think his driveway goes all the way to the street. You didn't tell me we're dealing with a nut case."

"I can't believe you just let him walk away like that."

Coop clamps down on his cigar, almost bites it in half. "You can't, huh? What would you like me to have done, cuff him spread-eagled on the ground? I have no warrant, no jurisdiction, no probable cause, nothing. He didn't have to even show us the trumpet case. How *did* you get the trumpet, by the way?"

I have a hard time meeting Coop's eyes. "I took it from Perkins's house the night of the murder."

"Wonderful, just fucking wonderful," Coop says as we step off the walkway and head for the street doors. "You remove evidence from a crime scene, and you have to tell me about it."

"Well, you asked."

"Didn't it occur to you there might be prints on that trumpet? Cross's prints. Las Vegas would have had a big jump on this if they'd had Cross's prints. And now we don't even have the trumpet."

"I didn't think about that, but I bet he didn't touch it anyway. Perkins is the one who showed it to me. Cross is too careful."

Something else besides the trumpet being missing is bothering me. Connie Beale said it was stolen. Cross said, and had proof, that he bought it from Mojo, who told me he had bought it at a garage sale.

Coop's car is where we left it, still being watched by the skycap, who asks, "Did you get him?"

"Not this time," Coop says.

We get in the car. Still seething, Coop slams his door so hard the window almost pops out. We sit there for a few minutes while taxis and cars swirl around us.

Where is the trumpet? Something Pappy said bothers me. He saw Cross come out of the pawn shop with the case and followed him to the airport, where he lost him, but of course—it wasn't Cross.

"Cross switched the trumpet when Pappy lost him at the airport."

"What?"

"Sure, that's how he did it. He must have guessed somebody would be waiting for him here. He switched it at Las Vegas, passed it off to somebody there who carried it for him to L.A. Pappy described him as a little weasel dude. That doesn't fit Cross."

"Maybe," Coop says, "but who?"

"Anybody, it doesn't matter. The point is, Cross still has the trumpet and the other tape."

"You mean you think he'll still go ahead with this, try to sell the tapes and the trumpet?"

"Why not? There's nothing to link him to Perkins's murder but me. Everything is my word against his. He still thinks the trumpet is genuine, and I know how to get it back."

"Good," Coop says. He starts the engine and skids away from the curb.

"I want to nail that sonofabitch."

"How about lunch in Malibu?" I ask Natalie.

"Malibu? Yeah, sure." She sees there's nothing in my hand. "I guess we're not celebrating getting the trumpet back."

"No, we're not."

While she changes, I tell her about the airport fiasco, but not about what I have planned. Not yet, anyway.

We eat at Gladstone's on the Pacific Coast Highway. The air is still chilly, but there are no rains, no mud slides. Just sun and the Pacific and lots of good fish served on wooden platters heaped high with french fries and small loaves of warm sourdough bread. Even the waiters cooperate by not bugging me every two minutes to ask if everything is okay.

After lunch, I surprise Natalie again by suggesting a drive farther up the coast.

"What's really going on here? You should be depressed and frustrated. Instead you're taking me to lunch and a drive up the coast."

"Just something I want to check out."

"This isn't going to be dangerous, is it?"

"Not this time."

We drive through Malibu, past the pier, the Colony, Pepperdine College, then down the grade to Point Dume and Zuma Beach. At the traffic light I turn on Trancas Canyon and wind up through the hills a half mile or so to Tapia Drive, where I pull up and park. Natalie looks around.

"Why have we stopped here?"

"This is where Raymond Cross lives. C'mon, let's take a walk."

If I wasn't holding her hand, I don't think Natalie would have come with me. We walk through a common area of the condominium complex that comes out near the pool. A sidewalk runs alongside, affording a view of the homes in Trancas Canyon below. Around the corner is a vista of the ocean that residents on that side must have paid heavily for. Cross's unit is about halfway down.

"You're not going to just go up to the front door and knock, are you?"

"No, we're not even going to walk past. Well, you can if you want."

"No thanks. So why are we here?"

I shrug and stare out at the ocean. "I just wanted to check out the place, get a feel for it."

Natalie turns toward me, one hand on her hips. "So if you break in here and have to make a quick getaway, you'll know the area."

"Something like that. Actually, whether I do that or not depends on you."

"Me?"

"Yeah, how are your acting skills?"

It takes the entire drive back to Venice to convince Natalie I'm not crazy. Another hour later, she makes the call from my place. I stand right beside her as she dials the number I give her.

"Mr. Raymond Cross, please."

"Speaking."

"Mr. Cross, I'm the personal assistant of Rick Markham at Pacific Records. I'm calling on behalf of Mr. Markham to invite you to a Pacific party this evening."

"Could I speak to Mr. Markham?" Cross says.

Natalie looks at me. I shake my head.

"I'm afraid Mr. Markham is not available at the moment, but he would very much like you to come tonight. He also asked me to remind you about the tape and the trumpet? He said you'd know what he meant, and he apologizes for the short notice."

Natalie glances at me again. There are several moments of silence while Cross thinks it over.

"Am I to bring the tape and trumpet?"

"I don't know. I assume you'd know about that, Mr. Cross."

"Very well, tell him thank you. Tell Mr. Markham I'll be there."

"Good. I'll tell Mr. Markham. Seven o'clock."

She gives him the address and hangs up.

"God, I was nervous," she says to me.

"Hey, if law school doesn't work out, there's always acting classes."

CHAPTER

SEVENTEEN

RICK MARKHAM'S THREE-STORY HOME IN ENCINO IS enormous, taking up the entire end of a cul-de-sac. Burning torches are positioned around the main entrance and up the winding walkway to the front door. Four young guys in black pants, white shirts, and red bow ties are parking cars when we pull up.

"Just leave the keys, sir," one of them says as he opens the door. He's speaking to me, but his eyes are on Natalie.

She dazzles the entire valet crew when she gets out of the car. Her blond hair shimmers in the torchlight, and the short black dress and heels showcase her long legs and slender body.

I stand with Natalie for a moment, watching the parking arrangements. There are no tickets. The cars are being parked in a lot half a block away, and the keys are put in small manila envelopes in a box with the license numbers written on the front with marker pens. I file this information away in case I want to get to mine or somebody elses's car during the party.

Natalie and I make our way up the front walk with

other guests and are greeted by some of Rick's people. Taped music spills out of the entranceway, some of Pacific Records' artists no doubt, but once inside I see drums and a bass lying on its side next to a grand piano, so there'll be live music as well.

I quickly scan the guests already there, looking for Raymond Cross, but either I miss him or he hasn't arrived yet. Someone I do recognize is Barry Hastings, standing near the bar. Him, I'd prefer to avoid.

Just past the bar, a large glassed-in entertainment room commands a view of the valley lights winking at us from below. The room is a symphony of clinking glasses, too-loud conversation, and forced laughter. There are a lot of record company types and a few pop stars I recognize from PR photos, as well as some television actors and actresses. This must be at least Rick Markham's B-plus list. The record business is obviously good.

I spot Rick Markham about the same time he sees me. He breaks away from a group at the buffet and comes over, looking like anything but a happy host.

"Evan, I need to talk to you for a moment." He guides me away after nodding to Natalie.

"Get us a drink and something to eat," I call to her over my shoulder. Rick takes me into a small office and closes the door.

"Two things," he says. "Barry Hastings is here, and not too happy with you. I discouraged him from coming, but he is one of my people."

"I thought he was fired."

"I had to rethink that," Rick says, watching my reaction. "It was kind of a setup, wasn't it?"

"Yeah, I guess it was. I didn't want him to lose his

job. I just didn't want him in charge of Clifford Brown discoveries."

"Well, I'll try to keep you two separated, but he may have a few words for you sometime during the evening. Now what about this Raymond Cross character you invited? What am I supposed to do about him?"

I'd given Markham only the briefest sketch on the tapes, the trumpet, and why I wanted Cross here tonight.

"Cross is the guy with the tape and the trumpet, which I want back. If we confront him about the tape right here tonight, we might clear up a lot of things with the police."

"What are you doing, staging an Agatha Christie thing here? I don't know, Evan. As usual, you're not telling me everything."

He paces around a few steps. Obviously, he has some reservations; he'd have more if he knew as much about Cross as I do.

"Look," he says finally, "I'll help if I can, but I don't want things to get out of hand."

"Okay. Cross will probably seek you out if he comes. You need to convince him that I told you he was the one with the tape, and no matter what I've said, you'd like to talk with him about it while he's here tonight. Is there someplace we could listen to a cassette later?"

"Sure, I have a big music and screening room downstairs. He's not likely to start anything, is he?"

"No, I don't think so. He's just got to believe you're really interested."

"If he saw Barry on television, he knows we are."

"I just hope he brought the trumpet. Anyway, let's just play it by ear."

I hear the taped music stop then, replaced by the sounds of a live trio and a trumpet.

I look at Rick. He shrugs. "I thought a trumpet would be appropriate. C'mon, let's join the party. I have to make up for my rudeness to your date. She's a real stunner. Serious?"

"Very. I'll introduce you."

By now the bar and larger room are full of guests balancing drinks and plates of hot food. As I walk by the trio, I instinctively flex my right hand. It's been rested for nearly two weeks. I wonder how it would hold up for a couple of tunes. The trumpet player is a stocky guy with a red beard and hair. I can't place him immediately, but he looks familiar.

I find Natalie warding off two guys who look like they belong in a daytime soap opera. Expensive suits, ditto haircuts, and winning smiles. Both are being very solicitous.

"Oh, there you are," Natalie says as I come up behind the two heartthrobs. "Nice talking to you guys. Good luck with the audition."

They both turn to look at me. In loafers, Dockers, and a dark sweater, I'm probably the worst dressed at the party. They look back at Natalie, then at me again. Probably they wonder what I'm doing with her, but they drift away looking for new prey.

"I guess I'm a little underdressed," I say, taking a Scotch and a plate of food from Natalie.

"True," she says, "but you have your good points."

We find a seat near the fireplace. Looking at my plate, it looks like a Thai/Chinese offering. Egg rolls, tiny chunks of meat and chicken on sticks, hot sauce, and an ice-cream-scoop-size mound of fried rice, which for my money is ruined with a sprinkling of peas.

"What are you doing?" Natalie asks, watching me separate the peas from the rice with plastic chopsticks.

"I don't do peas in any form. It's a childhood thing. I'll tell you about it sometime."

"I'm learning more about you all the time. Anything else you don't eat?"

"Sweet potatoes. That's all you get to know for now."

We work our way through the food, and I get another drink for me and a white wine for Natalie at the bar. The little I catch of the trio sounds good. Maybe I'll give that a try later.

I bring back the drinks, and for a few minutes we just people-watch. Rick Markham comes over, and I introduce Natalie. Rick is charmed out of his socks.

"If I can make up for my rudeness earlier, perhaps you'd like to meet that gentleman over there."

We follow his gaze and see the star of a current TV cop show holding court with a small group of admirers.

"I certainly would," Natalie says. "Evan?"

"I'll catch up with you in a minute. Think I'll have a cigarette." I haven't seen anyone smoking or any sign of ashtrays.

"Through those doors," Rick says. "There's a deck out there."

"Thanks. See you guys in a minute."

I make my way outside. There's another couple on the deck as I take up a position at one corner, looking out over the San Fernando Valley. The air is January cool, but it feels good. The couple drifts back inside, and I'm just about to do the same when I hear a voice behind me.

"Trying to avoid me, Horne?" It's Barry Hastings, the itinerant surfer and trumpet expert.

I turn to face him. "Not at all. Why should I?"

He's on the way to being drunk, already slurring his words and a little unsteady on his feet. He sets his glass down on the railing so hard some of his drink splashes out.

"You almost got me fired."

"You did that on your own, Barry. I told both you and Rick we didn't need a leak on the tapes. Nobody told you to go on TV and make what was obviously a premature announcement."

Hastings just sneers. "You didn't think Rick would really fire me, did you? I'm too valuable to the company, certainly more than a broken-down piano player."

Against my will, I stiffen and flex my hand. For a moment I contemplate shoving Barry over the railing. "Why don't you just cool it, Barry? Go on in and enjoy the party."

"There aren't any tapes or a trumpet, are there?"

"There are tapes and a trumpet. They're just not the real thing. If you'd waited, you could have saved yourself some embarrassment." I lean back against the railing as Barry wobbles before me.

"You know what I think? I think you just want to, like, cut me out of the picture, and that's cold, man, really cold."

"There's nothing to cut you out of. Before the end of the night, I'm sure Rick will explain everything."

"Rick." Barry snarls. "I don't even get to call him Rick. It's Mr. Markham this, Mr. Markham that. I—"

"I'm not interrupting anything, am I?" Natalie says. She's come up behind Barry Hastings.

He whirls around and almost falls over the railing without my help. I grab him by the shoulders, but he shakes me off. "Let go of me, man." He heads back inside. "Don't get in my way, Horne," he calls back from the door.

Natalie and I watch him go. "Charming," she says. "Wasn't that the guy on TV?"

"None other. He's not too happy with me."

Natalie rubs her arms. "Let's go back inside. It's cold out here."

"Sure, I want to check out the band."

We make our way through the crowd to the bar area. I make a quick scan of the room, but still no Raymond Cross. Maybe this isn't going to work after all.

The band is just about to play a second set when I recognize the trumpet player, a studio session guy who plays good jazz as well, Steve Patterson.

He catches my eye and comes over. "Evan Horne? I thought that was you. Hanging out with the in crowd these days, huh?" As is often the case, Steve and the band, all in tuxes, are the most formally dressed at the party.

"Not hardly. I just happen to know the host. You guys sound good."

"Yeah, it's nice to get out of the studio for a while. I just threw this together for tonight. What are you doing these days?"

I hold out my hand and flex my fingers. "Still in rehab, but it's getting better."

"Cool, man, why don't you play a couple with us? Bobby won't mind," Steve says, nodding toward the pianist.

I hesitate for a moment. I'm dying to play, but I don't know how my hand will hold up or for how long.

Everything else about this evening is reckless though—why not this too?

"Hey, why not? Thanks."

Steve walks over and speaks to the pianist, who nods and waves and heads for the bar as I sit down at the piano. They don't roll their eyes, but I catch the bassist and drummer exchanging glances. I know what they're thinking; I've been there myself. I wish I could ease their apprehension, but that won't happen until I play.

Musicians are always wary of people they don't know sitting in, especially at a party. Good players get stuck with somebody's friend playing wrong chords and generally messing up a good gig.

I run over a few chords to check the action of the piano. "How about 'Stella by Starlight'?"

Steve nods. I play eight bars up front, and Steve takes the pickup notes. I start feeding him chords for the melody, substitute changes that everybody knows, and the bassist is right with me. We smile at each other, and everything is fine and relaxed. The drummer plays slightly on top of the beat and pushes us right along through three good choruses, Steve sounding great with his mute.

No pain, no tenseness in my hand. When it's my turn I manage to get through a couple myself before I turn it over to the bassist.

While I comp for him, I catch Natalie watching me over her glass. Suddenly, just behind her, dressed in a dark suit and tie, I see Raymond Cross, his eyes riveted on me at the piano.

I almost miss the restatement of the theme, but somehow manage to recover as Steve takes us out. There's some polite applause from the people nearby.

"All right," Steve says, grinning at me. "Another one?"

"Okay, one more." Cross has moved a little closer. "You know 'Jordu'?"

I can't resist seeing if Cross reacts to one of the Clifford Brown tunes, and I know Steve, like every jazz trumpeter, knows it.

"Sure," Steve says. He takes out the mute. Open horn on this one. There's a one-measure pickup before we join him on the theme. Steve is neither Clifford Brown nor Connie Beale. His sound is brighter than either of them, but he nevertheless reminds us that this was sort of how Clifford Brown did the tune.

While Steve winds his way through the changes, I keep one eye on Cross. He's nearly at Natalie's shoulder now. I try to signal her with my eyes, but she doesn't get it, just smiles in return.

Steve gets inspired and stretches out more than I expected. I take just one chorus, as I feel my hand begin to tighten up. By the time we finish the tune, I feel the first twinge of pain creep up my wrist. I could play through it, but not tonight. That's all for me. Two tunes.

"Thanks, Steve," I say, standing up and shaking hands. I wave at the bassist and drummer, who are friends now, and join Natalie. Cross has melted into the crowd, but I keep him in sight.

"That was great," Natalie says. She touches my wrist. "Okay?"

"Yeah, I'm good for about fifteen minutes. The guy breathing down your neck was Cross."

"Where?" Natalie says. She turns around to follow my gaze. "God, I didn't even know. I thought you were sending me some kind of secret love signal."

"No, that's flickering eyebrows. I'm going to look for Rick. It's time to get this show going."

"Should I be worried?"

"I don't think so. I just want to play the tape with Cross here, see if we can provoke him into something."

"Like what?"

"I don't know." Natalie looks worried. "Look, nothing is going to happen, okay? Keep an eye on Cross while I round up Rick."

I go back into the larger room and find Rick talking with a couple other record types. I catch his eye and he breaks away.

"Cross is here, so I think it's time."

"Okay," Rick says. "We can go downstairs to the music room. How are we going to play this?"

"Let me be the bad guy. Just act like you're very interested, and then follow my lead."

"Gladly. What do you want me to do?"

"For starters, just get him downstairs and occupied for a few minutes. Something I want to check on, then I'll be down."

"You're going to leave me alone with Cross?"

"Take Barry with you. He can hit him with his surfboard. He needs his confidence restored."

"Okay, but don't take too long. Where's Cross?"

I point him out to Rick. He goes over and speaks to Cross. He has a drink in his hand and some kind of leather dispatch case tucked under his arm, which I'm sure has the tape inside. No sign of the trumpet.

I go back out the front entrance. The valet attendants are huddled together, working their way through sandwiches and Cokes.

"Hey guys, I need something out of my car. White

Pontiac. Go ahead with your food. I'll just run down and get it myself. Got the keys?"

"Here you go," one of them says, holding up the envelope. He was too busy gawking at Natalie to remember I drove up in a Camaro.

I find Cross's car easily. Besides mine, it's one of the few that's not a Mercedes, BMW, or Cadillac. I check the trunk first, and right there under a blanket is the trumpet case, the trumpet inside. I grab it, close the trunk, and start walking back to the house, when I stop abruptly, knowing exactly how I'm going to get it out of here.

I toss the keys in the envelope to the valet guy and go back inside, looking for Steve Patterson. I find him at the bar, drink in hand, talking to a girl with a pile of blond hair in a skin tight black jumpsuit. She appears to be hanging on his every word.

Steve notices me come up beside them. "Hey, Evan. Gonna play again?"

"Not tonight." I look at the girl. "Can I borrow him for just a minute?"

"Sure," she says.

Steve gives me a look and notices the trumpet case. "Don't go away," he says to the girl. To me he says, "What's with the trumpet?"

I pull him aside and tell him what I want him to do. He frowns, doesn't really understand, but agrees. We go over to where the band is set up, make the switch, then I head for the front entrance again.

"I'll call you tomorrow and explain everything. Thanks, Steve. Good luck with Cat Woman."

Back outside I see the valet guys again. "Didn't need it after all," I say and grab the keys to Cross's car for the second time.

They probably think I'm just one of these crazy record types as I jog back to Cross's car and return the trumpet case to the trunk. Then I stroll back to the house, drop the keys in the box.

Now it's time to listen to some music.

The party has thinned a bit, but there's still enough of a crowd that I don't find Natalie for a few minutes. She's been looking for me.

"Where have you been? Cross went downstairs with Rick and Barry Hastings about fifteen minutes ago."

"Just taking care of a minor detail. Let's go."

We go down a hallway off the main party room and find the stairs. Rick Markham, Raymond Cross, and Barry Hastings are already there. Rick sees us come in.

"Evan, there you are. Join us, please. Let me get you a drink."

Hastings, standing at the wet bar, glares at me; Cross sits in an ultramodern chair with a satisfied smile, clutching his leather case. The room is an oversize den with a sound system on one wall and a large-screen projection television dominating the other wall.

Rick says, "Mr. Cross has been telling me how he came into the tape. We're just about to listen to it. You two have met, I take it."

"Yeah, at LAX. I bet that's an interesting story."

Cross smiles again. "I'm sure Mr. Horne omitted some salient points when he told you about the tapes."

"Tapes? I think there's only one. The Las Vegas police have the other one, don't they?"

"True," Cross says, "but only temporarily. That tape is my property and will be returned to me shortly once their investigation is completed." Not flustered in the least, he unzips his case, takes out a reel tape box, and hands it to Rick Markham. "Shall we?"

Rick hands it to Barry, who threads it on the machine while Natalie and I sit down opposite Cross. It's almost like the night at Ken Perkins's house, when I first heard the tapes.

Barry hits the play button, and the room is filled with the music of Clifford Brown, except now I know it's not Brownie. I can't believe how cool Cross is, sitting there with a satisfied smile on his face watching Rick and Barry's reaction to the music. He really thinks he's going to pull this off.

Rick gives Barry a signal, and he stops the tape about halfway through. "Very impressive, Mr. Cross. Pacific Records would be very interested in these tapes, provided the police release the other one to you and there are no—how shall we say—problems."

Cross looks at me first. "I assure you, Mr. Markham, the problem with the police is just a slight misunderstanding and will be sorted out in due time. The tapes are my property and are indeed Clifford Brown."

Rick looks at me. Natalie tenses beside me as I set my drink down and scoot up on the edge of my chair.

"Evan?" Rick says. He looks like he's waiting for a cue.

"Pacific Records would be making a big mistake putting much stock in this tape or the one the Las Vegas police have. The slight misunderstanding Mr. Cross mentions is much more than that. He's wanted for questioning in the murder of Ken Perkins, and both tapes were stolen from Cosmos Recorders in Hollywood several weeks ago."

"That's preposterous," Cross says, the timbre of his voice revealing the first crack in his veneer of confidence. His appeal is to Rick Markham, who isn't sure where I'm going with this. "I spoke to a Lieutenant Cooper when I arrived at LAX the other day. I was neither detained nor charged with anything, much less murder. Mr. Horne is simply disappointed that he will not play any role in the discovery of these tapes."

"Whether the tapes are stolen or not, Mr. Cross is a suspect. And there's something else." I get to my feet and take a cassette out of my pocket in a gesture that's become, in the past few days, as automatic as taking out my wallet. "May I?"

"Of course," Rick says.

I go over to the sound system and put the cassette in the machine, press the play button. It's the same tape I've played so many times for myself and also for Markham and Hastings. I lower the volume and turn to Rick.

"Cross is right. The tapes are genuine. They've been tested by the FBI lab and confirmed as being manufactured in the fifties. But this trumpet you're hearing is not Clifford Brown." Just for effect I raise the volume for a few moments, then lower it again.

Cross jumps to his feet. "Oh please, do we have to listen to this?"

Rick does a good job at looking surprised. "What are you saying, Evan?"

"The recordings were made in 1955, but the trumpet player is a man named Connie Beale. Both he and the pianist on the tape, Nolan Thomas, will submit affidavits to that effect if necessary."

Barry Hastings's shock is genuine, since he's not in on any of this. "You gotta be kidding, man. That's Clifford Brown. Nobody could imitate him that well."

"Connie Beale could and did. In 1955, he was a very

talented trumpet player who idolized Clifford Brown. He learned all the solos and had the technique and sound to imitate Brown precisely."

"I don't believe it," Hastings says. "It can't be done."

"Yes it can, Barry. The more distinctive the sound, the easier it is to imitate, and Clifford Brown had one of the most distinctive, original sounds in jazz. Connie Beale knew every nuance of Brownie's playing." I shut off the tape and take the cassette out of the machine.

"And where is this Connie Beale now?" Rick wants to know.

Cross has sat down again. He hides it well, but he obviously didn't know I'd found Connie Beale. He wants to know too.

"He's working at a club in Hollywood. I heard him play the other night. Nolan Thomas, the pianist on the tape, teaches in his home."

There's a minute or two of silence as everybody digests what I've said. Markham is not quite sure what to do. He clears his throat and looks at Raymond Cross.

"Ah, Mr. Cross, we seem to be at an impasse here. Evan has raised some significant questions that will have to be answered to our satisfaction before we can proceed further with this."

"This whole thing is ridiculous," Cross says, for a moment allowing his facade of calm to break. "You're going to take the word of this—this—piano player who thinks he's a detective. Horne is trying to convince you of something that is just not true. I also have something else that will prove these tapes are genuine." He pauses for a moment to make sure he has everyone's attention. "I have Clifford Brown's trumpet to go with the tapes."

Barry Hastings is suddenly very interested again. "Wow, man, I'd like to see that."

"You will, you will," Cross says, "and then we'll talk further. I don't know who this Connie Beale is or where Horne came up with him. I suspect it's something he's totally fabricated."

"The trumpet is Connie Beale's, too," I say, "and no, it's not stolen, at least not from Beale."

"Of course it's not stolen," Cross says. "I have a bill of sale. I bought it from another collector." The half-truth has restored some of Cross's confidence.

"Well, I'll leave you to it," I say to Rick. "I'd go very carefully here if I were you. Natalie and I have to go."

As I walk past Cross, he half whispers to me. "This is not over yet, Horne."

"No, it's not."

Natalie and I go back upstairs. The party has thinned even more, and the band is on their last set. I wave at Steve Patterson on the way out. He tilts his trumpet toward us in response.

"C'mon," I say to Natalie. "I want to beat Cross out of here."

"Me too," Natalie says. "You really rained on his parade."

I get my car from the valet guys and drive halfway down the block, then stop and back into a driveway that gives me a clear view of the front of Markham's house. I turn off the engine and lights.

"What are you doing?" Natalie says.

"Just want to check something."

A couple of minutes later Cross emerges from the house and asks for his car. There's a brief conversation with the valet attendant, who probably wonders why Cross doesn't look like me, but his car is brought around quickly. Cross gets in and drives off, comes right past us.

I didn't need to make the switch after all. Cross never even checks the trunk.

"Sometime later tonight or tomorrow, he's going to be even more pissed at me when he discovers that once again he doesn't have the trumpet."

INTERLUDE
June 26, 1956

CLIFFORD BROWN DIDN'T KNOW HOW LONG THEY HAD been out of Philly—a few minutes, a few hours. He stirred on the seat, shifted his position, and opened his eyes slowly. He could see the top of Richie's head against the window, Nancy's hands on the wheel, and spots on the windshield. Rain. He didn't want to see that.

The back window was cracked open a couple of inches. He could smell the rain, see the dark sky, the blur of headlights passing them on the opposite side of the turnpike. He hunched down farther in the backseat, seeking the darkness, closing his eyes again.

He couldn't tell if it was minutes or hours before he came awake again, not sleepily this time but instantly wide awake. Everything about the rhythm was wrong. The car was moving too fast. He opened his mouth to speak, but for some reason he couldn't call out to Nancy, tell her to slow down. The rain was heavy now, slashing against the car, the wipers whipping back and forth with their own relentless throb, the tires slapping against the wet pavement.

His whole body tensed, anticipating something. He saw the blur of a yellow sign streak by them as they headed into a curve. Then he felt something beneath him, the rear wheels breaking loose, the car sliding. It wasn't his imagination. He glimpsed Nancy's hands gripping the wheel tighter, saw her in profile, her face tensing, eyes opening wide, Richie suddenly sitting up.

"Watch it, baby," Richie said, putting one hand on the dashboard as if to steady the car, but it kept sliding.

Nancy said, "Oh," then, "Richie!"

"Slow down, baby, slow down," Richie said, his voice pitched higher.

Brownie was upright now, feeling the car suddenly slow, his heart pounding in his chest as Nancy jammed on the brakes, but the tires gripping only water, sliding farther sideways until they were facing the cars behind them.

Brownie gripped the seat with both hands, his eyes wide as the car spun and spun and spun, completely out of control, then ripped through the guard rail, the engine sound suddenly becoming a high-pitched whine as the car left the ground and plunged downward over the embankment.

Brownie saw the trumpet case pop off the seat beside him and fly out the window, felt his head hit the roof of the car, rain on his face, saw Richie upside down in front of him as glass shattered and the car made its agonizingly deliberate descent to the embankment.

All their voices screaming in unison as the car smashed into trees, but by then Clifford Brown didn't know anything.

The car rolled over again and again, then reached its final resting place upside down, the wheels spinning in the rainy Pennsylvania night.

CHAPTER

EIGHTEEN

LIKE A GUY WATCHING FOOTBALL, NATALIE IS STILL glued to the TV, totally mesmerized by the O. J. Simpson trial, when I call Steve Patterson.

I've already run some errands, walked on the beach, and gone through the motions of scanning the want ads for a new place to live, but my heart is not in it. I want to stay in Venice.

"It's research," Natalie says. "I'm getting some tips from Marcia Clark."

"Whatever. You'll probably be watching it in class all next semester."

"Yeah, if it's over by then."

I've waited till noon to call Steve, to give him time to recover from playing Rick Markham's party. His phone rings several times, then there's a click, followed by a different pitch to the ring before he answers.

"Don't worry, man," he says when he picks up. "I had a ten o'clock session, TV thing for one of these cop shows. Another date at one. What do you want me to do with the trumpet?"

Car phone. I can hear traffic noises in the background. "Can you bring it with you to the session?"

"Sure. I'll be at Sunset Recorders. Just going to grab some lunch. Funky old trumpet. Whose is it anyway? It's got *C.B.* engraved in the bell."

"Not who you think. It's a long story I'll tell you sometime. Thanks, Steve. See you at one."

I hang up the phone, thinking by now Raymond Cross has certainly discovered the trumpet missing and knows I have it. All I can do now is report in to Danny Cooper and wait for something to happen.

Natalie clicks off the television, stands up, and stretches.

"Noon recess?"

"Yeah, but I've had enough for today. Are we doing anything?"

"Lunch and two stops. Want to tag along? Someone I'd like you to meet."

We get to Sunset Recorders right before Steve's session begins. I leave Natalie in the car and run inside to find Steve amid a cacophony of dissonant noisy conversation as thirty musicians tune up and compare notes.

Steve is busy showing the horn to the rest of the trumpet section. They're passing it around, offering their guesses about the inscribed initials.

"Count Basie," says one.

"Naw, Chet Baker."

"It could be Bix Beiderbecke," another one says. "Wasn't his real name Charles?"

"No, that was Buddy Bolden, but this isn't a cornet. Buddy played a cornet."

"How about Charlie Brown?" the guy on the end says.

The horn finally ends up back with Steve.

"Here you go, man," he says. "I put it in an old gig bag." He hands me the trumpet in a soft vinyl case with no room for anything but the trumpet.

"Thanks, I really appreciate it, Steve. How'd you do with Cat Woman?" I still remember the girl at the party dressed in the black jumpsuit.

Steve's eyes flick to the music on the stand in front of him. "Aw, she hooked up with some producer before I finished the last set."

The studio suddenly quiets as a voice comes out of the speakers. "All right, gentlemen, I think we're ready to begin." The conductor mounts the podium and glances at the score. Behind him in the glassed-in booth, the recording engineers have their eyes on the control board.

"Well, I better get out of here," I say to Steve.

I stop at the door though, and listen to them run through the first cue. Must be a chase scene and car crash. The tempo is way up, with the horns falling off at the end of the phrase that only last a few seconds. Makes me wonder how my own will turn out.

I nod to the pianist. He looks at me and shrugs. "TV," he says.

I flex the fingers on my right hand. No residual pain from last night. This is where I should be. Seated at a ten-foot Steinway playing, not chasing around L.A. trying to provoke a killer the police suspect but can't arrest.

I let myself out as the red light comes on and go back to the car.

Natalie is glancing through the newspaper.

"Want to meet a hip old lady?" I ask, getting in the car.

"Sure." She sees me check my watch. "What's the matter?"

"It's okay. She's had lunch."

"Who?"

"The hip old lady."

"We haven't."

"Right after this. I promise."

Gladys Cowen *has* had lunch, but not her soap. By the time we get to Cosmos, she is very annoyed.

"Canceled it for that damn trial," she says. "Waste of time."

Natalie is instantly charmed. The two of them get into a discussion about soaps and trials on TV and generally forget I'm there.

I let them go for a few minutes. "Excuse me, ladies," I say.

They both stop talking at once and look at me. "Let's humor the boy, Natalie." She turns to me and lights a menthol. "You found out something?"

"I tracked down two of the musicians on the tapes."

"Did you find the tapes?"

"Well, I know where they are. Getting them back is another story. The police have one, and somebody else has the other one."

"The police? Well, they can just give it back, then, can't they?"

"It's not quite that simple, Gladys." I glance at Natalie for support.

"Evidence," she says.

"These tapes are part of a murder investigation in Las Vegas," I tell Gladys.

"My tapes?" Her eyes get big. "My God, people killing each other over music."

"Gladys, can those tape reels be identified? Did your

husband use any kind of marking on them? Or was there something out of the ordinary?"

"No, I don't think so," Gladys says. She thinks for a moment. "Wait, yes, there was. Tom pasted address labels inside all the blank reels. You couldn't see them from the outside, but sometimes we shipped tapes. He thought it was a good idea in case the box got lost or damaged."

"It's a wonderful idea. If necessary, would you be willing to testify to that in court? It might make it easier to identify the tapes and get them back."

Gladys sits up straight in her chair. "I certainly would. You just tell me when and where." She turns to Natalie. "He's a good boy, isn't he? I knew he'd find my tapes. You take care of him, darlin'."

"Oh, I will," Natalie says smiling.

We have lunch at Johnny Rockets in Westwood. Somehow a fifties-style diner seems appropriate. There's a crowd of UCLA students and a scattering of tourists. We wait our turn for two seats at the counter while oldies but goodies blast out of the jukebox.

The fare is simple: great hamburgers, plates of french fries, little paper cups filled with catsup, and cherry Cokes, made at the fountain and served in paper cones set in black pedestals. Somehow I managed to resist one of the thick chocolate malts that come with the sweating stainless steel mixer.

"Oh God, this is wonderful. Do you realize how un-L.A. this is?" she says, finishing off the last of her fries dipped in catsup. She leans back in her chair, sucks on her straw until there's a gurgling sound, and sighs contentedly. "It's just like high school."

She looks around. There are still people waiting for tables. "Well, what happens now?"

"I guess we pay the check and get out of here."

"No, I mean with Cross, this whole thing?"

"Well, I've blown his cover as far as him being able to peddle the tapes to anyone, certainly Rick Markham. But we're no closer to an arrest for Perkins's murder."

"We?" Natalie still can't resign herself to my Lone Ranger strategy. "Isn't he going to be awfully mad at you for taking the trumpet again?"

When I don't answer, Natalie studies me for a few moments.

"That's the idea, isn't it? You're making yourself a target."

"I'm not making myself a target. Let me see what Coop says. Maybe Cross will do something stupid, something they can get him on."

"Evan, you exposed Cross as a thief, ruined his chances to pull off a hoax with a record company, and accused him of murder. I was there, remember?"

I put up my hands in surrender. "Well, you got me there."

Natalie isn't mad, just worried and serious. "You've set everything in motion, now let Coop handle it. Promise?"

"Promise."

"If you don't, then it's you who's doing something stupid."

We leave Westwood and drive back to Venice, but Natalie decides to go home for the rest of the afternoon.

"My place is a mess. I've got laundry and housework to catch up on. I haven't done a thing since midterms," she says.

"This from a girl who has a Just Say No to Laundry magnet on her refrigerator."

Natalie ignores that one. "I also have to go shopping for groceries."

"Really? Should I call later?"

"You'd better. I'm cooking tonight for a piano player who thinks he's a detective. Don't be late."

I find Danny Cooper in his office doing police lieutenant things—paperwork, phone calls. He glances up, apparently glad for the distraction, when I walk in.

"I was just about to call you," he says. "Cross called, wants to file a complaint against you. Says you stole his trumpet last night."

"This guy is amazing," I say. I sit down opposite Coop. "We were at a party at Rick Markham's, the guy from Pacific Records."

"And a good time was had by all, no doubt. How did you do it?"

I tell Coop about the switch I made with Steve Patterson and about listening to the tape Cross still has. Coop sits there, hands folded across his chest, occasionally shaking his head.

"Clever, you jazz musicians, aren't you? Always helping each other out. Well, let's see. You got back an old trumpet that is not valuable to anyone except perhaps to its owner, which you removed from a crime scene in Las Vegas, embarrassed and exposed a murder suspect who knows you're the only one who can put him in Ken Perkins's house the night of the murder, and generally pissed him off. What's on tap today?"

"You tell me."

"Okay. You're not going to like it, though." Coop leans forward on his desk. "You're going to have to give the trumpet back."

"You've got to be kidding."

"Sorry, sport, that's the way it is. Cross has a bill of sale for the trumpet. He showed it to us at LAX, remember? He says if he gets the trumpet back he won't press charges."

"*He* won't press charges? I hope you told him what to do with his complaint."

"I said I'd look into it. I stalled him for a while, but if he wants to push it, I have no choice."

I get up and walk a few paces around the office. "C'mon, Coop. This is crazy. The trumpet is a minor thing. We both know Cross killed Ken Perkins."

"Maybe," Coop says, "but we can't move on him."

"What would it take?"

Coop stands up and stretches. "I gotta get some coffee." He looks at me staring at him, still waiting for an answer. "Get Cross to come in and confess. That's about the only way it's going to work. Want to join me?"

"No, I've got things to do." I start for the door, but Coop calls me back.

"I want that trumpet."

I drive away from police headquarters with no clear direction in mind, just letting the surge of the traffic flow carry me along to Ocean Avenue. On impulse I turn left and head down the California incline to the Pacific Coast Highway. I still haven't decided where I'm going by the time I reach Santa Monica Canyon, so I just keep heading north toward Malibu.

A light rain begins to fall, and I wonder how much of the cliffs will fall on the highway this year. There was heavy rain last night, so mud slides are not out of the question. I turn on the wipers and notice oncoming cars on this curvy, two-lane stretch have turned on their lights. I do the same, but nobody slows down.

To my right expensive homes, precariously perched on stilts, jut out from the cliffs, apparently ready to slide across the highway and into the dark gray Pacific at any moment. I push the cassette I've been carrying around for days into the deck. I laugh out loud when the first tune comes up: "It Might As Well Be Spring."

By the time I get to Malibu Pier, I realize I know exactly where I'm going. I can't wait any longer for something to happen, I have to make something happen. Don't give up, Cal said. Okay, here goes.

Passing Pepperdine College the traffic thins out, probably mostly Malibu residents trying to make it home before the highway is closed. I ease down the long grade past Point Dume to Zuma Beach. In the summer the beach is packed with thousands of sun worshipers, but now one lone fisherman casts his line into the ocean while the wind whips around a boarded-up lifeguard station.

I turn right at Trancas Canyon, drive up the hill to Tapia Drive, and park in the visitors' lot. I get the trumpet out of the trunk and jog around to the front of the condos, rain dripping off my head. One glance at the ocean churning up white foam below, crashing on the beach, then I ring the doorbell.

Raymond Cross opens the door and stares at me for a moment.

"You."

"I have something I believe is yours."

I enjoy the moment, catching him totally off guard. Just the look on his face is worth the trip. From inside I hear music, the tape that started everything. The sound of a trumpet that never was Clifford Brown.

Cross at first looks past me, to the rain-slick side-walk that overlooks the canyon, as if he thinks there's someone else there. His eyes, full of questions, come back to me, then go to the trumpet in the vinyl bag I have tucked under my arm.

He doesn't say, "Come in." Instead he says, "I've been expecting you." He steps back, holds the door open, nods for me to enter. He too knows it's come down to this, just the two of us.

I stand in the entranceway while he shuts the door. To the left is a kitchen-dining area with sliding glass doors affording a view of the coastline. On my right are stairs leading to the second floor.

"In there," Cross says, nodding toward the living room.

There's a fire crackling in the stone fireplace, the pungent smell of wood chips wafting about the room, clashing with some kind of air freshener. Two large chairs face one another in front of the fireplace. An ebony-lacquered coffee table squats between them. On one wall, from floor to ceiling, are glass-enclosed shelves that extend under the staircase and must house thousands of records. On the opposite wall is an elaborate stereo system that includes a reel tape player. A video cam on a tripod lurks in the corner, its eye pointing toward me. I watch the tape reel turn slowly, listen to Connie Beale's trumpet fill the room with a Clifford Brown solo.

It's the Duke Ellington song, "What Am I Here For?"

Good question. Like almost everything else I do, I'm improvising, seeing where this tune takes me without knowing the ending.

Cross, still unsure of how to proceed, regards me for

a moment. Then a slight smile comes over him. "Sit down," he says.

I take a seat in one of the chairs, feel the warmth of the fire sweep over me. There's coffee in a mug on one side of the table. Cross notices me look at it.

"Would you like some?"

"Sure, why not?"

I set the trumpet case on the floor while he goes off to the kitchen. He returns in a minute with a mug of coffee for me and sits down opposite in a tall, dark green wing chair.

"This belonged to Bette Davis," Cross says, patting the arms of the chair. "I got it at an auction. The chair you're sitting in came from the estate of Humphrey Bogart." Cross smiles. "I can never resist unusual or rare things."

"You should have stuck to buying things rather than killing for them."

"Oh please, I'm disappointed. Is that why you've come all the way out here? By the way, how did you know where I live?"

"It wasn't too difficult for the police to find your address."

"Yes, your friend Lieutenant Cooper. A simple but, I gather, rather efficient man." Cross's expression is almost a smirk. "Please don't tell me this house is surrounded."

"No, I'm not trying to tell you that. No one knows I'm here." I watch him for a moment, trying to anticipate his reaction. "I want to buy the trumpet."

He looks as if he hasn't heard me. He just stares for several seconds. I hadn't noticed it before, but now that he's more relaxed, on sure ground, I catch an audible intake of breath each time he speaks. It reminds me of

Raymond Burr or Rod Steiger. "You want to buy the trumpet?" he says.

"Why not? It can't mean anything to you."

"It means a great deal to me. It's the—excuse the pun—instrument of this entire adventure. Don't you understand that? No, I'm not going to sell you the trumpet, for a number of reasons."

Cross gets to his feet, goes to the tape deck, and stops the music. "We've both heard this many times, haven't we? How about something new?"

He rewinds the tape and removes the reel from the deck. All his movements are measured, meticulous. He puts the tape in its box, then pauses to look at me. "We could trade, I suppose, couldn't we?"

"Trade?"

"This tape for the trumpet. You did take it from my car at Markham's party?"

"You know I did."

Cross shrugs. "As I told you when I got the pawn ticket, valet parking is not very secure, particularly at a private home."

I realize Cross is enjoying this. He's more secure now. I'm on his turf, and he's in control, at least for the moment.

"No, on second thought, I guess we can't trade, since you have nothing to trade. The trumpet and tape are both mine." He smiles, raises one finger in the air. "But I have a better idea."

From the shelf near him, Cross takes a foil-wrapped roll of antacid tablets, puts one in his mouth, and watches me while he chews on it. A strange look comes into his eyes, a vacant stare. It's what I couldn't see the night Ken Perkins was murdered. It's some kind of inner excitement rising inside him, ready to bubble over. His eyes go to the video camera.

"Your coming here has provided me with an excellent opportunity."

I have no idea what he means. I take a sip of coffee and watch him. It's almost as if he's unaware I'm sitting in his living room.

I watch him open a new box of videotape and put it in the camera. He presses the record button, taps on the mike, and adjusts the levels. He carries it over near the coffee table, till it's at an angle facing his chair. He looks through the viewfinder, checks everything, then satisfied, he comes over to sit in his Bette Davis chair.

"Now, I think we're ready," he says.

"Ready for what?"

"To record, of course. I'm going to tell you everything. How I came into these tapes and the trumpet, and of course, how and why Ken Perkins was killed."

I look toward the camera, then back to him. I don't know if I'm in the frame or not. Cross enjoys what must be a look of utter astonishment on my face.

"You see," Cross says, "no matter what I tell you, it will remain my secret. Even if you were to tell the police about the tape we're going to make, there's nothing they could do about it. It's still your word against mine. Yours is not too good at the moment, even with your friend Cooper."

"Then what's the point? Why make the tape?"

"The point is, I will have a videotape recording of a murder confession. Something so rare, so unique"— Cross speaks the words with genuine enjoyment— "something I know for sure no one else has. It's the dream of every collector."

He holds up his hands and smiles again, as if he's surprised I don't get it. "Besides," he says, "I'll—"

Cross looks at me, sees something in my expression that causes him to smile again. He knows what he sees is fear, disbelief, and the realization that I'm looking at a man over the edge. He wallows in it. I stare at Cross, watch the pure pleasure spread over his face as my own registers the ingenuousness of his words.

It's the same look I saw when Coop and I stopped him at the airport. He was getting away with something, knew nobody could stop him.

I look once more toward the camera, imagining myself the host of some surreal talk show.

"Welcome to *Obsession*. My guest tonight—Raymond Cross."

CHAPTER

NINETEEN

"You know about the elaborate practical joke Ken Perkins played on some of the collectors? The phony record he manufactured?"

"Yes, another collector told me about it."

"Perkins went too far on that one. He humiliated us all."

Here's what else Cross has been obsessed with. This is his weak point, the compulsion that pushed him over the line.

"The others didn't take it quite so badly."

"No, that's true, they didn't," Cross says as if the thought has just occurred to him. "Oh, it was very clever. I'll give Perkins that. Finding the old vinyl, the label paper, hiring the group. Very elaborate." He pauses, shakes his head. "We all went for it, far too easily."

Cross's body goes tense. I can almost feel it, sitting across from him. He squeezes his hands tightly, stares into the fire as the shadows flicker on the wall.

"When Perkins confessed that he had made the whole thing up, we didn't believe him at first. None of us believed it was possible for someone to fool us, experienced collectors, with a totally bogus record, one that had never existed. But he did."

Cross relaxes somewhat; the pitch of his voice changes. "Well, we had to accept the truth. We'd all been duped. But I made a vow right then, at Perkins's little celebration dinner when he broke the news. Someday, somehow, I would get even. I would outdo his little escapade."

Cross turns to me and smiles. "And then one day, it happened, right in court while I typed up the details of these sloppy criminals and their sordid little crimes. The means for my revenge dropped into my lap, in my court."

"Sammy Dell—Spinner."

"Precisely. A petty thief who was fond of records and tapes. I took it as a sign. When I went to see him, it was so easy. He had this box of tapes. They could never be traced to me. After all, Dell had stolen them, hadn't he?"

I watch Cross replay the whole scene in his mind, see the pleasure it gives him. Somehow, once he's finished, I have to get out of here, get this tape to the police.

"Well," Cross says. "I don't know jazz very well, but I saw the names, recognized a few, but what was important was that these tapes had obviously never been released. They were genuine fifties recordings. I didn't have to manufacture anything. Let the tape be analyzed. I welcomed it. And then I saw the note."

"The note?"

"Yes, someone, whoever had supervised the recording, had written on a card, a note to himself. 'If this isn't C.B., it's his double.' I was fascinated. It didn't take much to learn that of course C.B. was Clifford Brown—dead since 1956. It was perfect. I bought some of his records, compared them with the tapes, and even to a nonmusical person like myself, it was astonishing how perfect the imitation was." Cross glances at me again. "Well, you know, don't you. We fooled you, certainly that night at Perkins's house."

Cross has me there. "Yeah, I guess you did, at least for a while."

He gets up to check the tape. The fire is dwindling, and for the moment the rain has stopped. It's nearly dark now as Cross returns to his chair and continues.

"Everything fell into place. I realized what an opportunity this was, how I could use Perkins himself to effect my revenge. He was very respected in the field. Together we could go to a record company, make a considerable deal. But Perkins wasn't entirely convinced we could pull it off, and of course he thought it was just for a joke anyway, that if we did succeed, we'd give the money back, just like he had done earlier."

"And that's where I came in?"

"Exactly. We had to be very careful. Perkins had a friend—Buffington, wasn't it?—who knew you. Perkins insisted we hear your reaction to the tapes. He agreed that if we could fool a musician, he might go ahead with the plan."

"But Perkins still thought it was a stunt, right?"

"Yes, and of course I hadn't told him everything. I had already decided that if you didn't think the tapes were genuine Clifford Brown, we'd drop the whole thing right there. I'd figure out something else to get even with Perkins. But you, you were adamant. Do you remember what you said?"

"If that's not Clifford Brown, it's his double?"

"Exactly what the man had written on the tape box." Cross holds out his hands, palm up. "I took it as another sign. Do you know why you were fooled so readily? Granted, the imitation was excellent, but you wanted to believe, didn't you?"

How many times had I asked myself the same question? "Yes, I guess I did."

"Why?" Cross really doesn't understand. "What difference would it have made to you?"

I have no answer for Cross, at least not one he'd understand.

"How did you figure it out?"

"Little things only a musician could possibly know—playing the tape for some friends I respect. Gut feelings, instinct. I began to have doubts; then I found two of the musicians who had made the tapes. What about the trumpet? That took longer after I found the postcard."

"Ah yes, the trumpet." Cross suddenly looks at me sharply. "Postcard? What postcard?"

"I found it in the trumpet case, under the lining. It should still be there."

Cross is trying to decide whether I'm serious. He gets up and presses the pause button on the video cam. He goes to a closet near the stairs but hardly takes his eyes off me. The trumpet case is inside. He takes it out, brings it over, and sets it on the coffee table.

"Show me," he says.

He watches as I peel back the edge of the lining and pull out the postcard. He takes it, reads it, doesn't really understand; he was obviously, until this moment, unaware of its existence.

"It's from Duke Ellington," I say, "written to the

trumpet player on the tapes, Connie Beale. He kept it as a souvenir, for good luck or something."

Cross slips the card back into the case. He stares into the fire for a few moments. "It was inevitable, I suppose."

"What?"

"There are always some things that can't be anticipated."

"You thought the musicians on the tapes were already dead?"

"It was a good possibility, wasn't it?"

I don't answer. Over the crackling of the fire, we both turn toward the video cam. There's an audible click sound as the camera restarts itself.

I take the trumpet out of the vinyl case and put it in the original battered case that Cross has. "This really goes in here," I say. I toss the vinyl case on the floor next to me.

"Now, where were we? Yes, the trumpet. It's been all over, hasn't it? And now you bring it right to my home. How convenient. You have to admit, the trumpet was a nice touch, wasn't it? I still remember the look on your face that night at Perkins's house.

"Bernie Dalton got it for me. He owed me money. I told him what to look for, had him check around; he finally found what I wanted from Mojo." Cross smiles again. "Can you imagine, Dalton came back and told me there was just one thing about it. The initials, inscribed in the horn." Cross holds up his hands again, tilts his head upward, and smiles. "Clearly, it was the ultimate sign."

And just as clearly, by that time Raymond Cross was a man on a mission, savoring his opportunity for revenge on Ken Perkins, seeing things that weren't there until it was too late.

"But then it went wrong, didn't it?"

"No," Cross says, "not at all. It went perfectly, as perfectly as I envisioned. The only hitch was Perkins, and you of course. He got nervous, wanted to bail out. If we succeeded, even temporarily, this was a serious hoax, fraud. When I wanted to keep you indisposed until we made the deal, he panicked. That's what we argued about. He threatened to go to the police, expose everything."

Cross gets very quiet then. His voice drops as he remembers, replays it in his mind. "I simply couldn't allow that."

"The gun went off, and, well—" He shrugs. "A pity. It would have been such a great joke, topping even Perkins, since I would have made a great deal of money in the process. I have you to thank for all of that."

"I didn't kill Perkins. You did. What happened to the gun?"

It's time to push now, or I'll be on the video as well. Cross is getting to the end of his story. He's lost now in the thrill of recording his confession, but he'll remember, realize he can't let me out of here.

"The gun?" Cross looks at me puzzled, as if he's forgotten I'm there. "It's not here, if that's what you're thinking. I had it with me when I went to the pier." He pauses and smiles, to let me know there's one more thing I don't know. "Yes, I followed you when you met Cooper. The pier seemed like a good place. The gun made such a small splash off the end."

I try to cover my excitement. This is what we need, solid evidence.

"Now," Cross says, "we have to find a place for you."

He leans in closer, turns his face directly into the camera, and speaks slowly, relishing each word: "I killed Ken Perkins."

And now was he going to kill me? Or could I just get up and walk out of here? Was Cross so confident that, even with me as a witness to his taped confession, it would never be seen or heard by anyone?

"What are you going to do with this tape?"

Cross looks surprised at the question. "Do? Nothing. Keep it, know that I have it."

He gets up and goes to the camera to stop the tape, then rewind it.

"But that's not really enough, is it?"

"What do you mean?" Cross presses play and peers into the viewfinder, checking the playback.

"I mean, part of the kick of being a collector is letting other people know you've got it. You can't tell anyone about this, even anonymously."

"What are you suggesting?"

Before I can answer, we both freeze as the doorbell rings. Cross presses the pause button on the camera and walks quickly to the front door. I watch him peer through the peephole, then spin around toward me.

"You lied. It's Cooper."

"I didn't call him. But what are you worried about? Remember it's my word against yours, right?"

Cross hesitates for a moment. The confidence is gone, replaced by agitation. The doorbell sounds again. He looks from me to the door. Then Coop is pounding on the door.

"Police, Mr. Cross. Open up, please."

I get up and walk closer to the door and stand behind Cross. He opens the door and flips on the outside light that causes Coop to blink.

"Lieutenant Cooper, how can I help you?"

"I spoke to Evan Horne about returning the trumpet, then I saw his car parked outside." Coop looks past Cross, but he can't see me yet.

"Why didn't you just call?" Cross asks.

"Is Horne here, Mr. Cross?"

"Right here, Coop."

Coop looks around Cross, sees me, and steps inside.

"Now see here, Lieutenant, you can't just barge in here and—"

"Yes, I can," Coop says, looking at me. "Barge in? The door is open, you're not stopping me. What's going on here?" He sees the video cam on the tripod and starts to walk into the living room, but Cross grabs him, tries to pull him around.

"You can't go in there. I know my rights."

"You're about to lose some," Coop says. He looks down at Cross's hand, then stares at him, challenging him. "Are you assaulting a police officer?"

Cross takes his hand away as if Coop's arm is a poisonous snake. "No—I—You have no right to be here."

Coop ignores him and looks at me. "You okay?" Coop asks. "What's all this?" Coop points at the camera.

"He just confessed, Coop. The whole thing— wanted to have the tape for a souvenir. He threw the gun off Santa Monica Pier."

Coop is trying to warn me with his eyes. Nothing could be more frustrating for a policeman to know someone is guilty of a crime and not be able to do anything about it.

For a few seconds, the three of us don't move. Then

the silence is broken by the clicking sound as the video cam starts to play. Cross's voice fills the room.

"The gun? It's not here, if that's what you're thinking. I had it with me at the pier."

Coop turns to the camera, bends over to look in the viewfinder.

"You can't do that!" Cross screams and charges past me, toward Coop. I catch him from the side, glance off, and spin backward into the sound system wall before Coop can grab him. My right hand collides with the edge of one of the shelves. Tapes go flying and I wind up on the floor, Cross on top of me, his hands digging at my throat.

Then just as quickly, he flys backward, as if someone had pulled a wire attached to his back. Coop has him by the back of the neck and pushes him facedown onto the Bette Davis chair. "Now you stay right here, Cross." Coop turns to me. "You okay?" Coop rights the camera tripod.

I nod yes, get to my feet, holding my wrist.

"You're under arrest, Mr. Cross. Assault and battery. You have the right to remain silent. You have—"

Coop finishes the Miranda routine while Cross glares at him. He cuffs Cross and calls for backup to take him in.

We both look at the video camera and wonder. "How did you know I was here?" I ask Coop.

"Natalie called me. You're late for dinner."

"You better tell her to meet me at the hospital. I think my wrist is broken."

Cross is silent and sullen as he's taken away twenty minutes later by two uniformed cops. Coop removes the video camera, looks around the room.

"Well, look here," he says, picking up the trumpet case. "We better return this to the owner."

Outside, we stop to put the case in my car. I ride with Coop to Malibu Emergency, cradling my arm against my chest. There's some swelling now, and a strong, throbbing pain.

"I'm not going to condone what you did," Coop says, "but I'll call Trask, tell him about the tape. That should be enough, but let's hope we get lucky and find the gun."

Coop waits until they admit me to be x-rayed. "You better do a psychiatric workup as well," Coop tells the doctor. "This guy is nuts." He looks at my wrist and shakes his head. "Jesus, it had to be the right one, didn't it? See you, sport, I've got a video to watch."

Natalie arrives as the doctor puts the finishing touches on the wet-wrap cast that fits over my hand and wrist like a long glove without fingers.

"Oh, my God," she says, putting her hand to her mouth.

"We'll have that off in four weeks," the doctor says. "Bad hairline crack, but you'll be all right. What did you do, try to karate-chop a brick?" He tears off a page from the prescription pad. "Take two of these before you go to bed."

Natalie walks me outside, and we stand for a moment listening to the ocean, audible even across the highway. We walk to her car.

"How did Coop know where I was?" I ask her.

"When you didn't call or show for dinner, I called him. That's where you said we were going. I told him we had been to Cross's place the other day. He didn't wait for any more. He just hung up. He must have gone right out there."

She stops, turns to face me. "What did happen out there?"

"I just spent the evening with a madman, I think. Come on, you can take me to my car."

"Can you drive with that cast?"

"Yeah, you need two hands for the piano, not for driving."

The Camaro is in place, glistening with rain. I slide in, carefully holding my right hand in my lap. The cast is rock-hard now. I drop the keys twice, trying to get the ignition key in, but finally get the engine started. I have to reach across my body with my left hand to depress the shifter lever button and slide it into drive.

"My place or yours?" I say to Natalie.

"Mine. Remember? Gladys Cowen told me to take care of you." She looks at the cast. Her eyes glisten in the streetlight.

"Come on, I'm fine."

Natalie's headlights behind me, I guide the car back down the coast highway. The road is slick and wet, but the rain has stopped. To my right, the sky is dark but for a narrow light strip on the horizon. Tomorrow will be a good day.

A couple of miles before Santa Monica Canyon, two lanes are closed, and the Cal-Trans crews are clearing away mud and debris from the most recent slide. Otherwise the trip is fine.

I take two of the Percodan at Natalie's and stay awake long enough to tell her about Cross's video confession.

"We've got him now," I say, feeling my eyes getting heavy. I drift off then. Natalie's face fades into blackness.

* * *

I wake up from a dream. I'm playing the piano, comping fine with my left hand, but my right, still encased in the cast, bangs against the keys, hitting meaningless clusters of notes. I try to reach across with my left to play the solo, but it won't reach.

"Evan," Natalie says. She's looking down at me, holding a cup of coffee.

I blink, look at her, then at the cast. I sit up on the edge of the bed and take the coffee, try to clear my head. I keep hearing Cross's voice, seeing his face on the video.

I take a shower, holding my right hand over my head so the cast doesn't get wet. Natalie helps me get dressed, and around noon I call Coop.

"Cross walked," he says.

"What? How?"

"His lawyer got down here bright and early, and given his record of no priors, his job, he made bail. I showed the video to the DA. They won't allow it now, but the bail was high. Cross may have to sell some of his records to come up with it."

"What about the gun?"

"I've got divers in the water now. We'll find it, we might even get prints."

"Prints?"

"Yeah, unless he wiped it clean, the water won't erase the oil residue from his fingers. Trask is on his way down from Las Vegas now. With the tape and the gun they'll get an indictment. I'll still need you to file the assault charge and a statement, but the Las Vegas murder charge will take precedence."

"I'll be down this afternoon. What if Cross takes off?"

"Let's hope he does. That'll be another charge to add to the list. How's the hand?"

"It hurts. Four weeks in a cast."

I hear Coop sigh over the phone. "Evan, get back to the piano."

"I'm going to try."

CODA

"FOUND IT," BLACKBYRD SAYS. *"ARRIVAL—EVAN Horne.* The guy claims it's mint-minus condition, only played twice, but they always overestimate."

It's been a couple of weeks since I talked to Blackbyrd. I'd nearly forgotten about my request. "How much does he want for it?" What I really want to know is, How much is Evan Horne worth on the collector market?

"That's the best part," Blackbyrd says. "It's a freebie."

"Have you got a name?"

"Yeah, got it right here somewhere. Hang on a minute." I hear him shuffling papers. "Here it is. Guy's name is Calvin Hughes."

I almost drop the phone. A few moments, and I can't say anything.

"You still there?" Blackbyrd says.

"Yeah, you know what, I changed my mind. Tell the guy thanks, but I'll pass. Tell him to keep it."

"Okay, you're the boss."

"Do I owe you anything for the search?"

"No, I heard on the grapevine you helped the police nail Ken Perkins's killer. We're square. Raymond Cross—who would have thought?"

"Yeah, who would have thought. Well, thanks, Blackbyrd."

"Willis."

Ace sent me clippings from the Las Vegas papers, and I saw the story in the Santa Monica paper. Coop's divers hadn't found the gun, but a fisherman on the pier hooked it one afternoon, and turned it in. Cross's prints were still on it, and everything matched.

I returned Gladys Cowen's tapes, and I've been helping her with the process of going through them to see just what her husband had recorded all those years ago. We aren't going to find Clifford Brown, but there is some good stuff that stands a chance of being offered to a record label. Rick Markham, however, says he's not interested.

Natalie is back at school, struggling with contracts, torts, and real property, and I got a reprieve on my apartment—an official notice that the developer's plans are postponed. So I still have my place in Venice for a while longer. Tim Shaw doesn't think much of my one-handed typing, but I got the cover of *Blue Note* magazine.

Now I look forward to a rubber ball, getting the strength back in my hand, and getting reacquainted with my piano. There's only one thing I still have to do before I go back to practicing, hoping, wrestling with my dreams.

It's Sunday afternoon when I call Connie Beale, ask him if I can come over.

"I've got a surprise for you."

"Come on over, man. We're fixin' to have lunch," he says.

When I get there, his granddaughter opens the door, smiles at me shyly. She's in jeans and a T-shirt, an apron tied around her waist, a large wooden spoon in her hand.

"Grandpa Connie's back there," she says, pointing down the hall where the music is coming from.

I knock and open the door to what is obviously Connie's music room. He's nearly lost, sunk in the plushness of a huge leather chair. His small frameless glasses perched on the bridge of his nose, he looks up from reading the notes to a CD. *Clifford Brown with Strings* is on the stereo: "Embraceable You."

"You heard this one?" Connie asks when I come in.

"Yeah, many times." The ottoman in front of Connie is the only other seat. I pull it away from the chair and sit down. Connie pretends not to notice the trumpet case.

He glances at me and holds up the CD booklet. "Some interesting shit in here." He carefully refolds it and replaces it in the CD case. For a few minutes we listen to Brownie turn the song into a cry of loneliness, a man who hasn't seen his girl for a long time.

"I could do that once," Connie says, as the tune ends. He eyes the trumpet case I've brought along. "What you got there?"

"I know. You did it on this." He pushes the glasses up on his forehead and takes the case from me, lays it across his legs.

He opens it, takes out the trumpet. "Never thought I'd see this old horn again." He presses the valves, feels their stickiness, and shakes his head. Setting the case on the floor, he gets up and goes to the shelf near the stereo and takes down a small plastic bottle of A1 Cass valve oil. He squirts a few drops on the valves until they work to his satisfaction.

Watching him handle the trumpet, it's like being a witness to the reunion of two old friends.

From another trumpet case he takes out a mouthpiece, inserts it in the horn, and for a few bars plays along with Clifford Brown. "Yeah, it can still play," Connie says.

"You said it was stolen."

"Naw," Connie says, smiling shyly. "Just didn't like to tell the truth, kind of embarrassed."

"What do you mean?"

"You know how things go sometime. My old lady told me she'd sold it at a garage sale. I was on the road, didn't use it much anymore. I had a new horn, she wanted to clear out things, she said. I think she did it on purpose. We wasn't getting along too well in those days. She wanted me to give up bein' Clifford Brown. She couldn't understand why I was so mad. She never knew."

"Knew what?"

"That this really was one of Brownie's horns."

I stare at the horn for what must be a full minute. Connie nods, sees the shock on my face.

"I didn't tell you about that. I met him one time, when he was out here at the Lighthouse. He and Max Roach had a place together. You know how kids are, no fear. I went over there one afternoon. I could hear him inside, playing scales. He was real nice, invited me in. We talked for a couple of hours, then he asked me to play. He had a bunch of horns lying around. 'Try this one,' he said. I played his solo on 'Joy Spring.' He was really impressed, then he just gave me the horn, just gave it to me. Man, I left there flyin'."

Connie looks inside the bell of the horn for the *C.B.* inscription, nods his head slowly. "Yeah, this is it."

He runs his hand over the horn. "That's how smart I was in those days," he says. "I played so much like Brownie, I had the same initials. I never told nobody this was Brownie's horn or that he gave it to me."

"Did you think they wouldn't believe you?"

"Hell, no reason not to."

Of course there wasn't, any more than not to believe Clifford Brown was playing on the tapes. I stare at the horn again. Bought at a garage sale for twenty-five dollars, kept in the trunk of my car, in a Las Vegas pawn shop. Clifford Brown's trumpet.

Connie's expression suddenly changes to a frown. "Did you look in the case?" He sets down the horn, opens the small compartment inside the case, and stops when he sees the postcard is still there. He sinks down into the chair and readjusts his glasses to read the card.

"Closest I ever got to the big time. Three nights with Duke. Like my friend Tommy Hamilton, ballplayer. He knocked around the minors for a few years then got called up at the end of the season. Four at bats, got two hits off Sandy Koufax."

"And the other two?"

"Struck out."

"What happened after that?"

Connie shrugs. "He got hurt in spring training, never recovered. Went to work for the post office, I think."

We listen in silence to Clifford Brown. Several times Connie smiles and cocks his head at something Brownie plays, then the CD ends.

I take the cassette out of my pocket. "You can have this too."

He takes it from me, looks at the label I've hand-lettered. *The Connie Beale Quartet*. He nods, smiles, opens the box, and puts it in the machine. For a moment he's back in 1955 as the tape begins to play.

He stands with his back to me, listening to himself, how he used to sound. I know all about that. This was Connie Beale trying to be Clifford Brown.

When he turns around, he blinks a few times and smiles. "Thanks, man, I appreciate this." He busies himself with putting away the CD, looking at his watch. "You want to stay for lunch? My granddaughter can burn. Her mama taught her."

"No, thanks, Connie," I say, getting to my feet. "I've got a date with a young lady and she doesn't like to be kept waiting."

"I can dig that. Well, okay then." We shake hands. He hesitates, then awkwardly, he pulls me in for a hug. "What happens to those tapes now, the real ones, I mean?"

"They were returned to the owner, Gladys Cowen. You should drop by and see her sometime. I think she'd like that."

Connie seems delighted at the thought. "I just might do that."

I let myself out. I stand on the steps for a moment, light a cigarette and think about the life Connie Beale made for himself, pursuing Clifford Brown. My own seems always centered on my right hand. I pull up the sleeve of my coat and look at the cast. At least that comes off tomorrow, then it's back to squeezing rubber balls and therapy.

I start for my car. When I pass the music room window, I hear a trumpet playing over the cassette, note for note like Clifford Brown. I listen until the music stops. I start to go on to my car, but I stop again.

I hear Connie, solo now, haltingly at first, but gathering strength as his fingers remember the notes, the Benny Golson melody, the Jon Hendricks lyrics probably swirling through his mind.

Connie Beale could never have been Clifford Brown on this tune. It was one song Brownie never played.

"I Remember Clifford" was written too late for that.

Match wits with the best-selling

MYSTERY WRITERS

in the business!

SUSAN DUNLAP

"Dunlap's police procedurals have the authenticity of telling detail."
—*The Washington Post Book World*

SARA PARETSKY

"Paretsky's name always makes the top of the list when people talk about the new female operatives." —*The New York Times Book Review*

SISTER CAROL ANNE O'MARIE

"Move over Miss Marple..." —*San Francisco Sunday Examiner & Chronicle*

LINDA BARNES